Praise for Emily Winslow

'A masterful whodunnit.'
Lisa Gardner, *New York Times* bestselling author of
Right Behind You

'[Winslow is] brilliant at portraying the ragged fragments
of these lives. What emerges isn't a single killer with
motive and means, but a tangle of stories crossing and
colliding, stray intersections of incidents and accidents,
misunderstandings and misreadings, all thanks to the
myopia of individual perspectives and the self-centeredness
of individual desires.'
Washington Post

'[*The Red House*] is a triumph . . . [Winslow] handles
to perfection the multiple-protagonist viewpoints . . .
Time these excellent stories were snapped up by a TV
company.'
Books Monthly

Look for Her

EMILY WINSLOW

Allison & Busby Limited
12 Fitzroy Mews
London W1T 6DW
allisonandbusby.com

First published in Great Britain by Allison & Busby in 2017.

Copyright © 2017 by EMILY WINSLOW

A CIP catalogue record for this book is available from
the British Library.

First Edition

ISBN 978-0-7490-2266-2

Typeset in 11/16 pt Sabon by
Allison & Busby Ltd.

The paper used for this Allison & Busby publication
has been produced from trees that have been legally sourced
from well-managed and credibly certified forests.

Printed and bound by
CPI Group (UK) Ltd, Croydon, CR0 4YY

For Gavin
Your patience and support make each word possible

CHAPTER ONE

Annalise Williams (Wolfson College), University Counselling Service, recorded and transcribed by Dr Laurie Ambrose

My mother picked the name Annalise for me because of a girl who was killed. Her name was Annalise Wood, and she went missing when she was sixteen. My mother was the same age when it happened. Annalise was lovely, much prettier than my sister and I ever became. She was the kind of girl you look at and think, *Of course someone would want to take her.*

Don't look at me like that. I know that what happened to her was awful. It just seems a very fine line between being the kind of person that others want to be with and be like and treat well, and being the kind of person that some others, just a few, sick others, want to take for themselves. That's the same kind of person, isn't it? The loved and lovely. Isn't that from a poem somewhere? That's what she was like. That's the risk when you're the kind of person who's wanted. Good people want to be close to you, but the bad people want you too.

There were two photos of her that the media used most: her most recent school portrait, and a snapshot of her laughing, with the friends on either side cropped out. Taken together, they presented the two sides of a beautiful and perfect person: poised and thoughtful, and spontaneous and bubbly. The kind of person who deserves help and attention.

Realistically, if they wanted these pictures to help strangers identify her if they saw her out and about with the bad man, they should have used photos of her frowning or looking frightened. Either there weren't any (which may well be the case; who would take a photo of that?), or they couldn't bring themselves to advertise a version of her that was less than appealing. The narrative is important. If you want the 'general public' to get worked up, you have to persuade. Attractiveness and innocence must be communicated, even if emphasising those traits makes the real person harder to recognise.

In the end, she was already dead, so it's a good thing, I suppose, that they used the nice photos. They're the images that everyone remembers. My mum was a teenager when those pictures were in the paper every day for weeks, then weekly for months. Annalise Wood was the most beautiful girl in the world. Everyone cared about her. It's what any mother would wish for her child, to be the kind of person that everyone would care about and miss if she disappeared.

It wasn't until Mum was over thirty that what really happened to Annalise Wood was discovered. Until then, several theories had become legend:

1) That she had run away and was very happy somewhere, laughing at all of us thinking she'd been taken. Maybe her parents hadn't approved of her boyfriend and she'd got her own way and taken revenge in one blow, by leaving her parents forever regretful of having forbidden her.

2) That she was still alive but captive, chained in a cabin in the woods, or maybe in a harem in some other country.

3) That her parents had killed her and buried her in the woods behind their property. This was a cruel theory, and absolutely no one believed it except for an eccentric local writer who sold the story in booklets before he was 'spoken to' by the police.

None of these were true, and everyone knows that now, but local kids still tell all of these versions as if they had really happened. They no longer say it was Annalise, who is now known to have been dead from the day she'd disappeared, but instead 'some girl' from decades before, from the fifties or wartime or even Victorian days. They always describe Annalise, though, even if they don't realise it: long, dark hair; pale pink skin; smiling. They still have details from those photos in their minds, the origin of the composite image forgotten.

A book about the investigation came out when I was three. I remember my mother crying behind the locked bathroom door. The photos were reprinted in all the papers. Mum tells me that she found me staring at Annalise's smiling face. She took the paper away from me, but I howled and demanded it back. She says I blackened my fingers fondling the page. I used to wonder if Annalise had been captive for years and then died when I was born. Maybe I was Annalise herself, reborn and recognising her own face in the news.

I wasn't. Annalise had been killed still wearing the clothes she'd been taken in, within two miles of where she'd been last seen, and the corruption had progressed at the rate one would reasonably expect for an old but not decades-old corpse.

I did wonder, though, when I was a teenager, if we had some bond. I grew my hair long, though it wasn't as thick and dark as hers. I wasn't as slim, but I smiled. I mimicked her serene school-portrait expression in the mirror in my bedroom, and emulated her wide-mouthed laugh when in groups. I have a snapshot that's almost exactly like the one of the original Annalise: me between two friends, woolly winter hats on, red scarf. With my hair mostly hidden, and my face half-turned, I look almost exactly like her. I cropped the picture like hers, just me, only a friend's chin on the left and another friend's shoulder on the right as evidence of my sociability. I was really proud of that photo. I felt like I'd lived up to my mother's hopes for me. I was lovely (from certain angles) and popular (look! Friends!). If I were taken away, people would want me back.

I think it's absolutely normal to fantasise about what other people would say if you die. It's really not fair to act as if this is morbid or self-indulgent. I've even read it advised in a magazine to imagine what you might want said about yourself at your funeral. They meant for you to imagine the end of a long life, and consider what you want to be remembered for: work achievements, contribution to society, relationships with friends and family. There was no right answer, they insisted, just the opportunity to discover our own priorities while there's still time. I don't think what I imagine is all that different. Besides, we can't help what we think about. We sometimes believe we can, but I know it doesn't work.

In my experience, there are ruts up there in our heads, sometimes with very steep sides. Sometimes in my fantasies I imagined, like I wanted to, that they chose my best photos (the cropped one, and my year nine school portrait, which is still my favourite), and that the news speculated that someone was driven so mad with lust by looking at me that he had to have me, and that I fought back so bravely that he had no choice but to kill me. Other times (and this is still inside my head but I can't control it) no one cares. No photos are published, or a blurry one, or me in the background of a scene, looking lost. Everyone thinks I must have wandered off on my own, because who would actually bother to take me?

Did I tell you that Annalise Wood was raped? The forensics said so. Well, that she'd had sex and then been killed, so one assumes. She'd also had a baby, before she went missing. Have you heard that one? This was kept secret for absolute ages but it finally leaked out. Not everybody knows but it's talked about. She'd had a baby when she was fifteen, a year before she was killed, and put it up for adoption. Her parents had sent her on a six-month exchange programme to France, they'd said, which is how it had been covered up. They never had a French student stay with them in return, so we all should have guessed, shouldn't we? We all should have told stories about how it was the father, so enraged at having his child given away for adoption, who had punished her.

No, I don't think things like that all the time. I'm just telling you how it was. These are the kinds of things that most people think of, not that I think of just all by myself. We needed a story to make sense of Annalise dying. We still do. Another book came out last year. That makes two. Three, if you count the self-published booklet about the parents. People still care about her.

Sometimes, typing my own name into a search engine, her photo pops up among the results. That's how important her first name is; even with my surname, you'll get her picture, usually the school one. She's wearing a white blouse and the school jacket. In the age progression they made once, to try to make her look thirty, she was wearing a similar suit jacket, but she looked dowdy, like she worked in an office and was bored, like she celebrated her thirtieth birthday with a bunch of nice girlfriends from work but no boyfriend or husband or kids. I'm only twenty-four but sometimes I look in the mirror and it's like I see this age progression happening to me, and I just want to make them stop and go back to using my good photos. Go back to that year nine pic, or that winter snapshot. Sometimes I wish I could freeze there. Not stop there. I don't want to be killed, obviously. But I wish I could still be that person, that bright, bubbly person, and just stay there. I think that maybe the real Annalise is so loved because she hasn't had to age.

I went to my grandmother's funeral six years ago and I hated that they put a recent photo of her on the service sheet. It's not just that she looked old but that she looked broken. It was like if you stared long enough at it the tremor in her hand would act up, and her head would involuntarily bob, like it did near the end. I wanted them to use a photo from before, like when she was a young mum or when she worked at the arts centre. Mum pointed out that both of those were from before I was born, and didn't I want a photo of the grandmother I'd known? Mum didn't understand that *all of her* is the grandmother I'd known, even the bits I wasn't there for. I looked at her and I saw all of her. It didn't seem fair to reduce her to only who she was at the very end.

The real problem with age isn't just the whole falling apart business, though that's pretty fucking terrible. The thing about age, even just my age, is that a young person is judged so much more indulgently. A young person is rated on their potential. You get complimented for having interests and plans and the natural talent or intelligence to maybe act on them. For a child to want to be a doctor or an astronaut, for a child to be 'good at' maths or reading, is praiseworthy all by itself. But an adult has to actually hit the mark, not just aim for it. If you miss it, well, the wanting it, the having the potential to perhaps do it, doesn't count for anything any more.

I guess I'm feeling a bit at sea. Everyone's so clever here. I'm clever too; I know that I am. Clever just doesn't feel special here. You think getting into university is a kind of trophy, but it's not. It's just a door, and you walk through it and there's a lot of work on the other side, hard work, not a reward. The real trophy is graduation, right? Except perhaps it's not. Maybe that's just another door too, and then the trophy is getting a job, but a job isn't a trophy, it's more work too. It's all doors, doors, doors. I just want to get to where I'm supposed to go and just be there. I want to get to a room where there isn't another door for me to aim for, just a nice couch and a bookshelf and maybe a TV. And a phone. And a man, a really nice man who adores me.

No, no one in particular. Not right now. Of course I've had boyfriends. I'm not ugly. I have a very normal romantic life, overall. I'm only twenty-four.

We still don't know who killed the real Annalise. No one knows who the baby's father was either. Probably both the killer and the father (or maybe the father is the killer) were strangers, grown men, but maybe one or both of them was a boy from school. I think that's probably right. You know how boys are.

No, no one's ever tried to hurt me. Why would you wonder that?

Boys are just boys, like boys everywhere. Girls can't do anything right. When I was thirteen, if you wore a bra, you were teased for it. If you didn't wear a bra and needed one, you were teased for it. If you didn't need one, you were teased for that. There's that awful couple of years where the girls expand, not just get taller but kind of inflate in parts, and we're so much bigger than the boys, and then when the boys catch up it's just this huge relief for everyone. [Laughs.]

The first time was fine. I was at uni, in Warwick. I didn't get into Cambridge as an undergraduate, so I went there. Everyone was taking this chance to make themselves over, just to be who they had always wished to be, except that they'd been trapped by their hometowns into being who they'd been since they were born. So I did it too. I made myself new.

I was alone with this boy. Well, we were at uni, so he wasn't a boy. But he was a fresher, like me, so not a man yet either. He was this male person. His name was Jason. I told him about what had happened to Annalise, but as if it had happened to me, years before when I was younger.

Not the dying, obviously. Not the killing. But the taking and it mattering. I cried while I told it, which isn't surprising because it's sad, whoever it happened to. He put his arm around me. He comforted me, and touched me, and was indignant for me. I went from being this very ordinary person to being someone who'd been worth stealing, someone who was worth grieving, someone who'd been through so much and come out stronger. We did kiss that night, but nothing else. That would have been weird, don't you think? You don't tell a story like that and just jump in. But we did it later that week. He was very gentle. He kept asking if what he was doing was all right. He was my boyfriend most of the first year.

No, that doesn't matter. You're going too fast. It doesn't matter why we broke up but it matters a lot how we got together. I didn't pretend to be Annalise because I'm a rape fantasist. I know some women think about that sort of thing, not the real thing, but a titillating form of playing at it. It's not for me. I have never, ever asked any man to act out a rape scenario, and I don't do it in my head either. When I think of Annalise, I don't think of her on the ground, under that bad person. I think of her in that school jacket, or that red scarf. You know, she wasn't even wearing either of those when she died. It was too hot. But I picture her the way she lived, not the way she died. Actually, better than the way she lived. After she died she was, like, beatified. She became a perfect image of herself instead of her whole, messy, real self. I took on that image. Anyone would want to be just the good bits, wouldn't they?

No, see, that goes back to the imagination ruts. I can take away the being killed part from what's in my head, but not all of it, not the rest of it. I wouldn't even know who Annalise was without her having been attacked, so pretending to be just who she was before . . . It doesn't make any sense. She became 'Annalise the saint' when she was taken. Before that she was ordinary. Popular, but not famous. Not perfect. It's awful to think that we don't entirely make ourselves, that we get partly made by what others do to us, but there it is. It's true.

I told you, I'm not a rape fantasist. If someone did that to me I might even kill myself. I know two girls who've been raped, or mostly raped, one by a date and one by a cousin, and they were each a mess for, like, more than a year. I told you: I don't think about what happened to Annalise. I think about what it would be like to be loved that much. That's all.

Rhoda! [Laughs.] I've never met anyone called Rhoda. If my mother had called me that . . . No, I know. You mean if she had called me anything else, like Jennifer or Christine or Alison. I imagine I would be different, but . . . I don't think you understand where I grew up. It's not my mother naming me for Annalise that makes Annalise important to me. It's me being born into a town where everyone, including my mother, is haunted by her memory to the point that my mother wanted to call me that, that's what makes Annalise important to me. Change my name, and I still would have those images in my head. Maybe everyone from Lilling does. Have you ever known anyone from there? No, I suppose you can't admit it if you did. Privacy and all that. But if you did, you'd know.

I researched it once. The two years after Annalise went missing, the name doubled in popularity

17

nationally. It's never been a top 100 name, so that's not a lot, but still . . . I'm not the only one.

I *am* talking about myself, Doctor. Don't be obtuse. You can't describe anything without comparing it to something else. You just can't.

I had a children's book about that. The first page showed a skyscraper. It was a photo of a cut-out piece of silver paper, rectangular with a point at the top and two columns of punched-out squares for windows. The next page was a photo of the same cutout, surrounded by cutouts of small village houses. The word TALL was printed on top. The next spread showed the same silver skyscraper dwarfed by cutouts of even bigger skyscrapers, so big we don't see their tops. That had the word SMALL, describing the same silver building. It went on like that, with the moon being both bright and pale, depending on the sky, and a cape being both blue and purple, depending on the colours close to it. The last pages were of the silver building, the moon, and the cape on neutral, empty backgrounds, with the questions, 'Tall or small? Bright or pale? Blue or purple?' You couldn't pick what each item was without also choosing a context for it. You couldn't judge it just by itself. Is it tall? Is it small? Compared to what?

So I talk about myself compared to Annalise. I'm pretty sure I'm allowed to do that.

I told you why I came here. I have anxiety about graduating. It's not the usual worry about wondering if my thesis will be accepted. I'm confident that it will be, and that's what upsets me. I'll have a master's, and then what? You know that room I told you I wish for, the one with no new doors? Graduating just seems like it will spit me out into a room with a thousand doors, and if I choose the wrong one I'll regret it. I may not even know that I regret it until a dozen more doors in, and then . . .

I never told Jason (my uni boyfriend) that I'd lied to him that night, about me being attacked when I was younger like Annalise Wood. I always let him believe that what I said had really happened to me, and of course he didn't betray my privacy by telling anyone else. Sometimes I brought it up again, just the two of us. I'd share a little detail, and he'd get this emotional, pained look. He'd become very protective and it just . . . it fed me. I don't know how to explain it. It made me feel closer to him. I was strict with myself; I never brought it up more than once a month. We were together eight months, so I suppose I talked about it eight times. I haven't told that to a man since.

No, I don't mean . . . Of course I have. I had a boyfriend the summer before starting here. I never said anything about Annalise, though. I thought I'd grown out of it.

Look, it's just a comfort thing. It's like a child who has to learn to not suck his thumb so his teeth don't get wonky. He's not doing something fundamentally wrong. Sucking his thumb isn't objectively bad. But it can have a bad consequence, so you gently tell this person, this small person, 'Sorry, you have to stop this now. I know it feels good, and you've done

19

nothing wrong, but it has to stop.' If you yell about it, if you go on about how wrong it is, you just add to the need to do the comforting thing that you want him to stop.

I know I have to not lie about that again, but the more I get stressed about graduating . . . It's just a comfortable story. I know it so well. I just . . . I can just put it on, and make a man feel sorry for me. It feels good. It feels safe.

Not anyone in particular. Not yet. Just men that I look at, and who look at me.

Oh! Sorry. Of course I understand. I should have looked at my watch.

Yes, in two weeks. Thank you, Dr Ambrose. Thank you. I feel better already.

CHAPTER TWO

Laurie Ambrose

The office door fell shut behind her. I didn't lean back in my chair until I heard the outer door open and close. She was on the pavement, my view striped by the blinds on the window. She was shrugging a rucksack over her shoulder and heading towards the Fitzwilliam. Typical student; typical twenty-something. But she was the second client to bring up Annalise Wood to me within months.

I shimmied my shoulders in a dismissive little shiver. Ms Williams had been my last appointment of the day. I was eager to leave but needed to wait for Blake. He's always been late, ever since coming into the world two weeks after his due date. I tidied the desk. I checked my phone for texts and missed calls. None. Nothing to be done; adult children have their own minds.

Ms Williams wouldn't have known this, but I grew up not far from the Annalise murder. Not in Lilling itself, like she did, but I'm almost twice her age so was alive when Annalise was killed. I was five then, and then nearly graduating from Cambridge when her body was found.

Even sixteen years after the disappearance, that was big news. That day I had been in a charity shop buying a shimmery purple wrap to go with a party dress I was planning to wear, and the woman at the till had been the one to tell me. She'd said, 'They found Annalise,' without context or explanation, but it was the very bareness of the statement that had made it clear that she was talking about *the* Annalise, not just someone who also happened to have that name.

I should clarify that this was true only because of geography. I was home for Easter break at that time. At home, just the name Annalise is enough. I was surprised when I then returned to Cambridge how few people were discussing it. It was in the national newspapers, of course, but not the local one. In Cambridge, one had to say 'Annalise, that girl from Hertfordshire who was killed ages ago' or, at least, 'Annalise Wood'. Just fifty miles away from Lilling, less than an hour's drive, and the public wasn't on a first-name basis. I grant that this is mostly to do with Cambridge having so much of a student population, constantly leaving and being replaced, often from much farther away. Still, it was one of the first times I can remember feeling suddenly foreign so close to my own home.

Back in that charity shop, the woman behind the till had looked blank and stunned and that's how I'd known that Annalise was dead, not found alive. I must have naturally assumed that that would be the case by then, but knowing it for certain was terrible. It really was. She wasn't the girl in the school uniform any more, or whomever that girl would have grown into. She was just a body, not even a whole body by then, surely. She would be bits and pieces.

I wrapped my arms around myself. The heating in our office hadn't yet caught up with the autumn chill.

My phone rang, quivering in my pocket. I snatched it up. 'Blake?' I said, without first checking that it was actually him.

'Sweetheart!' Dad said, and he sounded unstressed, ready for a chat. I gave in, to give Blake more time.

Mum was fine, Dad told me. Everything was the same. We talked about my sister, Helen, and how Dad used to come to all of my tennis matches.

'Dad, do you remember Annalise?'

He hesitated. 'Sure! Uh, who? Was she a friend of yours?'

I hesitated too. Maybe Dad's memory was going, like Mum's. *No*, I assured myself. *Maybe just not everyone is wrapped up in collective concern for a singled-out and taken-down teenage girl.*

'Never mind. She was just a girl I . . .' I almost said 'knew'. That's what it feels like sometimes, when you grow up in the shadow of something like that. I had forgotten that. This new client was bringing it all back.

'I can look in your mother's phone book. I can see if her parents are still—'

'Aw, Dad, that's sweet but it's all right. I don't need—'

'Did she play tennis with you?' Dad asked, not letting go.

'She was a school friend, Dad,' I said expediently. It was easier than trying to explain. But even in lying I didn't take the simpler road of saying, 'Yes, yes, we played tennis together.' I've never seen a picture of Annalise playing tennis or any reference to sport in her life at all. It didn't feel right to lie about the dead more than strictly necessary. 'Remind Mum that we'll all be coming for Christmas.'

'Christmas!' he said, sounding pleased and surprised, but I'd told him weeks ago that we'd be there for the looming holiday. It was already November; not long now.

And November is a busy time at the University, first term of the new academic year. No sense waiting any longer for Blake, or chasing him up. I should be relieved he has better things to do than meet his mum for dinner.

'I have to go, Dad,' I said, ending the call with just a few more back-and-forths, and fumbled in my handbag for my car keys, which reminded me of taking away Mum's car keys last Christmas, and how it had shamed her. But she would have kept driving if we hadn't. Nothing short of an accident was going to convince her she wasn't able to any more. Now Dad has to keep his keys where she can't reach them. It was one of the most difficult things I'd ever been part of; thank goodness for my sister and father. I don't know if I could have resisted her tears and pleading by myself.

As I stepped outside our old Victorian office building, and breathed in the sound and smell of the rush-hour traffic on Trumpington Street, the office phone inside rang brightly, chipperly. I wouldn't have been able to get in fast enough to pick it up, so I waited a few minutes at the door and then dialled into the office voicemail from my mobile.

'Dr Ambrose?' said a young, female voice. 'This is Anna, from today. Annalise Williams?' She paused as if we were talking together, waiting for me to fill in the blank with an acknowledgement. 'I just want to say thank you. I'm already thinking of what else I'd like to tell you. Well, everything, really. It's good to talk. Sometimes everything is all tangled up inside but when it comes out in words somehow the mouth has funnelled it all into a straight line that makes sense. It makes a proper story. I can't wait to see you again.'

There was no click, just a hanging-on. I listened to that airy sound of being connected for about twenty more seconds before there was a staticky *clack* and the recording cut off. I wasn't sure if she'd hung up, or if it was the system that had automatically limited the message. It was discomfiting, the way the message had stopped but not properly ended. Sometimes clients get a little too close. It was best to take care.

I looked around before descending the steps. It was darkish already, the normal but somehow always surprising autumn early dark, and thoughts of dead Annalise made me stupidly anxious. The murder had never been solved. Her body had been eventually found, but not her killer. I wondered if any police were still looking.

Once in my car I made a note of the client's call, to put in her file. I abbreviated her name as 'Anna', which is how she'd booked the appointment. The full 'Annalise' felt taken.

CHAPTER THREE

Morris Keene

I'm used to every new door I approach belonging to a witness or suspect or family of a victim. It should feel good to make a social call, but I didn't know if I'd be welcomed. I stopped to check the address on my phone again, to put off arriving a little longer.

I was in the right place.

Damn.

The house was pressed down by heaps of big, ball-like blossoms clinging to the end of summer. They climbed up from below and then up and over the roof, like the ropes pinning Gulliver.

Chloe is no gardener. Neither is Dan. They'd just moved in; that's why everything was still alive. By this time next year, there'll be weeds choking the flower beds.

No, don't underestimate her, I reminded myself. *Who knows how she's changed?*

She'd had a baby. Maybe she was nesting. Maybe Dan was nesting. He was the one who chose the place.

The bell was a little brown button on a porcelain circle. It looked like a nipple. I turned my head to avoid staring at it while I pressed it and waited.

It was almost a year since the back of my right hand had been slashed in the process of apprehending a murderer. At first I'd been relieved to be alive; the slash to my abdomen had scared me a hell of a lot more. Then the loss of my ability to grip had affected, well, nearly everything: driving, writing, even using my phone. It was frightening, but at the same time a convenient distraction from the psychological trauma reaction, which was much more embarrassing than mere physical incompetence. *You thought getting stabbed in the belly was bad? Wait till you see the effects of the seemingly minor hand injury! You thought the hand injury was incapacitating? Wait till you see what it's like when your mind betrays you!*

But both my hand and my panic attacks were now under control. I had adaptations to my car, and I'd trained my left hand to pick up some slack. I'd learnt to recognise my physical stress reactions as artefacts of the attack and not necessarily as evidence of present danger. I wasn't 'back to normal' but I was good enough. I pressed the bell again, with my impaired right hand, just because I could. I kept track of such little normalities throughout each day and stacked them around me like sandbags against a flood of self-recrimination. *Points for me*, I thought, and even smiled.

From inside the formerly silent house, a baby wailed.

Dan answered, wearing an apron around his waist and a little towel on his shoulder. He raised his finger to his lips as the baby continued to cry in the background.

I shrugged to mean 'sorry about the bell.'

The wailing came nearer, in a bouncing, hiccuping sort of journey. Chloe appeared in the doorway. There must have been a baby on her somewhere, but it was hard to find among the layers of ruffles hanging off her pale pink dressing gown. I'd never seen Chloe wear pink of any shade.

'It was a gift from my mother,' she explained, a tinge of defensiveness in her voice. 'It's convenient for breastfeeding.'

The baby, too, was dressed in pale pink, presumably another grandmotherly gift. She'd gone quiet but wriggly, squirming and yawning.

'Do you want to hold her?' Dan offered.

I waited for Chloe to nod, then reached out towards the frilly nest on her chest.

Chloe hesitated, for only a moment, her glance falling on my compromised right hand before offering the baby up. I slipped my palms under the little one's shoulders; Chloe's gown gaped to reveal a complicated beige nursing bra and black leggings. No matter. We've both seen each other at our worst.

My still-functional thumb and the palm of my hand made a secure V. My good left hand tucked the baby into my chest.

'Name?' I asked, automatically bouncing. There was less weight than I'd expected. My own daughter was fifteen; I'd forgotten how little and how light they start.

Dan sighed. 'Not yet.'

'He wants to call her Robelia,' Chloe said, plonking herself down on the clear space at the end of the sofa. The rest of it was piled with pillows and magazines.

'I don't. She's joking.'

'Robessa.'

'Chloe . . .'

'After his father, Robert.'

'No, I want to call her Robin.'

'That's a boy's name.'

'It's unisex.'

'Christopher Robin,' Chloe said. A Pooh-bear on the floor at her feet emphasised her point.

Dan flung his hands in the air. 'This is where we are.'

'What do you want to call her?' I asked Chloe, decanting the now-fussy baby back into her arms.

Chloe arranged cushions under her elbow and around the unnamed baby to make a complex sort of fort and got a breast out. Somehow the baby found it among the ruffles. 'I don't know.'

Chloe usually hates not knowing something; that's what makes her a good detective. But she said this contentedly. She didn't seem to mind.

I looked around, to give her privacy. The living room and dining room were piled with boxed plastic toys, the wadded-up wrapping paper in which the toys had arrived, still-packed moving boxes, and unwashed coffee cups. Only Dan's slanted drafting table was pristine, but empty. He's an architect. He was taking some time off.

Chloe was also taking time. She'd had to leave work earlier than she'd planned, after a physical fight with a suspect. She'd had to go on bed rest. She must have hated it.

That was months ago. This was the first time since that I'd visited.

'Dan, could you please get me a cup of tea?' I asked. He

tactfully left the room. I knew he could still hear us, but that was all right. There was at least the illusion of respect and privacy.

I sat on the edge of a soft chair that was otherwise occupied by a stack of neatly folded baby clothes, tags still on. 'I'm glad you're all right.'

'You can move those,' she offered, meaning the clothes.

I didn't care if I had the whole chair or not, but I moved them to accept her kindness. I sat back.

'I'm glad that you're all right,' I said again.

She nodded.

I waited.

'How's Dora?' she asked.

'How do you think?'

Dora's my daughter. Chloe had let her be arrested. Dora had then been cleared but she'll never forget it. I'd ridden with her in the back of the police car. It had felt inevitable and frightening and like the end of the world.

'I'm going back to work,' I announced. This was what I'd come for. I had something to prove.

Chloe's eyebrows rose. 'Really?'

I deserved that. The last time we worked together, she'd seen me utterly fall apart. But I was past that now.

'Back to Major Investigations?' she asked.

I shook my head. Chloe's place in Major Investigations was being held for her, as is proper. Mine had already been filled.

'Cold case.'

Again, 'Really?'

'Yes, really,' I snapped. The dedicated 'Review Team' was new, since Cambridgeshire County police had combined with Bedfordshire and Hertfordshire. We look at cold cases, current-but-stalled cases, and cases with 'bad outcomes' such as domestic violence that has escalated to death. The brief fad of calling forensic investigators 'CSIs' has mercifully been overturned, but we in the Review Team emulate a different TV show: as in *New Tricks*, we're all technically retired officers, partly paid by our pensions. I'm the youngest in the group, retired by injury not age. As Chloe knew full well. *If she thinks me ridiculous, or unfit, or undeserving of work, or perfectly deserving of an old man's job . . .*

'Fine,' Chloe said, wide-eyed, as if it were *my* tone that was unreasonable. She moved the baby over to the other side. The first breast, still exposed, glistened. 'I'm sorry,' she said, tugging the ruffles around to cover everything except the baby's downy blond head.

'For what?' I demanded. I needed her to say it straight out and not pretend that we were talking about her tits. I don't give a fuck about modesty.

'I did the job right, Morris, but I'm sorry it hurt Dora. And I'm sorry that that's the best I can give you. If you want me to fall on my sword, well, I can't.'

'And I'm glad that you're all right and I'm glad your baby's alive but I'm not sorry that I didn't visit you. I couldn't have looked at you. I would have been sick with anger for what you were part of, what you did to my family. I thought you might understand that now.' The baby was between us, forcing us to keep our volume at a civil level.

'I do understand it. I would hate you for it too. You're allowed to hate me, Morris. No one's stopping you. I won't try.'

31

The baby must not have been hungry, just tired and in need of comfort. After that brief suckle, she was suddenly finished and asleep, her head lolling over Chloe's arm. Dora used to sleep like that, utterly loose, utterly at rest. She has insomnia now.

Life is long. That phrase had been bubbling up over and over again in recent weeks. Life is long and there's a lot in it. I do hate Chloe for having let that investigation go so far in the direction that it did. I hate her more than Spencer, the detective sergeant who did the arresting, because Chloe knows me. She knows Dora. She should have stopped it at any cost, for me.

And all of the reasons that I thought she should have done that for me, all of the reasons that I hated her, are the same reasons that I didn't only hate her. We'd worked together for years, and she was the best of my partners. I hated her, but I also trusted her. The past few months, I'd missed her. Her baby could have died. She could have died.

'I'm glad you're all right,' I said, again. I meant it.

Dan brought in a tray. I cleared the coffee table of board books, a box of wet wipes, and a plate of flaky croissant crumbs. I took a cup in my good left hand.

'When do you start?' Chloe asked me.

'This week. I'm reviving a case.'

'Anyone I know?'

'Before your time.' I'm ten years older. 'Before mine too. Annalise Wood.'

Chloe laughed too close to her teacup, making it slosh. 'That old chestnut? Who are you going after next, Jack the Ripper?'

'Old Jack didn't kill in Cambs, Beds, or Herts. And his case hasn't had new evidence pop up.'

Chloe sat up straighter, jostling the baby, who curled in the other direction but didn't wake. 'New evidence? From . . . when was it? '78?'

'She went missing in 1976. Body found in 1992.'

'What's come up?'

I hesitated. I wasn't supposed to tell anyone; the press would be ready to run with anything about Annalise if the new information leaked. But this was Chloe.

'Well?' she pressed.

I think I'd come knowing I would tell her. In my self-indulgent imagination, I did it to impress. Getting to close a famous case was a pretty good start to my return to work. But what I wanted when actually sitting in front of her, baby snores and her ridiculous ruffles and my fucked-up hand between us, was different. You can't impress someone who knows you, really knows you. You can only share.

I smiled conspiratorially, and lowered my voice. 'DNA match.'

Her gasp was gratifying.

'Wait . . . didn't they try DNA testing years ago?'

I nodded. 'They did. It worked; they got a result. But there was no match to it in the national database. Not then.'

A different voice, sceptical instead of excited: 'I thought the body was too far gone for that.'

I'd forgotten that Dan was there. He was absently stacking plastic rings on a tall cone, one of those toddler fine-motor-skills games that could, at a pinch, double as an executive stress toy.

33

'The sample didn't come from inside her. It came from the inside of her skirt.'

Dan's hands were hypnotic. The purple went on top of the blue; the red went on top of the purple.

'Look, Chloe, the baby's asleep. Do you want to come along?' I said, without having planned to.

Her face twitched in surprise. 'Come along where?'

'To interview the bastard. You wouldn't be official. It wouldn't be paid,' I added hastily.

She and Dan caught eyes. 'I haven't pumped,' she said.

'There's some formula in that box your sister sent,' Dan suggested.

'I haven't showered in three days,' she noticed, in a tone of wonderment, as if this were the first she'd realised the fact.

'You showered last night,' Dan reminded her. 'It was two in the morning.'

'Did I?'

I remember those days. Everything a blur. 'You don't have to . . .' I said, to take the pressure off.

Chloe got up and flounced out, trailing a wake of incongruous lace.

'She hasn't been out except to go to the pharmacy and Sainsbury's,' Dan explained.

I nodded, plopping a yellow ring onto an orange one. We were almost at the top. 'Working on anything new?' I asked him.

'I'm joining a firm. It'll be more consistent. I'm set to start when the baby's six months old. Chloe will go back to Major Investigations then, and the baby – she'd better have a name by then – has a place with a childminder at the end of the road. We had to register her as "Baby Matthews", can you believe that? I'm not even insisting that she be called Robin. I'd like it, but I'll take anything. Chloe won't budge.'

I wasn't sure what was going on with that, but I remember having a hard time choosing a name. I didn't want to accidentally call my daughter after someone I'd arrested, or someone who'd been a victim in any case of mine, or a traumatised relative or witness. You work this job long enough, that's harder than you'd think. I'd vetoed my wife's first choice of William when we didn't yet know if we were having a boy or a girl, because of Will Teague, a Peterborough murderer of prostitutes. It hadn't been my case personally, but it was in Cambridgeshire while I was a young cop and it had been huge. Some names just get ruined.

Chloe reappeared, transformed. Her hair was brushed; she was dressed in a suit. She was no longer wearing pink, but the colour was in her cheeks.

'I hope it is him. Wouldn't that be something? We'd solve Annalise Wood,' she said once we were in my car, with doors closed, belts clicked. She was giddy enough that she looked like a kid herself. It didn't feel like preparing to interview a suspect; we might as well have been going to Legoland. I started the car.

'DNA makes it almost too easy,' she joked, as if her earlier years as a detective had involved samples of mastodon wool and analysing cave paintings.

'You've always had DNA,' I pointed out. It makes me either experienced or old that I remember, just barely, when tests for blood type were high-tech. 'It hasn't put us out of a job yet. I'm sure there'll be something left for us to do.'

I joined the motorway towards St Albans, heading to Lilling.

* * *

35

The man's name was Charlie, which is a name it's easy to say dismissively. It's a nickname that's easy to use to push someone around.

His parents answered the door. They were both upright and healthy-seeming, which meant Charlie was living at home at age fifty-two because of his own lack of resources, not for their sake. He'd grown up here, at the edge of Lilling, and had been in the school year below Annalise.

'Charlie home?' I asked.

His mother looked worried. 'No . . .' she said cautiously. Her husband stood behind her, hands pressing down on her shoulders.

'Are you police?' he asked.

I smiled that they'd recognised it in me. I waved my Review Team ID, which is technically not a warrant card, but looks near enough and gives me most of the same powers. 'Are you expecting police?'

Chloe looked pointedly at the empty place where a car would park in front of their terraced house. 'Is Charlie out?'

'He's at work,' the father allowed, seemingly ignoring the inference but clearing his throat awkwardly. The reason Charlie's DNA was in the system was for persistent kerb-crawling, that is, soliciting street prostitutes. He'd been cautioned, then fined. The last incident, combined with a stupid traffic violation, had seen his driving privileges banned for six months. Less than six months ago.

Just as his mother started to stammer excuses, a modest blue sedan, about ten years old, pulled into the parking space next to their small, scraggly lawn. The vaguely muffled narration of a rugby match emanated from the radio within. It must have been a tense moment. The driver leant over the steering wheel, and left the car idling. As a crowd cheered in the background and commentators crowed, Chloe rapped on the driver's-side window and pressed her warrant card up against the glass.

Charlie flinched, wagged his head from side to side looking for escape, and could have shot the car into reverse if he'd wanted a chase.

His quick surrender instead, and his so-fast-as-to-be-reflexive explanation of 'only to work and back', didn't strike me as coming from someone with a guilty conscience over rape and murder, even from a long time ago. Nevertheless, we had his DNA from the corpse.

'C'mon, Charlie,' I said. 'We're going to have a chat.'

As giddy as we were over getting to bring in the murderer of Annalise Wood – well, a significant suspect in the murder of Annalise Wood – there were sobering obligations attached. Our every move would be subject to legal scrutiny. The media would jump as soon as they were signalled. Catching him driving was a gift; we let him think that was why we'd come.

I told him, 'We just need to have a conversation. We can talk here if you like . . .' while sliding my eyes towards his parents. I couldn't, in my new role, personally arrest him, but I could make him want to come away with us to talk.

He got into my car sheepishly and, I think, even blushing.

The nearby police station was expecting us with a duty solicitor waiting in an interview room. I let them wait a little longer and took the long way, through Lilling proper and past Annalise's old house. I drove slowly.

Estate agents cite Lilling centre's 'charm' and 'history' to justify its house prices. Back in the 1970s, it would have been just another village full of Tudor leftovers, inconvenient to any major city. Now, with longer commutes normalised, house prices have leapt. Those who can afford it get to live a few centuries in the past and pay for it with income from jobs in London and Cambridge.

Annalise's former home, now managed by a rental company, was likely to have been upgraded inside, but the historic outside – all plaster and beams, as though a corner of Stratford-upon-Avon had been chipped off and dropped here – must look much as it did then. Chloe swivelled round to watch Charlie seeing the house.

He didn't oblige. The rear-view mirror showed him head down.

In minutes we were through and out. Away from the centre, simpler homes, still with a tinge of the sixties and seventies about them, lined the road, giving way to fields and a railway track roughly parallel to this section of road. Annalise's body had been found buried along that stretch of railroad. Not here, not this close, and not visible from the car, but along this route.

Charlie was looking out the other side.

Outside it was autumn, but in 1976 Annalise had gone missing from a legendarily hot summer. It was June when she disappeared, still term time, with classrooms in her Bishop's Stortford secondary school (which Lilling's teens still attend) boxing the temperature in. That heatwave is one of my earliest memories. The air had been still and heavy and damp. Opening windows had done nothing; there had been no breeze to catch.

Annalise had left school on her bicycle. She would have been sweating. If she'd made it home she likely would have showered and changed, but she was eventually found still wearing her school uniform.

'I feel sick,' Charlie blurted from the backseat.

'You'll be fine,' Chloe dismissed him, without turning around, deliberately declining the invitation to be motherly.

'I think I'm going to . . .' And he did, all over the seat beside him.

I focussed on the driving, breathing through my mouth to avoid the sour smell. Chloe swore and turned around. 'Keep your eyes on the road,' she admonished him, presumably to keep his travel sickness from repeating itself, but sounding as though she were telling him off for staring impertinently.

Shit. This was going to delay his processing. He'd have to be seen-to by a doctor before we got to question him.

At the station, while Charlie was examined and hydrated and asked to choose standard, halal, or kosher fare should he be in long enough for a meal, Chloe and I cleaned the car. A young Sergeant McMartin showed us where to park within reach of a spigot and brought us a bucket and sponge.

'Shame to see Charlie in here again,' he commented, leaning over us, his hand on the car roof.

Although there was no room for him to help, and certainly no obligation, I didn't appreciate him towering over me while I was on my knees scooping sick. Chloe was inside the car, in the clean spot where Charlie had been, wiping after me. 'You see him often?' she asked.

'Not here. Out there. Kerb-crawling, yeah? We cautioned him. We even fined him. We thought a night in would do the trick, but I s'pose not. Where'd you catch him?'

'He was driving,' I said. 'Unlicensed.'

Chloe backed out of the vehicle and asked Sergeant McMartin face-to-face over the roof, 'You've been the one to pick him up? When he's been soliciting?'

'Every time. Poor sod.'

'What's his type?'

'Type? The women? Not you, if you're interested.'

Chloe waited out his trickle of a laugh.

'Just a joke. Never mind. He likes long hair, is all.' Chloe's hair is short. 'Dark hair, but always white women, I think. Never Asian. That's not really narrow enough to count as a "type", is it?'

I stood and brushed off my knees. 'Any of those women ever come to harm?'

McMartin lifted his chin as his glance slid back and forth between us. 'Not that's been noticed . . .'

'Would you check for me, please?' I emptied the bucket out over a narrow bed of gravel and weeds alongside the wall.

'Not Charlie. He's pathetic, not . . . not bad.'

'We'll be in the interview room,' Chloe said, rolling down her sleeves and pulling her jacket back on.

McMartin shrugged, and accepted the bucket of soiled towels that I handed over. 'Shit, Charlie,' he said, swinging the bucket, back and forth, back and forth, as he led us in through the back door of the station.

Charlie, who inspired protectiveness in the sergeant who regularly arrested him; who had blushed and stammered and seemed sure he'd been brought in for unlicensed driving; who had seemed unaffected by Annalise's house: this Charlie, who, on the other hand, had also vomited out

40

of nowhere, as if perhaps he knew deep down that this was bigger than he was letting himself consciously think it was, waited for us meekly.

The interview room had a built-in recording system and a panic button in case of violence, but not nearly enough room for two detectives, a suspect, and a solicitor. At least we didn't need to squeeze in a translator.

Charlie and I eyed one another across the table, which was, of necessity, hardly big enough for the paperwork. Chloe, in a chair just off the table corner, held most of it on her lap. The solicitor sat just behind Charlie's shoulder.

I pressed record and recited all of our names and the date. As soon as I finished a repeat of the caution, Charlie said, 'I had to get to work. I had to. If I didn't work and didn't pay my bills, you'd be arresting me for that.' He folded his arms and leant back.

Chloe spoke as if idly, while flipping through a file: 'You do like paying for things, don't you, Charlie. You pay for things that most men can get for free.' She looked up, and smiled.

The solicitor intervened: 'Paying for sex is not a recordable offence.' *Trawling for it by car is, but never mind*, I thought. 'As for driving while banned, my client will accept the fine, and appeal through the proper channels to have his driving privileges restored.'

Charlie nodded along, sweating.

I nodded too, as if our rivers were all flowing in the same direction. 'Tell me about them, Charlie. The ones you choose. Emma the last time, wasn't it? And Tracy?' This had been in the file, the regulars he'd been caught chatting up from his car window.

41

'I don't know their names,' he answered, at the same time that his solicitor told him not to say anything.

'But you'd know their pictures, wouldn't you?' Chloe asked brightly. 'I have one here, I'm sure of it.' She made a show of shuffling papers, then slid a photograph across the table.

Long dark hair, dark eyes, pale skin, a smile. Surrounded by friends, but she was the only one looking at the camera. That orangey tone of seventies film made the mood of it feel dreamy and faraway.

Charlie sucked in a breath. The solicitor asked what exactly was going on. I pushed back in my chair; maybe I sensed what was coming.

Charlie turned his head and was sick in his solicitor's lap. The solicitor jumped up and back, skidding his chair up against the wall. Chloe put her head out the door to call for the doctor and a cleaner.

I leant forward over the table, over the photo of Annalise, towards Charlie's sour, panting breath. 'She's who you like, isn't she, Charlie?'

He shook his head. He wiped his mouth.

'Charlie?' I said again, but the doctor put his hand on my shoulder.

I left the solicitor in the men's room, wiping his trousers with wet paper towels. Chloe had gone into the ladies' room with a complicated-looking breast pump and a determined expression. I was in an interview room identical to the first, waiting, eating a chocolate granola bar from the jail kitchen.

We were all attending to our bodies. That's at least half of

42

life. There are psychological needs too, and swaying emotions, but bodies are the relentless foundation of most actions.

It had been assumed from her disappearance that Annalise's murder was a sex crime. Maybe he hadn't even meant to kill her, or had only had to in order to keep her quiet about the rape, if there was a rape. There's more than one way to get semen inside a girl's skirt; maybe that part was consensual, or after death. At any rate, Charlie had been there, and he knew something, something he'd never told police, even when Annalise was just a missing person and there was supposedly a chance of getting her back. That's something to answer for all on its own.

I said 'come in' to the knock on the door. It was Sergeant McMartin. 'The women that we know Charlie's been with, they're fine. They're drug addicts, but they're accounted for.'

I nodded and thanked him. He left me alone again.

If Charlie had deliberately killed Annalise, I'd expect his violence to have seeped out through other aspects of his life. But this wasn't a man who lashed out when cornered; he made himself sick with fear. He was more the type to piss himself than to attack.

Or if Annalise's death had been a covered-up accident, I'd expect more dramatic remorse and control from her killer. Religion, maybe, or obsessive-compulsive mannerisms, not this casual, emotional Charlie.

Chloe opened the door without knocking. 'Never breastfeed,' was all she said, darkly, as she took her same place in the chair just behind me.

'I'll bear that in mind,' I agreed.

Then the solicitor and Charlie came in, and we were all

43

as we had been. I wonder if that's what it's like to feel guilty about something. You keep trying to leave the room, but every next room is exactly the same.

'Where did it happen, Charlie?' I asked.

'Where did what happen?'

'Your DNA has been matched. We know you had sex with Annalise Wood. Was she your girlfriend?'

He looked around the room, as if to share his wonderment with an agreeing crowd. 'Girlfriend? No. We were friends. Why do you think that we . . . ?'

Chloe backed me up. 'We know you did, Charlie. You don't need to hide it. You were a lucky man. Well, boy. It was a long time ago.'

He shook his head. 'No. I never had sex with her. I would have, but I never did because she didn't think about me that way.'

'Maybe not to start,' I offered, 'but women can be persuaded. Sometimes they don't know what they want until you show them.'

'No. That's not true. You're saying that to make me agree with it, but I know that's not right.'

The solicitor interrupted. 'He has denied having sex with her. Are we really talking about a forty-year-old crime?'

'His semen,' Chloe explained, pulling out a lab report to back her up, 'was on the inside of a dead teenager's skirt. You know, the wet spot.' She handed it over to the solicitor.

'That's impossible,' Charlie said.

The solicitor shook his head and gestured for Charlie to stop speaking while he looked over the report.

Chloe prodded, 'Are you saying that's not your DNA? Our lab thinks it is.'

'I know it is,' he said, going pale.

'Do you need to get to a toilet?' I asked quickly. But he looked shocked, not sick.

'So it's your semen,' Chloe summarised. 'But you didn't have sex with her. Is that right? Is this a semantic thing? Maybe you didn't get it all the way in so you think it doesn't count?'

'I never touched Annalise. Never. Not with my hands, not with my body. We never kissed, we never fucked, and we never did anything in between.'

'You're saying you fucked her skirt, then?' Chloe laughed at the end, a short, direct 'ha!'

Charlie closed his eyes. He whispered something to his solicitor. The solicitor whispered back. This is precisely where our caution is superior to the American 'Miranda warning'. In America, the right to silence is absolute. In this country, silence can be judged as evidence of guilt. That difference is motivating.

'I was in her bedroom. I jerked off into one of her skirts.'

I laughed like Chloe. Well, that was quick thinking, if nothing else. Now to ask for details and get him to trip over himself. 'What was the point of that, Charlie? Were you hoping she'd not notice and then wear it? Was that exciting?'

'Are you fucking crazy? She was dead. She was never going to wear anything again.'

We all froze for a moment, even the solicitor, who was the first to regain enough composure to ask, 'When was this, Charlie?'

'1979. Annalise's parents kept her room like a shrine. Everything was still there: her schoolbooks, her make-up, her clothes. Everything dusted and kept nice. Mrs Wood kept in touch with all of us, all of Annalise's friends. She'd do these teas and things. I was there one time with Cathy and Andrew and Liam and Pru. I went upstairs to the loo and I peeked in her room. It was . . . See, we'd all got older. And her room hadn't. In that room, she was still studying for O-levels, while Pru and Liam and I had jobs, and Cathy and Andrew were home from university. We'd grown up and Annalise was still sixteen. Her clothes were all school uniforms that none of us wore any more. It was . . . it was really fucking heartbreaking, if you must know. I was really fucking sad and I really fucking missed her. And I just . . . So I did it and then I went back downstairs.' He rapped the table with a closed fist. The solicitor tapped his shoulder and he drew his hands back into his lap.

'Are you saying,' I recited for clarity, 'that three years after her disappearance, or more, a hidden Annalise Wood, or her corpse, was dressed in a skirt taken from her wardrobe and buried in it. Is that what you're saying? You may wish to consult with your solicitor about whether that's the lie you want to stick with.'

'It's not a lie!' he shouted, which was the angriest we'd seen him get. Even in that anger, though, he didn't seem on the offensive. Instead, he was bent forward, pleading.

'Charlie,' I said, leaning forward myself. 'I have to put this together. Do you see my trouble? I have to put this together for a courtroom and a jury to understand. They'll understand, Charlie,' I lied, 'if you had sex before she disappeared, or if you snuck into her room and messed on her skirt while she slept nearby. That will make sense, Charlie. This, though? This isn't good enough.'

He didn't look like a liar. His posture was, for the first time today, open and unburdened. He held out his hands, then let them drop. 'I don't know how that skirt got on her, her, her *body* . . . I . . . It was in her wardrobe in January 1979.' He flung up his hands again. He seemed as frustrated as I felt.

Chloe took over. 'Let's say we take that, Charlie, we accept it. We still have a story. You took that skirt back with you, to where you kept her, dead or alive. You pulled it up over her legs, fastened the little snaps and zipper. You're still in the story, Charlie. Let's say we accept that you buried her three years later, fine; you can still be the one who took her too.'

Charlie covered his face, and his shoulders shuddered.

'No crying, Charlie boy,' Chloe admonished him. 'It's too late for that.'

He uncovered his face, which was wet, yes, but also smiling with a big, open mouth. 'You don't even fucking know. Can you believe this?' he asked the solicitor.

'I find it's all too believable,' I said. 'I think a jury is likely to think so too.'

'You don't even know!' he shouted, and stood up, but the solicitor tugged his sleeve and brought him back to his seat before I could hit the panic button.

'What don't I know, Charlie? Tell me. I want to know everything.'

'*Comment ça va?*' he asked in an execrable accent. '*Comment allez-vous?*'

'Interview suspended,' I said into the microphone, but before I hit the stop button Charlie grabbed my hand. Chloe stood. The solicitor put his hand on Charlie's elbow.

'That's all I remember from my six months in France,' Charlie said. 'January to July 1976. It was an exchange programme through our school. You can ask anyone. I was in the Alps when Annalise went missing. My parents told me on our weekly call home. Those calls were the only time I was ever allowed to speak English. I had to find a way to tell my host family what had happened in French. That's not exactly the vocabulary we'd been given, you know? I told them that my *amie* was *perdue*. I told them that she was *absente*. They thought that she was my girlfriend and that we'd broken up. I finally had to say that she was *morte*, just to make them understand. We didn't know yet that she was dead, but it felt like she was. It felt like she was going to be. It was one of the worst times of my life. I didn't have anything to do with what happened to her, not when she disappeared, not when she died, not when she was buried, not when she was found.'

'Interview concluded,' I repeated. He didn't object this time. I pressed the button.

'Do you think he really was in France?' Chloe asked from the passenger seat. We were on our way home in my car, which still smelled of soap and sick.

'We'll have to check but, yes, I think he was really in France.'

'He could have done it before he left. The skirt thing.'

'He could have, but that would have been almost six months before. Surely Annalise or her parents would have washed it between when he left for France and when she disappeared.'

'France is close. Being there doesn't mean he couldn't have come back. Schools do day trips all the time.'

'We'll check. His host parents may still be alive, and will have had same-age children as Charlie. Someone will be able to tell us if he buggered off at any point.'

'But you don't think he did.'

'Do you?'

'No.' Chloe looked out the window, dragging her gaze along a wide flint wall, jagged and sharp, like magnified sandpaper. 'If he's telling the truth about the skirt . . .'

'. . . then she was buried by someone who wanted her to look like she'd been killed the day she disappeared. In her school uniform.'

'Which in turn means that she probably hadn't been killed that day, and that she was wearing something different by the time she died, or maybe the same thing still, just . . . tattered, perhaps.'

'And maybe she wasn't raped. Maybe there was no sex at all.' Jesus, was the skirt all there was to that? I didn't even know if there was flesh left when they dug her up . . .

'We can hope,' said Chloe, meaning we can hope that there was no rape. That would be good for Annalise, who would have suffered less on her way to death, but bad for finding her killer. Without semen, there were not a lot of options for DNA after all these years.

'Are you free tomorrow?' I asked.

'Why, are you sending me to France?' she joked, smirking.

'How about the local charity shop? We need to know what happened to the clothes from Annalise's wardrobe. The parents are dead, but some of those friends Charlie mentioned . . .'

'Pru, Liam, Cathy, and Andrew,' Chloe recited. Cathy

49

was the most important; Charlie had told us he'd been married to her for a few years a couple of decades ago. 'You want to meet here?' she suggested.

I shook my head. 'I'm going to talk to someone in Cambridge.' We needed to know more about the body.

She was already typing into her phone, presumably tracking down the old friends.

'Don't you go and get carsick now. I can't take it again.'

She laughed, and kept pressing buttons. 'Who's in Cambridge?'

I just smiled.

'Someone I know?'

Someone we both knew. He retired from forensics and got work as a porter – those combination receptionist/security/administrative gatekeepers at the colleges. A fair few ex-police end up in those jobs as a quieter retirement. 'Jimmy,' I said.

Chloe laughed. 'I'll trade you Lilling for Trinity.'

That's right; he's at Trinity, the largest, wealthiest college. 'I once dated a girl at Trinity.' I smiled.

'Good memories?'

I shrugged. 'She was fine. The dates were fine. Being young, though . . .' That had been superb. I'd had no idea at the time how special it was. Being twenty was a good memory.

'I was an idiot when I was an undergraduate. Not sure I like remembering that.'

'But you didn't know that you were an idiot. You thought you were brilliant, didn't you?' That's the sum of age twenty: cockiness.

'You still think you're brilliant, even when you're not,'

she averred, lightly, but we both knew that wasn't true. The past year had rattled me badly.

But I played along: 'I'm not cocky, just always right.'

'Me too,' Chloe agreed. 'What are the odds that it's two perfect cops who end up working together?'

It was better this way, better than apologising, or arguing, or explaining. We'd been at odds a lot over this past year, Chloe and I, but maybe our differences are why I trust her: if I can get her to agree with me, or she can get me to agree with her, well, then we must be on the right track.

We'd left Charlie in for the night, based on his driving violation, to give us a chance to look into his French alibi. If he had indeed been away on a foreign exchange when he said he was, we'd have to let him go, even while we double-checked the details.

I didn't think that Charlie would advertise that we'd questioned him about Annalise. The details would only embarrass him. All that sergeant knew was that we were interested in a potential pattern involving white girls with long, dark hair. The solicitor knew, but he wouldn't breach confidentiality.

Thank God we hadn't done this more publicly. Thank God there had been no press conference, no fanfare. The fact was, we didn't have Annalise's killer.

I tamped down the familiar feeling of a panic attack stirring. *Breathe, Morris.*

We had a skirt that proved that her burial and possibly her death had taken place years after her disappearance. We had leads to follow. It was less than I'd thought we'd had this morning, but more than we'd had yesterday.

'I've got one,' Chloe announced. 'Prudence Greene. Ah,

and Liam Taylor or Liam Henley.' She scrolled, and pressed the screen, and squinted at tiny text.

We drove around a bend to an abrupt view of open fields and it felt very seaside all of a sudden, very rented-convertible-with-the-top-down. I felt excited. We didn't have the answers yet, but we had work to do. That was more than I'd had a month before. It was a salt-in-the-air, sand-in-the-car feeling, here on this road deep in landlocked Hertfordshire at the chilly start of autumn.

'You mind if I put music on?' I asked Chloe, who was still bent over her phone.

'It's your car.'

I pushed the volume up. I rolled my window down. I drove.

'Did Gwen work when Dora was born?' Chloe asked, when we were almost back to her home.

That was not a question I expected. 'No, she didn't. This job . . .' I shouldn't have had to explain it to Chloe. 'She made up for my schedule being unpredictable. And overbooked.'

'Was that hard for her?'

'Probably sometimes . . .'

'But she wanted to? It wasn't just because she thought she should?'

'She did want to. She always had. What are you—'

But Chloe changed the subject back to the investigation. 'Andrew, Cathy, Liam, Pru . . .'

That recitation put me in mind of her nameless child. 'You need to name that baby,' I prodded her as her fairy-tale cottage loomed into view. 'Aster, Daisy, Rose?' I suggested, plucking random names from her lavish garden.

She waved her hand vaguely in the flowers' direction. 'They're not going to last. Dan and I are shit gardeners. But he fell in love with it, with the idea of it, that somehow we'd become the kind of people who can keep up a house like this. Or the kind of people who can afford a gardener. Christ, my tits hurt. Where's that baby?' She got out of the car.

Before I pulled away from the kerb, I wondered if that's what I was doing, if that's what I'd always done: liked the look of something, followed my gut, and just crossed my fingers that I'd live up to it. Isn't that exactly what I was doing now, back at work?

That's bloody everybody, I reminded myself. That's the difference between forty-plus and twenty: we see through ourselves at forty, sure, and we see through everyone else too. Somewhere, the person who killed Annalise Wood had got older too, more aware of his weaknesses, maybe more vulnerable. I was going to find him.

CHAPTER FOUR

Laurie Ambrose

Dad had eventually figured out which Annalise I'd meant, and phoned me back, worried and disapproving that I was asking about a dead girl. He hadn't appreciated it when she had come up in conversation last Christmas either.

It was Helen, my sister, who'd brought her up, specifically the semen sample that back in the nineties had failed to yield a DNA match with any known criminals or match any other open cases. DNA testing had been impressive and almost science fiction back then, but it hadn't been able to do anything without a suspect to match it up to. Dad had walked out then, taking his cup of milky coffee elsewhere. In Mum's younger days, she would have chided Helen for mentioning semen at breakfast. Mum, though, had already started to loosen her social standards. (Helen apparently never had any to begin with.)

I must have been frowning because Helen had chided, 'Oh, don't be so serious, Laurie.'

Mum had then changed the subject to laundry – possibly

making the leap from semen stains to stains in general; it doesn't bear thinking about. But the fact is that Annalise is talked about. That's normal, or at least not abnormal, especially from our little corner of the country.

I had my mini-recorder and headphones in bed. Simon was already asleep. I never thought I would be with a man who smokes. I suppose he never thought he'd choose a woman who snores. Our younger selves would be amazed at how forgiving we'd become in middle age.

Hannah-Claire Finney is the other client who had talked about Annalise months ago, an education officer from the Fitzwilliam Museum. The museum is part of the University, which is why she'd come to me. She looked in her thirties, with a Canadian accent, and her crossed leg had bobbed up and down, up and down, throughout almost the entire session.

I clicked the little triangle representing 'play':

Hannah-Claire Finney (Fitzwilliam Museum), University Counselling Service, recorded and transcribed by Dr Laurie Ambrose

Both of my mothers are dead.

I don't mean two mothers as a lesbian thing. They weren't together. They were each my mother, separately. Depends who you would ask, and when.

[Laughs.]

Can I have a glass of water? Please?

[Drinks.]

Thank you. Sorry. You know what? I could even say I have three dead mothers, if you looked at it a certain way. Three! How many people get to say that? Or do you hear that a lot? Maybe I'm terribly, terribly normal. Boring, even. How amazing that would be.

Sorry. I know I have to explain. That's the point, isn't it? Explaining? And the act of explaining it is going to make everything fall into place, even without you making sense of it for me. Right? That's what I've been led to expect.

[Clears throat.]

I was raised by my grandparents. I always thought they were my grandparents. Their daughter, my mother, had died. It was a drug overdose. (They didn't tell me that, but I found it out myself later.)

They moved us all to Canada, for a 'fresh start'. Our extended family rarely visited us, and we never went back to England. Knowing what I know now, I suspect that Mum and Dad were protecting their hold on me.

See, their daughter wasn't actually my mother. They just said that she was, but really I had been adopted by them in their grief when she died. And that girl who'd really given birth to me, who like their daughter had been just a teenager, had, like their daughter, then also died, a year after I was born. She was murdered. I think my parents – June and Oscar, the ones who adopted me and said I was their daughter's child – had been worried about my biological grandparents then wanting me back. Those grandparents had been glad to see me go when I was the ruin of their daughter's chances at university, but when she was so suddenly dead, and she'd been their only child, well . . . They might have wanted me then, mightn't they?

All four grandparents are dead now, from natural causes. I'm past forty years old. Lots of people have dead grandparents at my age. June, who raised me, died of breast cancer and Oscar died of a different cancer the next year. It was then that a cousin told me about my other grandparents, and my other dead mother. My cousin said that, with June and Oscar dead, she was the only one in the family who knew, and that it wasn't fair to keep it from me in case anything happened to her. She said that I had a 'right to know'.

But there wasn't much to it besides just knowing. There was no one to reach out to. The dead girl's parents were already dead themselves by then. They had died together on a ferry crossing the Baltic Sea. You probably heard about it in the news; fourteen people died. More than two hundred survived, which is good. I try to think about the survivors sometimes. When I find myself imagining my grandparents in the cold water, struggling, maybe one of them watching the other die first, I try to make myself switch: I think instead about the people who were rescued, and then hugged their families at the dock, or hospital, or wherever they were taken. Sometimes my imagination has helicopters and uniforms in it. Sometimes whole families, with babes in arms and wagging dogs, march down to the water's edge and pull their loved ones out themselves. I know that's not how it happened, but it captures the spirit of it, I think. It's like when things are arranged in a painting not to represent what would have been caught if there had been a camera there, but to create a single, technically false, moment, that represents the truth of a busy event over time. Like putting all of the disciples in *The Last Supper* on one side of a long table. They do that in the theatre too, so that the audience can see everyone. It's a necessary falsehood to make truth more accessible. That's different from a lie. A lie has malice, or at least selfishness, behind it. Its purpose is to deceive. This kind of falsehood is generous. It wants to reveal, not hide. Besides, it's aimed at no one but myself in my own head.

I've always been optimistic. I used to imagine my mother – June and Oscar's daughter, because, remember, for most of my life that was all that I knew – as a popular, happy girl trying something naughty for the first time. It was a bad batch or lot or whatever you'd call it, and her friends did everything they could to help her. That's what I assume happened. Why would I consider alternative scenarios? That's a good one. I don't need more.

Of course I'd still love her if things were really different from that. If she was an addict or even a dealer, if she stole the drugs or sold them to kids younger than her. I'd still love her. Even knowing she wasn't really my mother. She . . . she's my sister, I suppose. Her parents adopted me, so she's my sister, even if we never knew each other. It's part of loving someone that you put the best spin you can on the information you have. That's love.

I wish I didn't know so much about my birth mother. There are even books about her, though I've never read one. I read some magazine articles, and things online. I look like her. When I first saw her picture, I felt sick. I cut my long hair short with paper scissors that night, which wasn't easy. I hacked my hair into a ragged bob and got my hairdresser to fix it later. I'm not ashamed to look like her, but it was scary. That school photo of her, looking right at the camera, with headlines underneath it like 'Remains Discovered' and 'Sex Crimes of the Seventies'.

I've never looked for my father. My parents – June and Oscar – they always said that he didn't matter. All he did was fuck her, right? It's not like Jenny – that's June and Oscar's daughter – or Annalise even had steady boyfriends, at least to public knowledge. It's not like they were halves of an acknowledged couple. They were just themselves, and, apparently, slept with someone, and had a baby – well, Annalise did. Jenny was never pregnant, I don't think, though it's hard for me to undo years of assuming she'd been pregnant with me. The person my mother spent an hour with nine months before I was born doesn't seem particularly important.

I do want children, but it's probably too late to do it the usual way. I could get pregnant, I suppose. I haven't got my hot flushes and freedom from the tampon industry yet. I think I've always pictured myself adopting one day, when I finally feel settled, but that feeling hasn't happened yet. And, yes, I am aware that adoption laws frown on 'older mothers'.

Honestly, honestly, this whole 'someday' thing is probably just my way of avoiding saying out loud that, while I like the idea of raising children, the reality is not actually a priority. There, I've admitted something that I haven't told anyone else before: I'll probably never be a mother. Well done, Doctor. Is this kind of revelation the usual goal?

Fine. I'm here because since the museum was robbed I've been having panic attacks. It's ridiculous. No one was hurt during the robbery. The men have been caught. But the jades haven't been recovered. That's what was stolen: Chinese jades. It's that loss that triggers me. Everything was the same in the gallery, except these empty places where things just weren't any more. Someone's got them, hoarded and hidden. We've since rearranged things so that there aren't empty spaces now, but that's almost worse. The emptiness at least acknowledged that the jades had been there, and existed, and mattered. Now it's as if they've gone on holiday, or are just in the storeroom waiting their turn on rotation. But they're not. They're gone. They're gone and it's as if it doesn't matter that they were ever there . . .

[Cries quietly.]

All right. I see it myself; you don't have to say it. All these deaths are catching up with me. All these parents. June and Oscar, Jenny, Annalise, and her parents who might have wanted to steal me back after she died. All of them are gone. Most of my friends still have both of their parents. I had, what, up to six? And I've lost them all. How careless of me. [Laughs.]

[Cries again.]

It's not that I care more about artefacts than people. You know that isn't true. That would be monstrous. It just seems so much easier to grieve these small things than the big ones. I'm so angry that someone forced their way inside the museum and just took things, they took them. It's like they ripped them away. It makes me . . . Look, I'm shaking. This is what happens at work sometimes. It just overwhelms me, and I have to duck into the disabled toilet for privacy. One time I was in there, quivering, literally quivering, and someone in a wheelchair knocked. He just kept knocking, and when I finally got myself enough under control to get out, he swore at me when he saw that I wasn't limping, I guess, or maybe he would have preferred me to crawl. He asked me if I was done 'pissing and putting my lipstick on'. My colleague Liz heard him talk to me like that, and when she saw my face she assumed I was upset because of him. She said I could have her office to get myself together in.

Sometimes I feel like I can't breathe. I don't actually think I'll stop breathing – I know that would be stupid – but I feel like I might. Annalise was smothered, did you know that? I didn't want to know that, but it was in all of the articles. He pressed so hard down on her face that her nose broke.

Thank you. [Blows nose.] Sorry. See, this is what I'm trying to change. Trying to get control of. I can't change anything by falling apart. The museum was right to replace the jade display, and I'm right to move on in life. I'm right to do it. What's the alternative? What does it accomplish to cry to you and say that Annalise's nose was broken? That she struggled but he wouldn't let her breathe? That she was my mum? She was my mum, and someone hurt her. I can't fix that. I can't do anything with that. I look just like her and that is terrifying. Sometimes I think about scarring my face just to make it my face, not hers. Jesus Christ.

[Breathing.]

I don't really consider doing that. I think about it, but I would never do it. I would never cut myself anywhere.

You're not going to report me for self-harm, are you? 'Suicidal ideation'? I have never hurt myself, and I never will. It's just an abstract thought. You'll note that, won't you? I'm fine. I just need to keep up at work. The feelings catch up with me at unpredictable, odd times. I was leading a school group through the museum's armour room, and the weapons just . . . They were made to hurt people. That's their only purpose. It just hit me, the idea of creating something explicitly to hurt people. I never want to hurt anyone, and no one's ever tried to hurt me. I said that to myself over and over, in my head: I never want to hurt anyone, and no one's ever tried to hurt me. I forgot what I was supposed to say, about the armour and swords and guns in there. I just forgot. I handed out drawing things and one little boy, at least one, drew someone stabbing someone else. I had to sit down.

I prefer guiding through the upstairs galleries. There's one full of Dutch flower paintings, one still life after another, showing off each artist's skill with precision and detail. They're cheery. One little girl miscalled them 'still alives' because, she said, in the paintings the flowers stay alive for ever. You see? And it sounds sweet, but it was actually terrifying to me, the idea of being frozen in one moment, nothing happening ever again. Just for ever being alive but being only that one brief piece of oneself, stuck in that one moment with no new ones coming. That's not really alive, is it? Is it? Jesus, I can make even flowers depressing.

I'm never afraid for myself. I walk home at night, all the way home, for exercise, and no one has ever hassled me. I simply don't see myself at the centre of any of these danger scenarios. Liz, my coworker who let me use her office? Her husband picks her up in front of the museum if she has to leave after dark. She never walks alone at night. She thinks I'm crazy when I do it, and tries to give me a lift, but I won't let her. She gave me that self-defence book *The Gift of Fear*, which was a horrible, horrible thing for her to do. I threw it away. I don't want to be afraid. It's bad enough picturing Annalise like that, and her parents in the water, and my parents in the hospital, and Jenny choking on her own vomit. It's bad enough picturing all of my parents dead; why should I start picturing myself dead? If someone wants to kill me, they'll kill me. I won't hand my life over to the idea in little pieces, afraid to do this or that, giving up this or that. I won't give up any of my life. If someone's going to take it, they'll have to take all of it at once. I'll think about them when they're right in front of me, and not a moment before. They don't get any of me in advance.

Can you explain the goal here? I feel worse than when I arrived, so I don't really see how talking about any of this is supposed to help. I'm supposed to be at work in an hour. I'm not sure I'm going to be able to do that. I should have signed up for meditation or breathing exercises, something practical instead of talk therapy. I need yoga. Or sex. Something to relieve the stress.

I've started seeing someone. His name is Henry. We haven't progressed to that level yet. I'm lonely. I don't know who I'm going to spend Christmas with. It's ages away but I worry about it, I honestly worry about it. His family runs a hotel out of a stately home in Shropshire and I picture us there for the holidays, but I can't ask him yet. We haven't even slept together. I have no right to expectations. But he has all this family, and I feel like I have none, which isn't true. I have cousins, two of them. Sandy and Sadie. Sandy's the one who told me that Annalise was my real mother. She said that was where my name, Hannah, came from, as a secret form of Anna, and that she's been jealous of that all her life. But I've always been jealous that they were sisters. You know what I mean? They have each other, and who do I have?

God, listen to me. I'm alive. What's fair about

that? People die every day. I know all about that. People die, and it hasn't been me yet. Who am I to complain about fair? Life's been pretty generous to me so far. I'm still here and better people aren't.

Loved people die all the time. Needed people die. If I died, no one would be affected, not really. No one's life would change, except, I suppose, someone who needed a job would get mine. Henry might miss me, but we haven't even planned for Christmas. It's not like we've planned 'a future'. I would marry him. Honest to God, I would marry him just to have someone who has to miss me when I die.

Sorry, can I have another tissue? Thanks.

[Laughs.] I always imagined that you marry someone who's your soulmate, your best friend, and you can tell them anything. I can't even tell him that I want to spend Christmas with his family! I don't want to scare him off. He tells me that I'm beautiful. He laughs at my jokes. He asks me about my day. I told him that my parents are dead, but that's all. He doesn't know about my complications. He lives near London, and works all over, so our getting together has been erratic. There hasn't been a chance for him to 'walk me home' and for me to 'invite him up for a drink', or however it's supposed to work. He's in Florida on business this week, and I'm seriously considering phone sex. You know, 'This is what I'd do if you were here with me' sort of thing. But he might find it awkward. That would be embarrassing.

No, this is good. I'm starting to get the point of you saying nothing except a prod here and there, making me just keep going. I said that there's nothing to be done about my losses, but I think there is. I want a family. Not children, a family. I want to get married. Maybe to Henry, maybe someone else. I need to own that. If my interest pushes him away, then he's not the right man. Best to find that out and move on early. I won't do the phone sex, but I will invite him to spend a weekend with me. There's a really nice spa hotel in Bury St Edmunds. I'll suggest it and see what he says. Then I'll know how he feels. Well, how he feels about sleeping with me. Then, after a weekend, I can ask about Christmas. Then, after Christmas, the future. Come New Year's Eve, we could be engaged. My whole life could change for the better in that short a time. And, if not with him, maybe someone else. The world is full of people. I only need one. More than one person together, even just one more than one . . . well, that makes a family.

Thank you, Doctor. I think I'd like to go now. I'll tell you next time what he says about the weekend away. If he says no, you can help me pick up the pieces. [Laughs.]

Hannah-Claire had emailed me a few days after that session, saying that Henry had said 'yes'. She hadn't clarified what the 'yes' had been to, precisely: sex? Christmas? Marriage? But whatever it was had been enough that she'd felt she didn't need to come and see me again. She'd said that she was happy.

I hadn't replied. It's not appropriate to engage with clients outside of sessions. But I was glad that she'd told me.

I removed my headphones and discovered that my

mobile had rung while I was listening. Somehow Simon hadn't stirred; once he decides he's asleep that's it for the night. Blake had finally phoned, apologised. I heard a feminine giggle in the background. I wondered if he was in a group or on a date. Either would be good for him. Standing me up for a friend or girlfriend could be the best thing in the world for him.

It reminded me of Hannah's laugh, the last sound on her recording. I hoped for her. I hoped for Blake, for his sister, Clara, and all of us.

I shivered again.

Pyjamas tomorrow night, I chided myself, setting my computer aside, tucking my bare shoulders in tank-top straps under the duvet.

CHAPTER FIVE

Chloe Frohmann

I'd phoned first, with the baby wailing in the background.
How professional.

It was a receptionist who'd answered. They tend to come
in two types: chatty, and judgemental. This one was chatty.
She asked if the baby needed something. I said, 'Sorry about
that. Crowded office. She has an inattentive mother,' while
bouncing her up and down on my chest in my living room.

The Cathy we were looking for – Annalise's old friend
and Charlie's ex-wife – was still near Lilling, working as a
paralegal for her husband's small law firm. He appeared to
be an upgrade from Charlie: successful, exuding confidence
and good posture in his website photo. His receptionist told
me that Cathy would be in and out today, and that I could
leave a message. I suggested that I could pop in. She – her
name was Rosalie, I was informed though I hadn't asked,
and both of her children are in primary school – offered to
make an appointment. They're twins, by the way, Rosalie's
girls. Six years old. And Cathy doesn't like surprises, so we

settled on one p.m. Cathy might not be in at exactly then, but, if she was, my visit would be officially on the schedule. Rosalie seemed to be comforted by this. I wondered how often Cathy told her off for things that other people did.

As I rang off, the baby thudded her head into the crook of my elbow and suddenly, deeply, slept. I should have been used to her off switch but I marvelled each time. I had to glide into her little bedroom, careful to maintain her stillness as perfectly as I could, and lay her down in her cot. I wriggled out of my leggings into a pair of pre-pregnancy trousers as best I could.

'Morris's investigation?' Dan asked, leaning against the door frame.

I nodded, and held a finger to my lips. I cast about through the clothes heaped on the chair.

Dan pulled open a drawer and handed me a folded jumper. 'I put away the clean clothes,' he said in a not-whisper as we left the room and shut the door behind us.

'Can you please wait until the door is fully closed?' I snapped, still whispering, almost spitting.

'It's really not your problem, since I'm the one who's going to be picking her up when she wakes.' But he said it in a whisper.

'Sorry,' I whispered back, getting away from the bedroom. I changed my T-shirt spattered with baby sick for the warm fleece. 'Thanks,' I added at a normal volume.

'You think this case is going somewhere after all these years?' Dan asked.

'Looks like.'

'Everything all right now? Between you and Morris?' he asked.

'Of course. Everything was done the way it had to be done. He knew that, always.'

Dan shrugged.

'Morris and I have worked together a long time.'

'It was his daughter,' Dan said, doubting there was enough time in the world for Morris to get over it.

I rifled through the sock basket by the front door and defended myself in my mind: *She's not in jail. She's not charged. It was a mistake and it's over.* But I admitted, 'If it had been me doing the arresting, he would never forgive me. Never. But that's all at Spencer's feet.' My new partner, though whether we'll be assigned to work together again when I return is still open.

'Spencer did it with your approval.'

'Without my interference.' The basket was full but had no pairs, literally none at all that I could find. Frustration popped out of my eyes in two perfectly symmetrical tears. Tears happened at the most random times since the birth; not crying, not sadness; just tears.

Dan knelt beside me and magicked two woolly red socks together. He put them in my hands.

'Are you up for this?' he asked, meaning interviewing Cathy.

I answered, meaning that and everything else, every other thing that there is: 'No. But I want to do it more than I'm not ready for it. I want to do it so I'm doing it.'

He helped me put the socks on, something he'd had to do when I was late-stage pregnant, and which he did now sometimes out of affection. He pulled them up under the hem of my trousers.

'Boots?' he asked.

'The brown shoes,' I decided.

He slipped them on my feet.

'Dan,' I said, not asked, but there was an upwards inflection. 'You can call her anything you want. Robin's fine. Dan Junior is fine. Stephen Fry. Whatever you want.'

'"Stephen Fry"?' he asked, laughing. I like making him smile. Maybe I should have said 'Hugh Laurie'. We used to watch old *Jeeves and Wooster*s when we were first dating.

'I'm serious. Well, not about Stephen Fry. But you decide. Not right now; tell me tonight.'

'All right,' he said, but he sounded hesitant.

'It's not a trick! I won't be mad! I won't hate it! Really, anything. Anything.' *Except Chloe*, I thought. *Except Margaret*, his mother's name. But I didn't say either of those things. 'Anything,' I repeated.

Out in the car, I wondered if Rosalie, the receptionist and mother-of-twins, had ever hesitated for a moment. *She had probably picked out names before they popped out. She had probably had multiple combinations ready in case of unexpected genders.* I bet myself that I would learn their names before I would learn whether Cathy was in.

I plopped my handbag on top of the breast pump in the footwell of the passenger seat. I had decided yesterday that I was done. I didn't mind the sucking at home but I wasn't going to feed the machine again. I hated that bloody thing. Dan had formula in the cupboard for this afternoon. The only machine I wanted to feel at one with was my car. It felt good to drive. *This had better come to something*, I thought, because the other friends Charlie had mentioned were, respectively, in Australia, dead from cancer, and, as

71

far as I could tell, dropped off the face of the earth. Cathy was all we had.

Rigg and Loft, Attorneys-at-Law, occupied what had once been a large home just outside of Lilling. I pulled into one of three visitor parking spaces. The fourth space had a sign reserving it for Mr Rigg, Cathy's husband. I had no idea where Mr or Ms Loft parked, nor Rosalie. Perhaps there were more spaces around the back.

Rosalie was on the phone when I entered. She was very grateful for someone's understanding and promised that Livvy and Bayley (I'm only guessing that it must be spelt with two y's; *dear God, what if Dan chooses a name spelt with extraneous y's?*) will never be late to football practice again. I mentally awarded myself a point for being right and said hello.

'Ms Frohmann, is it?' Rosalie asked warmly, using the civilian title even though I had made it clear on the phone that I'm a detective inspector. She winked and slid her glance to the right. Someone was waiting in a little seating area next to a pitcher of water with a lemon in it. Likely a potential legal client and I supposed Rosalie didn't want to give away that I'm police. I allowed it; being in her good graces could come in handy later.

'Is Cathy Rigg in?' I asked, and added to ingratiate myself, 'Your daughters are gorgeous!' There were two separately framed photos of what appeared to be the same person. It didn't help that they were in identical school uniforms.

Rosalie beamed and nearly wriggled with pleasure. 'Thank you! Livvy cut herself a fringe the night before, so they'd look different in their photos this year. Bayley cried so hard she missed the bus and ended up cutting herself a fringe in the loo at school. They're both left-handed and so they both cut it with the same accidental slant.' She said all this with adoration, as if her daughters' identity crises weren't, at the least, worrying.

'My daughter looks almost exactly like me,' I fabricated, for something to say. 'Some days I think she'd shave her head to make the difference more clear.' I grinned, not sure if I sounded like a normal doting mother of a tween, or like half of a deeply dysfunctional relationship. 'Is Cathy in?'

'Mrs Rigg isn't back yet. You're welcome to help yourself to some lemon water. She shouldn't be long.'

'Thank you, Rosalie,' I said, grateful that she hadn't asked my child's name. 'I'll find out tonight!' would have been an odd answer, especially since I'd implied that she's about eight, or whatever the age is that mothers and daughters start fighting. *Why am I picturing us at odds?* I asked myself. Maybe steeling myself, just in case. I'd hate to assume that it's all going to be, well, licking cake batter off the spatula and good grades – *for heaven's sake, baking? Grades?* – and then be blindsided.

The stylish potential client in the seat beside me, the lemon water, and Rosalie's cheerful deference seemed together to aspire to a city skyscraper instead of a converted village house, however grand it once had been. In truth this old mansion was now tatty. I could see where two rooms had been connected to make this lobby, and where a toilet had been shoehorned in down the hall. It had been done well, about ten years ago. Maybe fifteen.

A woman pushed open the grand front door by hefting a large cardboard box against it. Rosalie jumped up to relieve her of it. 'So sorry, Mrs Rigg!' she apologised as she did so, as if she could have done anything about it before that moment. I noticed the careful 'Mrs', not 'Ms'. That difference usually wafts by unnoticed but Rosalie had emphasised it.

'Papers for Nigel,' the woman said, referring to the box Rosalie had thudded onto her desk, and also I assume referring to Nigel Rigg, her husband. This would be Cathy, Charlie's ex, certainly doing her best to live a very thorough distance from him in lifestyle if not in actual miles. 'Why are people waiting?'

Rosalie explained, 'Ms Sunden is here to give her signature, and Ms Frohmann would like to ask you a few questions.'

Just then Nigel Rigg jogged down the centrepiece staircase. 'Amanda!' he said, holding out both hands in apology for the wait to the woman beside me. An international phone call, he said, was the culprit. Rosalie had the client's papers ready and a pen uncapped. Nigel Rigg smoothly took them without a thank you and swept the client through a piece of the wooden panelling that I hadn't realised was an office door.

I noticed that he hadn't acknowledged Cathy.

'How may I help you?' the ignored spouse asked me.

'It's about Charlie.'

'Excuse me?'

'Charlie Bennet. We—'

She grasped my upper arm and steered me into what had once been a dining room. Old paintings on the walls looked darkened by years of atmospheric candlelight, from before a bright run of LEDs had been hung from a

74

metal wire strung across the ceiling. The enormous table could have been original to the house, only now used for meetings instead of dinner. 'Who are you?' she demanded, while shutting the door.

I identified myself and showed my warrant card; she touched her fingertips to her forehead and pinched her lips together. 'Charlie . . .' she muttered. I noticed her dark hair, now chin-length but perhaps once long. She was slim. She had a pretty face. She would have been Charlie's type back in the day. And, back in the day, they hadn't yet known what they'd all become. Maybe he was supposed to be a rock star by now. Maybe his attention had been flattering then.

'I'm sorry to bother you, Mrs Rigg,' I said, following Rosalie's lead. If Cathy Rigg liked her marital status emphasised, I could do that all day long. Or perhaps the emphasis should be on *Rigg*, in contrast to the previous *Bennet*. Keeping track of women's various names was always a pain in every investigation. *Jesus, I'm glad I didn't change my name.*

'What's he done now?' She flung herself into a swivel chair.

I remained standing. I could sit next to her if I needed to persuade something out of her; for now I started with authority.

'Your school in Bishop's Stortford had a French exchange programme when you were there, is that correct?' I was avoiding mentioning Annalise, though I didn't know how long that could last. I just wanted to keep off the deeply ingrained tracks of that old investigation as long as I could.

'What? France?' Cathy shook her head.

75

'Are you saying that there wasn't a French exchange?'

'No. Yes! Yes, there was. But why are you asking me? I'm saying that, no, I don't understand why you want to know . . .'

'Do you know if Charlie Bennet ever participated in said programme?'

'Charlie?'

'Yes.'

She laughed. 'Charlie! Yes! He did. It was . . . it was the year after I went.'

'Can you confirm the year for me, please?'

'He was there in 1976.'

Neither of us was saying the name that both of us knew defined that year.

'And the name of the programme?' I asked.

'I don't know. Something French. Well, obviously. Sorry, no. It was a long time ago.'

'That's fine. I can ask at the school. Do you remember the name of the teacher who ran it?'

'I'm sure she's retired.'

'Most likely. But her name?'

Cathy nibbled at the tip of one long finger. 'It was a long time ago.'

'Yearbooks?'

'I'm sorry, but you're going to have to leave. If you want to ask me anything else, I'd like a solicitor present.'

'We can ask your husband to join us,' I suggested.

She straightened up. 'I wouldn't dream of interrupting his work. And, actually, you know what? I divorced Charlie seventeen years ago. No, wait, eighteen years now. Eighteen years! Our divorce is now old enough to vote, or

76

buy a drink at the pub. I have nothing to do with him any more. If you have any further questions about Charlie you can ask his parents. Or his whores. It's up to you, really. But don't ask me.' She rose and manoeuvred me towards the door.

I could have argued, but chose to acquiesce for now. She escorted me past Rosalie and out the grand door. She watched through a decorative stained-glass window to check that I'd driven away.

I pulled over around the corner and jotted notes. I had wanted to ask her about Charlie's story of visiting with Annalise's parents and the accessibility and state of Annalise's old bedroom, but Cathy had mentioned something potentially more interesting. She said that Charlie had gone on the French exchange the year after she herself had gone. As I recall the gossip around the case, there had been some talk of Annalise and a French boyfriend from the year before she disappeared. It sounded like Cathy and Annalise may have been in France together. And Cathy certainly didn't want to talk about it. I needed to do some research before talking with her again.

And research wasn't too far away. I drove a mile or so onward to find a proper place to leave the car. I ended up pulling off onto some grass at the side of the road. This wasn't pavement territory, with shops and pubs and old unused phone boxes. This was nowhere.

The fields didn't belong to any farm; instead they hosted a train track cutting through in the distance, somewhat parallel to the road. I'd known that Annalise's body had been found near tracks, near Lilling, but I hadn't known exactly where. Someone on the Internet had posted GPS coordinates, and I'd marked it on my mapping app. The spot was only twenty minutes from here, not a bad walk through tallish grass. Once I got close, I didn't need the coordinates any more. There was a bouquet at the base of one of the two remaining poplar trees.

No card or explanation; just a handpicked bunch of wilting . . . purple I-don't-know-whats. I'm terrible at flowers, but I know that they sometimes mean something. I snapped a picture.

How is it that some crimes capture so much public imagination that people – strangers, even – still grieve them decades later? It's like historic ghost stories. Most deaths, even terrible ones, get let go of, but occasional ones, for being particularly surprising, ironic, iconic, or grisly, get remembered as spooky tales. If Annalise had been killed a hundred years ago, her death might be a ghost story now, and she a transparent, wispy figure wandering along the tracks, or riding her last bicycle journey on the way home from school over and over again. Or she might be just one of many deaths forgotten. She got remembered not just because of who she was or what happened, but because of a confluence of salacious media, well-chosen photographs, a super-hot summer, and a panic that England might have gained its own Ted Bundy, whose trial had been at that time so much in the news across the pond. But this wasn't a serial killer, not as far as we knew. He seemed to have killed only her.

Or she, I reminded myself. If Charlie's semen got on the skirt the way he claimed it had, it wasn't necessarily a man who had killed her, though that was still the more likely scenario.

I looked around. The road was in view. No cars visible at the moment, but that could change quickly.

Still, if a car did come along, and they bothered to look to the side instead of straight on, what could they see? Someone by the tracks. Even if they saw digging, they'd think 'train works', not 'body dump'. The bigger worry would be a train going by. Not so much from being observed (though, depending on the speed and type of train, that could potentially be a problem) but from the whoosh of it passing. Gusts from a train's motion are powerful. I wouldn't want to be next to a pile of dirt shovelled out of a grave when a train bulleted by.

I made a list: find out what trains used to travel along this route, and what their speeds were. Something tugged at the back of my mind, from secondary school history lessons: train strikes. I added that to the list.

As I pushed my booted feet against the dry yellow grass, I imagined the journey with a body. I couldn't think of an inconspicuous way to transport it. A wheelbarrow, perhaps? The walk would have been more of a danger of discovery than perhaps the burial itself. Dogs, I reminded myself. People walk dogs. That's how it was found. *Why take the chance? What was special about this place that made it worth it?*

A train going north jolted me out of my wondering, and a car whooshing south on the road sandwiched me between their rushing speed as I headed back to my car.

The road into Lilling proper was easy to follow. Well, almost inevitable to follow; there weren't other obvious options once on it, just occasional dirt tracks leading off.

I glanced at my watch when I arrived; perfect timing. An estate agent was waiting for me.

I wasn't moving house; I had an appointment with a woman called Marnie from Showcase Homes! to show me Annalise's old house, which was currently available to rent. Marnie was now nearing retirement age; she had been a newbie back in the eighties, being mentored by the agent who first sold the house after Annalise's parents died. Now it was her turn to be in charge.

At first, the house had been treated as if it were cursed. No one wanted it. There was talk of whether it should be burnt down or made into a museum, but the fact is, though it was Annalise's house, the murder hadn't (to anyone's knowledge or even suspicion) happened there. So, eventually, there was buyer interest. The neighbours had banded together and petitioned the relevant forces on the city council to prevent ghoulish thrill-seekers from getting it. It had finally sold to a family who were aware of the history but wanted no details. Marnie herself had helped fix it up, she had told me on the phone, so that you couldn't tell which room had belonged to Annalise. The buyers had explicitly asked not to know which room had been hers.

It was all fine for them until the body was found in 1992. They got tired of the renewed interest in the case manifesting in cars slowing down and people pointing up at their windows. They had sold to a single man who then lived an apparently staid and solitary life, and upon his death the house went to his three estranged adult daughters, who sold it again. The latest family to live there was from Finland and extremely practical about the tragedy. After three years, the husband's work contract was ending and they were readying to return to Helsinki. Marnie didn't mind showing me around.

I asked her to show me Annalise's room first. She brought me upstairs and sighed as she opened the door for me. Inside: posters on the walls, homework on the desk, make-up on the dresser. They'd unwittingly given their daughter Annalise's room.

I walked around. It was easy, if somewhat inaccurate, to think of Annalise at this desk, on this bed, in front of this mirror. The seventies would have had different bands on the posters, and different colours of lipstick, but the shape of the room and the placement of the windows limited the possible furniture permutations, so the main arrangements would have been the same. But it wasn't Annalise whose footsteps I was tracking today. I was after Charlie.

'Was this always here?' I pulled open the door of a bulky wardrobe.

Marnie quickly interjected, 'They'd rather you not open drawers or cupboards.'

'Sorry,' I said, pushing it shut. I didn't care about this girl's clothes. I just wanted to think about Charlie, at a tea party downstairs, coming up these stairs, crossing this room . . . There was a large window next to the wardrobe. *I hope she pulls her curtains when she changes her clothes.* Charlie would have had to take the skirt over to a more sheltered part of the room, or kept behind the wardrobe door, or taken a risk with the window. Or maybe it had had blinds then. I shrugged. What he'd done could have been done fast.

'Where's the loo?'

'Do you need to . . . ?' Marnie asked anxiously. I supposed she had been asked to keep buyers off of their toilets as well.

'I just want to know if it's upstairs or downstairs.'

'Oh! Yes. That's fine. It's right out here.' She walked me out into the hallway. 'Over the kitchen. The plumbing all in one place.'

So he asks to go to the loo, heads up here, is gone for five or ten minutes . . . That works.

'Do you have photographs, Marnie? I noticed that you're magic with a camera.' I had noticed nothing of the sort, just that Showcase Homes! had a good-looking website, but the flattery worked.

'I always think photos sell a house, more than a visit even. If the photos have captured the buyer's imagination, well, the deal is done.'

'Do you have the older photos from other times the house was sold? Maybe even photos from when the Woods lived here?'

'Well . . .' She shuffled her feet. 'Well, as I told you, we changed things around for selling. Max didn't like people trying to get a look at the Woods' private lives. Nowadays you would hire a stager, but back then we all just pitched in. Max – he was my mentor – felt it was important to let the house look like its future, not its past.' She nodded her head and enunciated the last words carefully. She had clearly thought them through and said them before.

'What was done with the Woods' things?' I asked, trying to sound casual and gossipy, which seemed more likely to get a response than if I seemed official.

Marnie shook her head. 'Max was very concerned. He didn't want people buying them at auction and making some kind of murder shrine out of them.'

The phrase 'murder shrine' had come out of her mouth

without any hesitation. I understood immediately what novels she enjoys and what TV she watches.

'And the clothes!'

My ears pricked. I hadn't even had to ask.

'Max didn't want anyone to be able to buy Annalise's clothes, and make some kind of obsessed sex shrine.'

I kept my face grave. I did not laugh. I would like a police commendation for this. 'What did he do with them?'

'The furniture he mixed in with bits and pieces from other places and sold them as-is, without *provenance*.' She said the big word with a carefully practised accent. Perhaps Marnie had also been on a French exchange years ago. 'People may be sitting on the Woods' sofa *right now* but they wouldn't know it.'

For a moment I felt as if I were in the audience of a horror film, shouting 'Don't sit on the couch!' to no avail. I did laugh a little. I covered my mouth. 'But the clothes?'

'He boxed them up and sent them anonymously to an organisation that collects clothes for charity and sends them overseas. Actually, I did the boxing up. He trusted me like that. He – well, just like you, he said I was magic.' She blushed.

Damn. Overseas. 'Magical Marnie, you wouldn't by chance have the name of that charity, would you?'

'Of course. I'll have to look it up.'

'And those old photos of the house? Of the way the Woods had lived in it?' I asked again, pushier. I didn't have anything in mind to look for in such photos; I just wanted to be sure that they matched what I expected.

'I may have. I'll check,' she said primly. I felt confident that this woman knew exactly what she had and just didn't

83

want to appear insensitive or like one of those thrill-seekers herself. 'I would have taken some, I think, so that we could defend the company if anyone claimed that the Woods' belongings had been damaged when they were moved out.'

'If you could email me when you find them, please.'

'Of course.'

As we walked down the stairs, I tried to picture the macabre gatherings Mrs Wood had thrown for friends, trying to keep her daughter's memory alive.

Marnie had an apparently congenital aversion to silence. 'You know, I'm really proud of my photography skills. This room, it wasn't so easy to capture the size. Because you see? If you stand over by the door – the obvious place – that wall there cuts everything off. It just looks small. But if you take it from up here . . .' She tugged my sleeve and pulled me up a few steps. 'Perfect! Even shows the garden through the window. Ooh . . .' She pulled out her camera. 'See what I did here?'

She handed the camera to me. I obligingly admired a series of shots of the room we were standing in, from various angles. She narrated the various qualities of the results: 'See how this makes the room look small, even though it isn't, and how *this* one makes you feel like you're right in the room?' I did, indeed, feel like I was in the room. *Magic.*

I scrolled backwards through kitchen shots, bathroom, the back garden, then . . . 'Oops!' she said. 'My nieces.' She took the camera back.

I recognised them: Livvy and Bayley, I'd guess about six months since the debacle with their fringes.

'Rosalie is your sister?'

'You know her? Small world!' she announced in delight. Then, 'She's not in trouble, is she?' She laughed. It was a joke, because I'm police. Of course I have never heard such jokes before, not at every social gathering I've ever attended since I joined the force. I made myself keep a smile and not roll my eyes.

Marnie continued: 'She's not my sister. We're cousins. But I call her girls my nieces because they're so young and I'm so old . . . Well, you know what I mean. They're family. I took these pictures for their birthday last month, in the law office building.' She whispered, 'We did it while Mr Rigg was out. He *doesn't like children.*' She wrinkled her nose judgementally.

She held the camera out to me again. 'I had to use some of the same tricks, to make the room look good and not so cluttered. It's that tower upstairs. They use it for storage. Well, Rosalie lets the girls use it as a playroom when she has to work during half-term. See, I angled things so that it feels like the room is spacious. You wouldn't guess that there are boxes of files piled up around the daybed. I think I was standing on one for this shot. And you want the light shining in on them, not silhouetting them. See how I did that? I managed to get the view too.'

What a view it was, framed in those windows: two lonely poplars next to a railroad track. Annalise's burial place.

I drove back to Nigel Rigg's law office. I didn't pull up to the house yet; just into the beginning of the drive to think. Of course this was near where Annalise had been found, in the sense that she had been found near Lilling. Everything in Lilling's environs was 'near' where Annalise had been found. It's just that the tower here goes up a level higher than most buildings in the area. And the windows face that direction.

I pulled further in and parked. I had been armed by Marnie with an excuse to return: some items she wanted passed on to Rosalie. I had some more questions and wanted them to appear idle.

Rosalie was hesitant when I entered. 'I'm sorry. Mrs Rigg isn't here. She's at the post office.' She sounded subdued. I wondered if she had been told off for giving me an appointment earlier.

'That's all right. I'm here to see you!' I rejoined heartily, and she perked up. I presented her cousin's delivery, which turned out to be hand-knitted jumpers.

Rosalie squeaked with delight. She explained that they had been knitted by Marnie's mother and . . . It doesn't matter. I let the explanation run its course. When sweater-related words stopped coming out of Rosalie's mouth, I confided, 'My husband's an architect,' which is true, though I would have happily lied if a different profession would have been more useful. 'He has an interest in houses with towers . . .' That's a lie, possibly an odd and transparent one, but—

'Oh, yes! The tower's a popular feature. Everyone comments on it.' Then her voice lowered. 'I'm sorry; I really can't show you up there. Mrs Rigg wasn't happy that you . . .'

I waved my hand affably. 'Of course. I wouldn't want to intrude. I was just wondering about the history; has this always been an office?' Obviously not, but I hoped that if I sounded stupid she'd give me more information.

It turned out that the house had been built by a Bairstow family that had resided in it for several generations. I wondered, *Could it really be this easy?* Had a member of that family been the one to choose Annalise's resting place so they could 'enjoy' it daily without having to risk returning to it?

But Rosalie's *Tales of the Bairstows* made that scenario seem less likely: in the seventies, the tower had been a nursery for little girl twins. Still, Charlie's bizarre assertion that the body actually couldn't have been buried until later opened up possibilities. 'When did the building change hands?' I asked. Rigg and Loft could be one in a series of business renters, or could be descendants of a long-established partnership. *Perhaps Annalise's murder could end up blamed on the father of obnoxious Mr Rigg; I wouldn't mind that at all.*

'Just six years ago. We used to be in St Albans.'

'And Rigg and Loft bought it directly from the Bairstows?'

Rosalie isn't stupid. 'Is this a police question or a my-husband-is-an-architect question?'

I think I like her. 'It's an I'll-leave-really-soon question. I just want to know the chain of ownership.'

'Mr Rigg doesn't like us talking about it.'

That made the information a hundred times more interesting than it was ten seconds ago. 'Rosalie, please.'

She leant forward. She whispered, 'It was a boarding house.'

My eyebrows squeezed together sceptically. 'Is that a euphemism?'

'No!' She looked horrified. 'But Mr Rigg likes to think of

the building as a family home. He's very family-orientated. He won't even advise on divorce cases if the client has committed adultery.'

The fact that Mr Rigg wouldn't like it prompted in me an urge to run out and commit adultery immediately, but I restrained myself. 'So, it was a boarding house in the eighties? Any old record books on some dusty shelf?'

'Mr Rigg doesn't like dust,' Rosalie said primly, eluding the actual question.

I pulled out a card with my name and information on it; crossed out the office number and circled my mobile. Before I could slip it to her, Mr Rigg appeared at the top of the stairs.

'Rosalie?' he said, awaiting an explanation of my presence.

'Mr Rigg, Mrs Frohmann had some questions about the architecture. For her husband.' Rosalie was a lot sharper than I had initially given her credit for. It's obvious why she'd glided around my police rank. I didn't even correct her that Frohmann is my maiden name and so 'Mrs' not appropriate with it; Mr Rigg was clearly the kind of man who prefers women my age to be married, so she had emphasised it.

'Yes,' I agreed. 'I was just wondering when it had been built and whether it had had many additions over the years.' Then I added, and this was possibly over the top: 'It's such a family-orientated building.'

Just then the phone on Rosalie's desk gave an old-fashioned jangle. She picked it up and her smile turned from automatic to genuine. 'Sorry, love! Your aunt isn't here right now. She's at the post office. But I know she's looking forward to seeing you tonight.' Pause; nodding. 'All right. I'll let her know. Bye, dear.'

Mr Rigg was nearly quivering with impatience. 'I'd prefer you not to use the office phone for personal calls during business hours.'

'Yes, Mr Rigg,' as if she could have stopped someone else from phoning for Cathy.

'And where is Cathy, Rosalie?'

Rosalie stiffened then forced her shoulders to relax. 'Errands, Mr Rigg. For the office.'

'It would be a better use of everyone's time for you to take care of such things during lunch.'

'Of course. From tomorrow onward, Mr Rigg.'

She held her bland smile in place until a door had closed behind him.

'I promise I won't call during office hours. But you can call me anytime, day or night. I'd like to know who lived in this house.'

She nodded, and tucked my card in with Marnie's gift of jumpers. In the right patterns, knots and tangles add up to something useful; my job depends on that.

CHAPTER SIX

Annalise Williams, second session, recorded and transcribed by Dr Laurie Ambrose

I did it. I know I shouldn't have, but I did.

There was this nice guy. I'd only talked to him a few times, and then last night I told him. He responded just like I knew he would: he was tender, and attentive, and angry on my behalf. When I told him that the man had never been identified or caught, you would have thought he was going to break his fingers he was making a fist so tight. I told him that it was all right, that it was a long time ago. He touched my hair and said that no one should ever be hurt like that. He just accepted me as damaged and scared and hurt and very brave, and held me. He made the bad feelings go away.

They are my own bad feelings. I was never hurt like Annalise, but I feel bad things just the same.

Everybody does. Victims just feel them bigger, and with more words to justify and describe them, and get to be fussed over, while the rest of us haven't earned that, what with our normal, everyday, boring 'bad feelings'. *God.* It's like when people with shitty jobs don't make enough to live on, but they make too much to qualify for benefits. I'm too lucky to qualify for sympathy, right? For understanding? Only real victims get that. The rest of us are supposed to take care of those poor victims. We don't get taken care of ourselves. We're not sad enough. *God.*

I'm going to see him again, on Wednesday. We'll talk about other things. We already have talked about other things: work and pets and parents, the usual. His father is dead. Then it was my turn to comfort him. See how it's fair? I don't just take. He's lucky to know me, just as lucky as I am to know him.

He says he likes my long hair. He pushed a bit of it behind my ear. That's bold, don't you think? A man doesn't touch a woman if he's not interested.

Are you married, Dr Ambrose? You've got a pretty ring, but it's not the usual diamond-engagement-and-wedding-band set. Why is that? Could he not afford it? . . . Oh. I thought that I could talk about whatever I wanted.

So long as it's about myself and my own experiences? Fine. I'll tell you more about my new friend. He's a bit younger than me but mature for his age. Do you remember being young, Dr Ambrose? I know it was a long time ago . . . Uh-oh, shame on me, that's about you again.

You know what? I had a great time with him last night, such a good time that I almost didn't come to this appointment today. I thought, why bother? But I decided that it was important to talk to you. I decided that you needed to know that I did it, I told him and don't regret it. I'm even a little angry that you almost took this away from me.

People say 'crutch' like that's a bad thing. Crutches are great! Have you ever sprained your ankle or broken your leg? You're not going to tell me, are you? Well, I have. I broke my ankle skiing and, shit, I fucking loved my crutches. Without them I couldn't do anything, but with them I could get around. You have something against me getting around? Why not use the crutch that's just right in front of me? It makes me feel good to tell part of Annalise's story as if it's my own, and it doesn't hurt anyone. Can you name one person who gets hurt by me telling this little white lie?

No, not him. I don't accept that. We were closer after we talked. It opened up big emotions between us in a contained and controlled way. He's happy. He wants to see me again. You can't argue with that. You can't say he's hurt. He's coming back for more.

Maybe, just maybe, if we were to get married and have babies and years down the road he discovers that I lied to him he might be hurt, but I really don't think that's what's ahead, do you?

Sometimes I do wonder to myself, what would I be telling in its place, if I didn't have this perfect story all prepared? Is there something better to say, something more important, that's being hidden by this? That opportunity cost is the only downside I can think of, but I haven't dug up any hidden secret yet. If I had my own story, my own molestation or whatever, I promise I would be telling that. There's nothing there. The fact is, everyone has insecurities and anger and even fears, but only those who've been through a trauma are allowed to admit them. So I give myself that permission. Telling Annalise's story gives me the opportunity to be honest about how I really am inside. I'm being more truthful in telling her story than I would be by putting on my happy-perfect date-face.

I'm using it only as a counterweight, only after I've established that I'm attractive and successful. Knowing that a man really likes me, admires me, or is even maybe intimidated, then I can be honest about the not-perfect underneath, to both his relief and mine. It makes him protective of me and careful. Every man should be protective and careful just as a matter of course, but we all know that's not the case. Right? You're a woman. If you're a straight woman, you know how men are.

I know what you're thinking. Why do I need this kind of coddling? What makes me so special and fragile? This is my theory: we all need it, but I'm one of the few stepping up and demanding it.

This is the stupidest fucking arrangement I've ever encountered. What is this silence? You're 'listening' like a plaster wall; really you're probably listing errands in your head, or song lyrics. This isn't

93

human. This isn't personal. There's supposed to be a back and forth, some kind of comment, not just prompts here and there, leading questions. There are supposed to be reactions.

Do you practise that blank face? Because, to be honest, it's a little too bland. It's a giveaway that something has hit home. Like in my last visit when I asked if you'd ever known anyone else from Lilling. You acted like that was meaningless. I almost laughed.

You don't need to say it twice. I'm off.

[Muffled sounds.] [Door slams.]

CHAPTER SEVEN

Laurie Ambrose

'Laurie?' Simon's voice wafted down from upstairs, along with lashings of coloured light from the pretty window on the landing.

'I'm here,' I called up to him, letting drop my handbag and keys. They thudded and clinked, respectively, on the wooden floor, just short of the hem of the threadbare rug.

Our house is full of old things, memory things. The rug has been mine since my first flat, handed down from an aunt who'd had it custom-made on a trip to Turkey when she was a young bride. The window was made by Simon's mother in her stained-glass phase, and fitted just inside the real window frame. It's of fat, happy birds on a flowering branch.

'You all right?' Simon blocked the birds with his body.

I didn't answer. The top of the stairs felt very far away.

'Laurie,' he said again, clattering down the steps and wiping his hands on his jeans. They were dirty. He must have been working on the plumbing in the upstairs bath. It'd been dodgy recently.

'One of my clients is dead,' I said.

His smudged hands touched me, leading me to the couch to sit down. He offered me a drink, but alcohol is only celebratory to me, or romantic, not 'medicinal'. Accepting would feel like making a toast to death. He got up and washed his hands, returning with a glass of water. I sipped, and set it down. The coaster was also of a bird, an American blue jay. His mother had given us them too.

He touched my hair and I thought of Annalise Williams and her creepy version of a date, her interest in my personal life, and her apparent spite. I try not to judge my clients, but thinking of her made me shiver.

'Tell me what happened.'

'One of my clients drowned. I heard it on the radio on the way home.'

'God, really?'

'You know that woman they found in the Cam yesterday? They've released her name.'

'I'm so sorry.' One arm behind me, the other on my knee. I leant into him, grateful.

Thoughts of my client Annalise, so keen to get off on a man's sympathy and attention, invaded my mind. It wasn't fair. I stood up. I walked across the room.

'Do you want to talk about it?'

'I don't think I should.' I can't share what I've discussed with clients except in the most general terms. 'It's someone I only saw once, a few months ago.'

It came to him and he snapped his fingers. 'Oh! Hannah something, in the river. I had the TV on in the background while wrestling with the plumbing,' he explained, clarifying that he hadn't been lazy today.

It would have been unethical of me to confirm the name. I changed the subject: 'I cut a session short today. It became personal.'

He tensed. I quickly assured him that it wasn't that kind of personal. There's a risk of attachment that, in the extreme, could become inappropriate or dangerous. 'Not like that. Just . . . strange. She knew where I lived.'

'What? She knows this house?'

'No. Where I was born.'

Simon shook his head in surprise. 'How did that come up?'

I looked up, at the plaster ceiling rose and the delicate, practical picture rail. This was home now. 'She made reference to an event from there.'

'Oh, that murder? Annalise Wood?'

It's peculiar to be from a village known foremost for a death. 'Yes, that.'

'And she knows that you're from Lilling? Is that on your LinkedIn?'

I thought. 'No.' I try to keep my personal life offline.

'Did you tell her?'

'Why would I tell her? In the first session, she asked if I knew anyone from there. Maybe I flinched or something.'

'Maybe . . .' He looked worried. I joined him back on the couch. I didn't want to let Annalise Williams' morbid relationship strategy affect me. 'Did she say anything else personal?'

It felt inadequate when spoken out loud. 'She mocked my age. She . . . she was hostile. I can't properly convey it.'

'But she's not the one who . . .'

'No. No. The woman who died only saw me once, then stopped.' *What if she'd come back to see me again? Had she still been having panic attacks? What if I'd been able to help her? Would she still be alive?* My thoughts must have shown on my face.

'Is there anything I can do for you?' Simon asked me. I felt a sweet pang in my chest at the sound of his voice. We'd been married less than a year.

'I . . .' I wanted to play him the recordings, to see if he thought I overreacted to Annalise Williams today. I wanted to play Hannah-Claire Finney's, just to hear her alive and hopeful. But I couldn't do that. Their stories weren't for me to share. But I wonder sometimes, when clients affect me – when they discomfit me, as Annalise Williams did, or emotionally touch me, as Hannah-Claire Finney did – at what point our interactions might become also partly mine.

Well, this was mine: 'I was five when Annalise Wood disappeared.' My mother was protective in my teen years, but I suppose most parents are. I don't think Annalise's murder caused that. I think the murder merely confirmed her fears, which were already deep. 'I was twenty-one when the body was finally discovered.'

'I remember it.'

'Why?' He'd never mentioned Annalise Wood before.

'Lilling isn't that far away. It was in the news.' We were both at Cambridge then.

I still rearranged memories of those years, when Simon and I knew each other but I was with Tom. University was the start of my and Tom's story; Simon was a background friend. Now, four years after Tom's death, those early memories were framed differently, zooming in on Simon's and my amiable, casual interactions as the start of our own story.

'She didn't like the ring you gave me,' I said.

'Who?'

'Annalise.' *Shit.* I didn't mean to say her name. 'The woman I asked to leave early today. She said that it was cheap to have a garnet instead of a diamond.'

He had too much confidence to let that get to him. His focus went elsewhere: 'Her name is Annalise? Like the murdered teenager?'

I'd already let her name out; it wasn't like I could snatch it back. 'That's how it came up in conversation. It's not a coincidence. Her mother named her after Annalise Wood.'

'Why?' His mouth frowned around the question.

I shook my head. 'She said that her mother admired how much Annalise was missed. She wished for that kind of value for her daughter.'

Simon whistled in amazement. 'That's a kind of popularity I could do without.'

'Not that someone stalked and killed her. The grieving after.'

'It's still morbid.'

I nodded. 'I know. It's a weighty name, especially for someone in Lilling.'

'So she's actually from there? Did you know her or her family?'

'No. I didn't recognise the surname. She's not necessarily from Lilling itself; all of the villages in that part of the county were affected by it; they all feed into the same secondary school. She said something odd,' I added, remembering. 'She said that the name Annalise had a spike in popularity after her disappearance was so heavily covered in the media. But I've never known anyone called Annalise. It always felt like a cursed name to me, like calling your child Desdemona or Lolita.'

'People die every day,' Simon mused. 'Why do we all remember Annalise? The name Hannah isn't going to become an anathema because your client was killed in the river.'

'Killed?'

'Wasn't she? You said . . .'

'I said she died. I assume it was an accident. Or . . .' *Suicide*, I finished to myself.

'Oh. All right. That's just as sad, isn't it? My point stands.'

He kept talking. I only half-listened, mesmerised by his assumption of murder.

He mused, 'I suppose the relative rarity of the name Annalise is part of the reason. Everyone already knows at least one Hannah, and probably several. That diffuses the effect. For many people, the murder story is the only time they've ever heard of an Annalise at all . . .'

I felt the tension in my face tightening my lips. I was offended by the suggestion of murder, just a further horror to add to Hannah's sad life. I also felt a tickle of selfish hope, and realised that I'd been feeling guilt: that this woman had been in my care and I hadn't saved her from herself. If someone else had done it to her, then it wasn't my fault.

Simon answered his own question: 'As for why some cases get famous, there's a titillation to it, I suppose. A pretty young girl, a mystery. All those years of wondering before they finally found the body.'

'They still don't know who killed her.'

'Really? After all this time?'

'It gets harder to figure out with time, not easier.'

'I suppose you're right.'

He waited patiently for me to go on, but there was so much that I couldn't say to him.

Even after Hannah-Claire's death, it would violate privacy ethics to tell him that she had also talked about Annalise Wood. That two people connected to Annalise Wood came to me within months; is that odd? Is that statistically unexpected? Lilling isn't so far from here. Her murder was famous. Was I being paranoid? I couldn't ask him.

I already edit myself, even in normal conversation, to cut references to Tom. I say 'my' instead of 'our': 'my savings' even though Tom had made most of that money, 'my children' (a boy and a girl, both grown-up and at university) as if they have no father. That blue photo album on the bottom shelf is now 'my trip to New Zealand', not 'Tom's and my fifth anniversary'. Simon had never asked me to be so careful, but I felt that I should, for my sake as well as his. I was learning a new 'our'. 'Our' now meant Simon and me.

My job added an extra layer of necessary editing.

'I need to talk to Prisha,' I announced. She's my boss, and ethics allow me to discuss clients with her. I could also talk about Tom without feeling disloyal. She'd known him.

Simon had known him too, which was a blessing with the children, who were, in a way, relieved that their new stepfather was someone that Tom had liked. It was possibly odd for Simon. I never knew his ex-wife. They had parted acrimoniously, and that unevenness hangs

101

over us. I had lost a treasured spouse to acute asthma after seventeen years; Simon had been divorced over a diagnosis of male infertility after five. I wonder if he, too, purposely edits her out of his conversation, for me . . . I always assumed his reluctance to mention her was for his own sake. Her leaving tainted even his happy memories of their marriage. I, on the other hand, have nothing but happy memories, magnified by their having been snatched away by unfair death.

'I thought Prisha was in Vienna this month.'

Shit. 'You're right.' Her youngest sister was having a baby there; the sister's husband was a minor composer in residence for a year at the opera house.

'You can't tell me, can you?' he asked, with an understanding smile.

I shook my head, agreeing that I could not.

'Shall I go for a walk? You can talk to yourself to your heart's content.'

He was starting a new company from home, so I rarely got to be in the house alone. He was conscious of that and was always offering to give me space. I rarely wanted it, but that day I said, 'Yes, please. I'm sorry. There's just something I need to work out, and . . .'

He kissed the top of my head. 'Shall I bring back a curry in an hour? Would that suit you?'

'How about something from the noodle place. Duck for me. Hour and a half?' I wanted to be composed when he returned. I wanted to be done thrashing out whatever was bothering me.

'The Dog and Pony,' he said over his shoulder as he exited. That's the pub down the road.

Tom and I had lived near the centre of Cambridge for the whole of our marriage. It was taking a bit of getting used to, now living in a satellite village: one pub, one curry house, one noodle place. A tiny library open only half-days. If I didn't have a car and an office in the city centre I'd go mad.

I'm not supposed to use words like that: 'mad', 'crazy'. Even in jokes or hyperbole they foster a mindset of otherness. I edited myself yet again, and said out loud, 'If I didn't have a car and an office in the city centre, I wouldn't like it very much.' I laughed. I did sound crazy, talking to myself and laughing at non-jokes.

I decided that, just for the next ninety minutes, I wouldn't edit at all.

I tried to conjure Prisha's presence: her calmness, her attentive posture. She would sit on the edge of the couch, balancing a teacup and saucer on her knee. But I didn't want to talk to her, not really, not if I had no constraints. It would be a sad thing if even in our imaginations we remained limited to what was possible.

'Tom,' I said out loud, then glanced over my shoulder, as if Simon might have heard that through the window. It's not that I prefer to talk to my dead husband; I'm just not allowed to share these things with my living one. 'Tom, I had a terrible day. No, that's not fair. I had a troubling day, but someone else had it much worse. Someone else is dead. No, not you – I mean, you are, but someone just died yesterday, someone I knew, a little, and I'm sad for her.'

Simon and I had bought this living-room set new, so it was hard to picture where in it Tom would settle himself. In the middle of the three-seater couch, arms spread over

103

the back? Or claiming the chair with the footstool? 'Next to you,' my brain conjured, in his voice.

How could I judge Annalise Williams for her manipulations and obsession, when I was indulging in an imagined conversation with my dead husband?

'I'm being very unkind,' I said. 'A woman came to see me twice. This is a different woman, not the one who died. I think of them both together, though, because they're both attached to an old murder, of Annalise Wood, back home.' 'Home' is a fluid word, meaning where I was born, where I grew up, where I used to live, where I live now, all at once.

'It's unkind of me to dislike her, but I do. Her name is Annalise, just like the murdered girl. She's obsessed with her. She tells boyfriends that she was raped and left for dead at some point in her past, and, instead of them running screaming, somehow this works for her. It gets them emotional, and, um, chivalrous, I suppose . . .' Two months into dating, I'd broken down in front of Simon over a cancer scare (the biopsy later revealed that the lump was benign). We'd been close before then, but that confession of fear, and his embrace of it, had deepened things between us. The only difference between that experience and Annalise Williams', I admitted to myself, was that her story was false, but I couldn't fault her reasoning: such vulnerability can, at a certain relationship point, raise the stakes. She didn't have a sob story of her own, so she borrowed one.

How does one get to twenty-four without some sad story to tell? She probably had plenty, I answered myself, but none so dramatic. I remembered that Simon looked at me differently after I told him, as if I were more precious for having been almost lost.

I was editing myself a bit after all. I only thought this part about me and Simon, and didn't say it out loud to imaginary Tom.

'Tom,' I said, coming back to the point. 'It's unkind of me to dislike her, because sessions are not analogous to real life. Real life has a back and forth, an equality in conversations. Sessions are, by design, narcissistic. I can't fault her for talking on and on, all about herself. That's what she's there for.' I sipped at the water Simon had brought me earlier. The glass was from a set Tom and I had bought at a charity shop for our first shared home.

'Sometimes it's tempting to imagine that the things that get admitted to in therapy are more real than the face the client presents to the world. You know, as if the public face were only a mask and that the private confession is what's really true. But that's not fair either. The public person is also true, just incomplete. You need to mix the secret things in with the public things to get the whole person, not just replace the public with the private.' Seeing as I was lecturing my imaginary dead husband, it was certainly good news that what's done in secret isn't the full 'me'.

'So, if her sessions make her seem self-involved and unpleasant, that's not really her, not in a complete sense. She shared with me a part of herself that she, wisely, shares with no one else. That kind of self-control speaks to wisdom, doesn't it? And self-understanding? So I mustn't judge her, or dislike her, because I haven't met "her". Not the full her.'

I retrieved my handbag from near the front door. 'Listen to this,' I said, and turned on the tape of Annalise Williams' first session. I'd brought it home with me.

I played the session on the mini-recorder, the volume pushed up as high as it would go through its tiny, tinny speaker. I commented as it went along, pointing out her wondering if I'd ever known anyone else from Lilling, and her mention of Annalise Wood having had a baby. 'That's strange to me,' I told Tom. 'I don't remember anyone ever saying that Annalise Wood had had a baby. I would have remembered that. And then there's this . . .' I swapped tapes, and put in Hannah-Claire Finney's tape, from her single session several months ago. Hannah had claimed to actually be that child. These two accounts were literally the only times I'd heard of this baby even as a theory, never mind as accepted truth.

Listening to Hannah's voice lulled me into grief. She'd never come back to see me. She'd been so hopeful for her future, possibly with Henry.

'She's dead now,' I explained to Tom. The tape continued to spin after the recording had finished. I clicked it off.

'Maybe the baby thing is a new theory of the case. Maybe there's been a new book. It's not as if I follow it in the news.' But my sister does, and she never mentioned it. 'Anyway, I'm going to transcribe these. Just to try to make some sense of them. This last one . . . Well, you tell me. I felt very uncomfortable, but maybe I'm overreacting.'

I played the tape of Annalise Williams' aborted session from that day. The tone of voice indeed conveyed the sense of menace I'd felt so sharply. 'See?' I said, as if proving my case. 'And she admits here that she knows where I'm from. Why would she know that? And if she did know it, why hide it in the first session? It's as if she'd been testing me.'

It had all taken longer than I realised. Simon fumbled

with his keys in announcement of his return. I clicked off the tape, and jumped up to open the door for him.

'Good talk?' he asked, hands full of takeaway bags.

I felt guilty, as if talking to Tom instead of just myself were taking unfair advantage of the solitude Simon had given me. I took his bags and smiled gratefully.

I set the table with proper plates and wine glasses. We'd chosen Simon's dishes over my chipped ones when we'd sorted through our aggregate belongings. I wondered briefly if it was him or his ex who'd chosen the pattern. I wondered if he had memories attached to these plates, of meals they had habitually cooked together, or of special dinners observing their milestones. *Does he talk to imaginary her when I'm not home? After all, I don't really think I'm talking to Tom's ghost. She wouldn't have to be dead for him to pretend she's here . . .*

He distracted me with gossip from the pub: our neighbours' daughter is getting married; our plumber is getting divorced. *Our.* Mine and Simon's. I felt present. The duck was pungent and the sauce was tangy. *I'm happy*, I thought, and I reminded myself that I'm not a hypocrite. I love Simon. Also still loving Tom didn't change that.

I'm happy, I thought, and I ached for Hannah-Claire Finney. I wished for her that she could be alive, about to spend Christmas with Henry's family. I wished for her that whatever drove her into the river was very recent, and that she'd had at least some months of peace before.

'I want to attend her funeral,' I told Simon. 'My client's.' I didn't tell him that it was because I needed to see who else would be there. I needed to see for myself that she had a family, even if it's just unlikeable cousin Sandy, who had for some reason told Hannah, after her adopted parents died, that her 'real mother' was a famous murder victim. How would cousin Sandy even have known that? What had Sandy expected Hannah to do with that information?

Simon's face froze.

'What?' I asked, fork hovering over the last of my noodles.

'The funeral might be delayed. The police are questioning the husband.'

My fork didn't move. My arm started to ache.

'Laurie? I'm sorry. I shouldn't have said anything. It was on the television at the pub.'

I could only choke out, 'What's his name?'

'Who?'

'The husband. Is it Henry?'

Simon's mouth opened and closed with no sound. 'It could be,' he said at last. 'I didn't register the name. Ware, I think? His last name is Ware.'

I tasted salt and realised I must be crying. I felt only anger. *If Henry had hurt her . . .*

'Laurie.' Simon rose, and pulled me up to meet him. He wrapped his arms around my shoulders. He rested his cheek on the top of my head.

'I didn't know they'd got married.' I leant into him. Our breathing synced.

My thoughts were full of Hannah, poor Hannah, having got her Henry and look how it went. But Annalise Williams intruded. She elbowed into my thoughts, jealous of this moment of loving closeness brought on by grief. This is what she seeks, over and over, with her false tale of victimhood.

It's not worth it, I wanted to explain to her. Real grief is never worth it. Comfort is a lovely, needed thing, but it's never bigger than the grief it seeks to mitigate. The grief always wins, even when the comfort is strong, even when the comfort is profound. I screwed up my eyes to squeeze out the last of the tears.

'Laurie,' Simon said, and he sounded like Tom. They both had kind voices, and they both loved me.

CHAPTER EIGHT

Morris Keene

Trinity is massive.

It's not just the wealthiest college; it's double the scale of even its nearest competitor. Its first courtyard is a ridiculous two acres. That said, its chapel is smaller than some. Grand, obviously, but, of the grand college chapels, not the grandest.

We ended up in there because we needed privacy for the conversation.

'See? No students!' Jimmy announced with pleasure, as our footsteps tapped on the stone floor of the lobby-like antechapel. Well, lobby-like if lobbies were where life-sized marble statues waited for chapel entry. I recognised only Newton and Tennyson; the rest were beyond my knowledge of the college's history. They looked alert, some even judgemental. It was under their eyes that we sat, on a long wooden bench, feeling small.

'I'd heard you left,' Jimmy said, holding his hand out in front of us, meaning that my hand was the reason.

'I did leave. I came back.' I held my hand out too. It was still here. Didn't work properly any more, but still here. 'I need to know more about Annalise Wood.'

He leant back, his bowler hat tapping a brass memorial plaque on the wall behind us, one of dozens. Trinity porters are among the smartest dressed; certainly better than me in my basic black suit and cheap grey tie. 'So you said. That was a sad case, Morris. A sad case. Before your time.'

It's not often that I feel young. 'I know, Jimmy. So tell me. What was it like?'

'It's the parents that I remember. Howlingly upset. At first trying to prove that the worst might have happened, just to get the police to do something; then desperately trying to come up with ways that maybe the worst hadn't happened, as years went on.'

I nodded. 'You were part of both investigations, 1976 and 1992?'

'I was the only one on both, officially. Unofficially, everyone who'd been on the case in '76 took an interest when the body was found.'

'Tell me as if I'm stupid. How do you even know that the body was hers? It had to have been far gone . . .'

'It was,' Jimmy began. He pulled off his hat, rubbed his head, stalling. 'Fresh bodies are bad. I know you know. They're close to life but just, stopped. It's wrong. It's uncanny. But long-gone ones . . .' He shook his head. 'It wasn't human any more. It wasn't a she, it wasn't a person. It was evidence that a person had once been there, like a footprint is, but it's not itself the person any more, not any person.'

Jimmy had retired after that investigation.

111

He shook himself and went on. 'We knew it was once her because of the clothes: black uniform skirt, school blouse with the crest on it, and the name-tape inside of the collar.'

'But the body . . .' I prompted.

He waved a hand vaguely. 'Right height, right hair. It was her. You sound like . . .'

I sat up straighter. 'There were people who didn't believe it was her?'

'It wasn't a matter of belief, Morris. It was hope. Some people get blinded by it. We're not supposed to.'

I nodded, agreeing with the sentiment, but still pressing the point. 'DNA?'

'This was the early days of the science. The parents were dead. There had been no samples set aside. We pulled out all the stops we had, but this was a long time ago.' The musical metaphor of pulling out stops was punctuated by the actual organ above us stirring to life with an arpeggio. From this point, the practising organist scored our conversation with pounding chords and a driving melody. I hadn't even realised anyone was up there.

'We had Annalise's fingerprints taken from objects in her bedroom. But the left hand of the corpse was too deteriorated, and the right hand had been carried off by scavengers. Before you wonder, the separation at the wrist appeared to be post-deterioration, so, no, there isn't a killer out there with a right-hand souvenir. There were most of her teeth, but there was nothing distinctive, just healthy teeth. But I felt pretty good about ID-ing a dead girl in a missing girl's clothes as the missing girl!'

He was clearly annoyed by what seemed to him to be criticism of his judgement. I tried to placate him over the volume of what I now recognised as a hymn. I didn't know the words but the tune was something I'd learnt at Christmas or Easter as a child. My chest vibrated with it. 'Jimmy, I trust you. That's why I'm here. You know better than anyone. I'm not asking because I don't believe you; I'm asking because I wasn't there.'

'You read the notes.'

'I read the notes. I make notes like that. I know that they don't tell the whole story.'

'Did you read the books?'

'Yes. But I want to hear it from you.' I hate 'true crime' as a genre. I don't trust it.

'I'm in the Martin book,' he said, nodding proudly. 'He quotes me.'

I nodded admiringly, which was what he seemed to be after.

'I'll tell you what I told him. Just because we don't know something doesn't make it a mystery, not in the way most people mean the word. People say "mystery" as if there's no possible answer, as if only the supernatural, or aliens, or some massive conspiracy were left. Something you don't know isn't as grand as a mystery. It's an ordinary thing that you just don't know.'

'You think Annalise's death was straightforward.'

'Of course it was. I hate to say this but you know it's true: sometimes people kill. Sometimes people rape. By "people", I mean "men", don't I. I say it as a man myself. And if you're going to kill someone, or rape someone, you'd want someone youngish, not too strong. But, unless you're a paedophile, you'd want someone pubescent, right? So it's not a shock that someone – some

113

man – who wanted to rape someone and then killed them (which may have been part of the thrill or maybe just a necessary evil or even an accident) chose a teenage girl. A pretty one. Well, most teenage girls are pretty. Maybe I didn't know that when I was a boy but it's obvious now. Young, riding a bike, long hair. It's a crime, but it's not a mystery.'

I anchored his musings in the practical: 'What do you think happened to her bike? It was purple, right?'

'Purple, with a stubborn souvenir sticker from a trip to Spain partly scraped off. If we'd found it, we would have known for sure.'

'And the rape? You're sure about that? Because in the notes—'

He slumped. 'The press treated it as a sex crime from the start. They shouldn't have. It was salacious. Unnecessary. But you know how it is. Ted Bundy in America was making headlines at the time she disappeared. Remember the Will Teague case, in Peterborough in the nineties? All those prostitutes? I swear my kids learnt the birds and bees from the coverage of those murders. It was everywhere, and it sold papers, just like this case. No doubt the coverage made it worse for Annalise's parents. But there was semen, Morris. I can't prove if it was a rape or a rendezvous, but, considering that he then smothered her, I'm going to stick with rape!'

I cleared my throat. 'Was any of the semen in her body, or just on her clothes?'

'"Just"?' He raised an eyebrow. 'Do you know how difficult it was to isolate it at all? This was a sixteen-years-dead former body, Morris. The pants were a total loss. The skirt had ridden

114

up and bunched in the grave, so part of it had been spared the fluids of decomposition. That we got anything useful at all was a bloody miracle.'

'So the semen you tested was exclusively from the skirt, not from anywhere else?'

'Meaning what?'

'Meaning that we know that someone came on her skirt, not that someone had sex with her.'

'The most obvious way to get semen on the inside of a skirt is to fuck the girl in it, wouldn't you say?'

The organist stopped abruptly, as if offended by a swear word in chapel. But, no, he must have been working through a difficult passage. He stopped and started several times, repeating a challenging flourish.

I tried to placate Jimmy. 'I just need clarity. You did the angels' work. I mean that. We're building on what you did then to now put this to bed.'

That worked; he perked up. 'You found him?' he asked, not angry any more. He looked hopeful.

'We're figuring things out. There might be more than one "him". We don't think the person who left the semen' – I deliberately phrased it that way – 'did the killing. What can you tell me about that? She was smothered? By a hand, or was there some kind of object involved?'

He shook his head and lifted empty hands. 'Blood vessels break in the eyes when someone dies like that, but we didn't have the eyes. All we had was a broken nose, and broken front teeth, as if from pressure. We had evidence in what was left of the flesh of her face that those wounds happened when she was alive, at least briefly. You get your face pressed in like that . . .' Here

115

he made a gesture, pushing with the heel of his hand. 'Over the nose and the mouth, well, you stop breathing. I don't know what was pressed there, if anything. There was nothing in the grave with her. A hand alone could have done it. A man's hand,' he clarified, meaning a large hand. 'There were only the clothes she went missing in, still on her. We sifted the earth around her body for days. There was nothing else. Nothing.' He squinted defiantly, daring me to criticise his meticulous work. 'Morris, if we'd found the grave closer to the time she went in, before her body . . . Well, if we're going to wish, we might as well wish that it had never happened!' He sounded angry enough to compete with the minor chords bouncing around the chapel walls.

This was going to be my professional life from now on, questioning my colleagues. Besides cold cases, our team's other work involved advising on stalled current cases and investigating domestic abuse investigations that had been handled badly. All, in a way, policing other police. I'd thought I'd been lucky to be handed Annalise as my first go, such a huge case; I'd thought it was a gift. Maybe it was a test. Maybe it was an albatross.

'What made the grave stand out?' I asked carefully, not engaging his indignation. *Just keep it flowing, just keep him talking*, like I do with suspects. It didn't feel right, treating my own people that way.

'It wasn't us that found her. It was a man walking his dog, one of those massive dogs, those kind that rescue people in mountains.' He didn't look at me and his voice was normal again. He knew this wasn't personal. I hoped he understood that in his bones.

'What about the tracks? Why there? Did anyone ask the locals about that spot, whether it had a reputation, why anyone would choose it?'

'She'd been laid near a copse of poplars planted in memory of a historic derailment. That's how she was found; a storm knocked down a tree and the roots brought her up.' He shrugged. 'Maybe it felt more respectful to choose a marked place, or maybe the trees gave some cover to the act of burial.'

'Did she look . . . ?' I hesitated. I've never seen a corpse that old. 'Did she look sixteen?' Hard to say if sixteen looks that much different from the years on either side, but Jimmy had seen her and I hadn't.

He reared back. 'She looked dead, Morris. Just dead.'

He stood up. I joined him. This was the job now: looking over the shoulders of earlier investigators, questioning their work and pissing them off.

He added, 'Someone else came to me about Annalise last month. She'd got my name from that true crime book.'

So not police. 'Family?' But Annalise had no family left.

'Well, that's the interesting thing. She looked a lot like those photos. Well, what those photos would have grown into. But I suppose quite a few people look like that. You get the hair right, and white skin and general Englishness, resemblance isn't that hard to achieve. She had it in her head that she was Annalise's daughter. You know what it's like.'

Oh, I do. Some people try to insert themselves into investigations, even to the point that they'll confess to things that can get them into trouble. To some people, attention, even in the form of trouble, is as necessary as oxygen.

'Except she wasn't trying to prove it. She was trying to disprove it. She brought me the book and said that there was nothing about Annalise having had a baby. She wanted to know if the autopsy had shown anything, you know, if her pelvis had shown she'd given birth. She wanted to know if we had any DNA sample left and if she could have a test done. I told her absolutely not. She suggested we'd covered it up for the parents' sake, and I asked her to leave. I'll be honest with you, Morris, if we had found evidence that Annalise had been pregnant, I'd've seen no reason to give that to the press. But there wasn't. I went and looked at the autopsy report again. There was nothing in the bones to suggest she'd had a child. Could have had a C-section, of course. Could have been pregnant and miscarried or aborted, but if she'd pushed a baby out, well, the pelvis would show it. No baby. That woman was a bloody lunatic.'

Probably. 'But Annalise could have had a baby by cesarean section. Yes?'

'You've read the interview with her family and friends. She'd never been pregnant.'

'She was in France for several months the year before . . .'

'There comes a point when you just have to trust your colleagues, yeah?'

Touché. 'Did you get the woman's name?'

'She didn't say.'

'How old was she?'

Jimmy squinted. 'Just a kid; about your age,' he joked.

He was right. If Annalise had had a child, that child would now be around forty.

'Thanks, Jimmy, for the information and the compliment.' Nothing like spending time with someone decades older to feel young again.

'I promise you that there's nothing in her story. She's just an attention-seeker. But if you truly want to chase your own tail, I sent her on to Peter Gage.'

I leant back, as if the name were a glass marble and I needed to get it to fall into just the right hole in my brain. 'I remember the name . . .'

'He worked the case in '92. He's a porter at Robinson now.'

'Thanks, Jimmy.' I tried to smooth things over. 'The case was lucky to have you.'

He thought about that for a moment, then tipped his hat. I felt forgiven for my necessary scepticism. He left the chapel.

I held still for a moment, trying to fit in with the statues. They represented men more important than I'll ever be. But they were dead, and I wasn't, which seemed to be more to the point than being special. I thought about the woman who'd sought Jimmy about supposedly being Annalise Wood's child. Probably, as Jimmy had divined, just an attention-seeker. But perhaps, just perhaps, something more interesting.

Robinson College wasn't far. I phoned ahead, asked if Peter Gage was working. He was. I walked.

The distance between Robinson and Trinity is ten minutes, but it jumps you forward four centuries. Robinson had been founded in the 1970s, tastefully choosing red brick over the bland concrete that curses most of the University's other late-twentieth-century additions.

Peter met me at the top of the long upwards path leading to the porters' lodge. At that point, the red brick gave way to a paved courtyard and, after that, lawns and gardens. Unlike in the more formal courtyards of the older colleges, it's permissible to walk on Robinson's grass. Peter Gage had offered me a walk in the gardens.

Peter was young compared to Jimmy, and a little older than me. So, not young to the students around us, but young in the new normal I was making for myself. He was cheerful, too, and seemed excited, rather than defensive, to have an excuse to talk about the case again.

He extended his hand to shake while introducing himself, so I knew he didn't know the details of my injury. I put my hand in his, gripping with my thumb but with the rest of my fingers slack. I could see in the quick flicker of his eyes that he noted the strangeness, but he didn't comment. Most people won't say anything so long as I handle it with confidence myself.

'Peter, I understand that you worked on the Annalise Wood case when her body was found. It's my case now. Is there anything you think was ignored at the time that should have been given attention?'

We were walking towards a pretty brook, which was crossed by a pretty bridge, and where a practical bright orange life ring hanging from a post reminded that bad things can happen anywhere.

'I'm not sure what I can do for you. Jimmy knows more about the case than I ever will.'

He was a few years older than me, within view of fifty while I was still recovering from hitting the forties, but had an earnest, youthful modesty. I assured him of his importance to the case. 'He's given me the forensic overview. You talked to witnesses, didn't you? I would really like to know what it was like.'

'It was like stepping into a legend. I'd grown up hearing about the case. I think it was the first case I was aware of as a child. It might have been what made me join the force in the first place. And then, when the body was found, somehow I was in the middle of it all. It had come out of nowhere. For something new to surface after so many years . . .' We paused at the centre of a long bridge, leant on the railing. 'Is there something new now?' he asked me, sliding his eyes my way without turning his head.

'Maybe.' I smiled. 'We thought we had something big that turned out to be something small, but might, just might, be something big enough.'

We were facing the sun, which felt good but made us both squint. He closed his eyes and considered out loud: 'After all these years . . . I'm betting either a deathbed witness confession, or DNA.' He opened his eyes and faced me. 'DNA, am I right? That's why you went to see Jimmy.'

'When you're right, you're right,' I admitted. 'But it's not conclusive. You can't say a word.'

'There wasn't much,' he recalled, thinking back. 'There was nothing to compare the body to. Her parents were dead. The original investigation had saved fingerprints but no DNA samples. Even a toothbrush, properly preserved, could have done it, but they didn't know that back then . . .'

'I can't say what it is.'

He carried on musing: 'So it can't be the girl; has to be the man. The stuff on her skirt. That's all they had. Right? I haven't lost my touch, have I?'

He said it as a joke, but at his age, and even at my age, the question has a manic tinge as well: *I'm not old yet, am I? Surely not yet . . .*

I had to be firm. 'Now do you see what the media will do with this if they catch it? Same as you. And I promise you it won't help. I have to keep what we have quiet.'

He acquiesced, apparently because the enemy of his enemy is his friend. 'The newspapers were appalling. The photographs they published! Actually published! And people came to the site. We had to have police at the body round the clock until it was fully removed. Some people brought their own cameras, which at least took effort then. Could you imagine it today?'

'What were the people like? You followed up on the original interviews, with whoever was still near Lilling. Any in particular that stood out to you?'

'It wasn't like interrogating a suspect, where an emotional reaction lets you know you've hit a tender place. This case was tender for literally everyone there, so a reaction didn't mean anything. Most of the people I spoke with had already heard the news, but there were some for whom I was breaking it. It took my breath away sometimes, I mean that. You'd think I was telling them about their own child. Well, they'd known her, some of them. Or at least known her parents. Or just remembered that she'd been one of them. None of my interviews did anything for the case, in the end. Just like this one won't do anything for you,' he added wryly.

We'd started wandering again, and I nudged away from clutches of students and from open bedroom windows. 'Is there somewhere more private?' I asked.

Sensing that this would be worth his while, he led me round a hedge to a grassy space he introduced as the college's outdoor theatre. We sat at the edge of the low stage, facing an empty audience. He offered me a cigarette; I declined.

I said, 'What if I told you that her body wasn't buried the day she disappeared? What if I told you it was buried three years later, or more?' Charlie hadn't messed with the skirt until 1979.

'Three years difference, out of sixteen . . . and now out of almost forty . . . You can't tell that with forensics.'

'What if I could? Would that make you look at any of your interviewees in a different way?'

His eyes followed fast-moving clouds as he savoured the chance to smoke. 'That would mean . . . she'd been kept before she was killed?'

I shrugged. 'Kept dead or alive. Went into the ground later than we thought.'

He demanded precision: 'Or was in the ground elsewhere first . . .'

'Possibly,' I allowed. 'But probably not.' It would be difficult to change the clothes of an unearthed corpse.

He shook his head; he let out a low whistle; those stereotypical signifiers of awe, as if he were playing them for someone in the back row.

He said, 'Lilling's full of big houses, especially at the edges of the town. Houses, fields, sheds . . . You think it was like that case in Germany?'

I shrugged. There have been too many cases of imprisoned women. Austria, Ohio, take your pick . . .

He continued, 'I don't know. There weren't any homes

where I wasn't allowed in. People wanted to talk.'

I pounced: 'Anyone who wanted to talk about it more than you'd expect?'

He wagged his head slowly for no. 'No one that made bells ring. Oh, there were the usual lonely people, who would have been happy to talk about anything. One cup of tea after another. But no one who seemed . . . voyeuristic. Well, at least not more than the whole thing naturally was.'

'And these were people who had been interviewed back in 1976 as well?'

'A lot of them. I'd been given the original interview list to use as a checklist. Sometimes it was the next generation on. Sixteen years, after all . . .'

And now almost forty. 'If you were going to do these interviews again,' I began, because that's exactly what I had ahead of me, 'where would you start? Who would you prioritise?'

We went over the obvious details that would pique interest: property, outbuildings, privacy, whatever would make it possible to hide a living teenager or her body for, say, three to ten years. Keep her any longer than that, and there wouldn't have been enough time in the ground for that level of decomposition.

He wouldn't let go of that time frame, and how I'd got to that first 'three years'.

'You can't get that level of precision from the body itself. It's insects, isn't it? Something that would have implanted itself at death and then hatched . . . exactly thirty-something years later?' He trailed off. Insects help in the scale of days and weeks, not years. Besides, the remains had been cremated.

He slapped his knee. 'It's the clothes, isn't it. Has to be. But she wore them the day she disappeared. I saw them myself, standard school uniform . . .'

I kept my face blank.

'We're back to his DNA. But you can't date DNA like dinosaur bones.'

'And if we could, it would tell us something within plus or minus a thousand years.'

'Fabric content? Was it a new style? But it had her name tape in the collar. I'm telling you, they were her clothes.'

I agreed with a bland nod. Then I wondered, 'What did the name tape say, exactly?' Because we hadn't yet touched on the route of the clothes.

'"AKW" for Annalise Katherine Wood.'

He remembered her middle name. I was strangely touched. 'Just the initials?' I clarified.

'Are you thinking we've mixed her up with someone else, some missing teenager from the county called something like Alice Kitty Walsh, and we were just too stupid to make a connection? The original detectives had been told that's how her mum had done her labels. We were looking for those initials.'

I believed him. My stress on the name tape wasn't mistrust of their work. If that label had been explicit, saying 'Annalise Wood' in full, then the clothes would have to have been used deliberately. But if there were only initials, someone could have got at the clothes, not knowing whose they were . . .

I shook my head. That was opening up more directions than would be easy to follow. All we knew about this body for sure was that she'd never had work on her teeth, and had long, dark hair. Actually, the hair . . .

'Peter, do you remember how long the hair was? On the corpse?'

'You think someone cut it?'

'Had they?'

He said no and stubbed out his cigarette on the bottom of his shoe, and put the butt into a little tin he carried in his pocket. 'You're wondering if her hair had grown.' He grinned, wanting approval.

'Had it?'

'It was long,' he said, holding his hands roughly two feet apart. 'Long, like in the pictures of her.'

'Which was the fashion in the seventies,' I noted.

'Exactly.' He took out the box of cigarettes again, offering again. He didn't expect me to take it; I think he wanted to know if we were going to keep talking long enough to get him through another. I nodded that he should go ahead. 'How fast does hair grow in three years?' he wondered out loud.

I looked it up on my phone. About half an inch a month, so about eighteen inches in three years. But I know from my daughter that hair sometimes reaches a terminal length. If it was long already, it might not have grown much more. Or someone might have been cutting it.

'Was it ragged on the edges?' I asked. 'Or clean across?' They would have expected clean across if they'd thought she'd died soon after going missing. They would have noticed a ragged cut or unexpected length, surely . . .

Peter thought so too, and chided me. 'The hair looked just like the day she disappeared. Where did you get this three-year business, anyway?'

From a prostitute's john who was driving when he shouldn't have been. From a boy who was in France when Annalise disappeared, and had an embarrassing story of masturbation at the ready. Was Charlie really enough to upend the assumptions of this case? *When it's his DNA, I suppose he is.*

'Thanks, Peter,' I said. His cigarette wasn't even half-done and he looked forlorn at my finishing. Good thing I had one more question. 'There's a woman who thinks she's Annalise Wood's daughter. Did she get in touch with you?'

He nodded, laughing and inhaling at the same time, which ended in a sputtering cough. He finally spoke, while knocking his chest with his fist. 'Her! Yes. She came here. We went for a walk, same as today. Except she didn't like that I smoked. Didn't say a word, but I could tell.'

'Well?' I prompted.

'"Well," what? She's a nutter. Annalise didn't have a baby.'

'But did she say why she thought that?'

'Wouldn't tell me. Wanted me to do all the talking. I didn't have much to say.'

'Did she give her name?'

'No. I have her number, though. She'd phoned the office to see if I was working. I wrote it down.'

I blinked. 'You're still a cop,' I marvelled.

'At heart,' he agreed.

I copied the number from a note in his phone into mine.

'Do you think the body's not her?' Peter asked as we stood and stretched our legs. We were at the middle of the front of the stage, and his voice seemed to carry.

127

'I can't say that,' I told him, meaning it deeply. *If that's not Annalise, we're worse off than when I took the case.*

'Oh,' he said, coming up with one more thing to use up the last centimetre of his cigarette. He inhaled then said, 'I think I know what you've got!' His eyes sparkled. He really wanted to prove he'd figured me out.

I looked away. 'Bet you don't.' It was a phrase that would inevitably egg him on, but I was confident that 'Charlie Bennet masturbated into Annalise's old clothes during a tea party in 1979' wasn't about to pop out of his mouth.

'The dog walker.' He lifted his eyebrows, waiting for me to admit he'd got me.

'Sorry?' I said, tilting my head in genuine lack of understanding.

'The one who found the body. We were all interested in him. A real character, as we would say if we were feeling polite. He was a strange one, and very interested in the case. We all wondered if he might have taken a souvenir before he called us. But . . .' He shrugged. 'He said he hadn't . . .' He stubbed out this cigarette, so I was pretty sure the conversation was about to end. 'It was worth a guess. A deathbed confession of some object buried with her, something not around before 1979?' Still a question mark at the end of his sentence, in case I might yet surrender to his cleverness.

'Peter, it would be a pleasure to discuss it with you, but you know I can't.' He's not police any more.

Technically, neither am I. But I'm *with* the police. He's with the University. It's different.

I wondered, as we walked back through the gardens, over the bridge, past the helpful but ominous life ring, if I would ever go this route. College courtyards have something over our overcrowded offices, but I could never do it. Not after having been a student at Cambridge. I couldn't imagine the way the undergraduates would look at me if they knew. *You were one of us, and now you're staff?* Never, I could never. *What does that say about me, caring what eighteen-year-olds think of me?*

I thanked Peter at the porters' lodge and took the ramp leading out. The slant of it, and the brick college walls behind me, made me feel like I was exiting the hold of a ship.

I headed into Burrell's Walk, a cycle path between Trinity's gardens and the University Library, and crossed another little bridge. I walked quickly, hands in pockets. The state of the case had me on edge. *If that body's not Annalise, I've got to solve it, or bury what we got from Charlie.* If all I contribute to the case is undoing what little they had, and the press gets hold of it . . . That's not what I came back to the job for.

Cyclists and students brushed past me as I stepped to the side of the path to phone the number of the obsessed young woman. Very likely a dead end, but not certainly, and so it was worth it to bother.

It rang six times, then went to voicemail. 'You've reached Hannah-Claire Finney. I no longer work at the Fitzwilliam. If you need to reach someone there, please call the main number. If you want to talk to me, leave a message!'

That name sounded familiar. A quick search on my tablet picked up fresh news stories. She'd drowned in the Cam, and her death was being investigated by Detective Sergeant Angus Spencer, the colleague who just months ago had arrested my daughter.

Breathe, Morris, I had to tell myself, again.

I have progress. I have possibilities, I reminded myself. *If our cases are colliding*, I decided, *mine is going to come out on top.*

CHAPTER NINE

Laurie Ambrose

I chose a light grey suit, not black, and compared hair-up to hair-down in the mirror. I planned to say that I was simply 'a friend', but what if someone asked me where from? I couldn't say from the museum; friends from the museum would likely be there and know that I'm not. I didn't know anything else about Hannah-Claire Finney. Well, I knew a lot, but nothing that I could say.

The body had been released. The husband, Henry Ware, had been questioned but not actually jailed. He was 'assisting police with their enquiries'. I assumed that there must have been photos of him and Hannah together, but the ones used by the media were separate: Hannah, exuberantly smiling in the local Botanic Garden (I recognised the glasshouses in the background), and Henry coming out of Parkside Police Station last week. Hannah looked happy, promising. Like Annalise Williams said of Annalise Wood: they chose an appealing picture. Henry looked angry in his, but anyone would be angry if, as they exited a police station, someone snapped a picture. Today I was going to see him look sad. I was curious to see him smile. Not today, but in the recent past. I wanted to see evidence of them having been together and happy. I wanted that for Hannah.

They had married quickly, which is usually due to either eager, naive enthusiasm, or pregnancy. No child or obvious pregnancy had been reported, so I dared to hope for the former.

Simon and I had been married almost a year already. I still sent him a little 'monthiversary' text when I noticed on the calendar that it was a 10th of the month. Two champagne corks from our post-ceremony family dinner were in front of my mirror right then, with my make-up brushes and straightening iron. Eventually I'll toss the corks as dust-catchers, or tuck them in a corner of my jewellery drawer. For now, they still caused a frisson of delight when I caught sight of them as I readied myself each day. Perhaps Hannah still had corks, or cards on the mantel, or even thank-you notes left to write. Just one month. It felt so short. Her life was too short. She was younger than me.

I dabbed at my eyes and breathed in through my nose. *Get ahold of yourself.*

I hadn't been to a funeral since Tom's.

Downstairs, Simon's papers were spread out over the dining table. He was applying for angel funding for his company. I could hear the fan in his laptop, a sign that it's been on too long. He'd been at this for hours.

'Don't forget to take a break,' I told him lightly.

Despite my chipper voice I must have looked apprehensive, because he looked at me and said, 'You sure you want to do this?'

I couldn't ask him to come with me. Two of us would be more obvious. I shouldn't have been going at all. Prisha would not have approved. Part of the confidentiality we owe each client is the fact of their being a client at all. 'I need to.'

'You look upset.'

'I'll fit right in, then. It's a funeral,' I reminded him. My voice quivered.

'Laurie,' he said, pushing out his chair.

I slipped into his embrace. The curve of my forehead rested against his neck.

Simon had attended Tom's funeral. I don't remember him there. He and Tom hadn't been close after university, but Tom, when a graduate student, had been Simon's supervisor one year. So Simon came. He'd told me about that when we were just starting to date, and that night at home I'd looked for his name in the service guest book, the first and only time I've ever opened that horrid memento. His signature was a scrawl, but he'd written a quote neatly in the 'notes' column: 'At the going down of the sun and in the morning . . .'

That's from a Remembrance Day poem:

They shall grow not old, as we that are left grow old:
Age shall not weary them, nor the years condemn.
At the going down of the sun and in the morning
We will remember them.

Tom had died in early November four years ago, just before Remembrance Day. Some people still had their paper-and-plastic poppies tucked in their coat lapels at the funeral two weeks later. That's why the poem had been in Simon's mind. No one in my family had died in either of the World Wars, so Remembrance Day has become about Tom to me, and to the kids.

When Blake was first at university, he'd stumbled on a formal Remembrance Day service there. He and Clara both chose Tom's old college, Jesus College, here in Cambridge. Simon and I had both been at Christ's College, practically just across the street. The college names are remnants of their history as religious schools, a theme now in name only. But for Blake, that service, beginning in the cloister at the centre of the college and then proceeding into the twelfth-century chapel, had stirred in him a longing for spiritual structure.

He began to attend evensong services, and discussion groups in the chaplain's rooms. He was eventually invited to take on the responsibility of chapel secretary, lighting candles and setting out hymnals. He's never tried to evangelise any of us, though he does invite us to special services, and I do go. Now that he and Clara are both at Jesus, we all attended the annual Remembrance service together last week. The ceremony is so moving that I'm almost tempted each time to become religious myself. The choir voices, the names of the college's wartime dead carved into the stone walls . . . It's difficult to resist the comfort of eternal life and eventual justice.

Hannah's funeral service was to be at the Catholic church in Cambridge, so I expected that there would be a similar emphasis on afterlife. But I wanted to know about her life.

'I'll be fine,' I assured Simon, stepping back and forcing

a smile. Looking at his face, my smile gradually became real. He still looked young to me, in his wire-framed glasses that he'd worn since uni. His inquisitive eyes and tilted head added to the studenty impression. It's only when I look at my children, now university students themselves, that I realise how old Simon and I really are.

'I'm going to see Clara afterwards,' I told him. 'She asked me to bring her her gloves and school scarf.'

Clara and Blake each have a room in this house, for holidays, but because the house is new to them there's no accumulation of childhood toys and teen posters. The rooms look like guest rooms, which I dislike. It makes me feel like they're 'visiting' when they're here, instead of 'coming home'.

The things she wanted were easy to find in an accessories box on her nearly empty bookshelf. All of her Harry Potters and Horrible Histories had been given to charity shops years before. Some picture books I'd saved for future grandchildren, but they're in a plastic bin in the attic, with special baby clothes and the toy dog she used to sleep with. Now she reads mostly on her iPad.

I decided that I'd stop at Heffers on the way, to buy her a book.

'Prisha called while you were in the shower,' Simon told me.

'From Vienna?'

'Baby girl. Eight pounds.'

'Aw, lovely. She must be thrilled.'

Simon was smiling, but I preferred to tiptoe around such topics. I worried that he felt badly that he couldn't father children. 'I'll get a present from both of us,' I told him, protecting him from shopping for baby things.

He kissed me, a deep kiss, his hand on the back of my head. Our mouths separated, and I kissed him in three quick, grateful bursts.

'I love you. I'm not sure when I'll be home. Do you have any calls tonight?' Time zones often forced him to do business in the evenings.

'None. I'm all yours.' His fingertip traced my jawline, then trailed off behind my ear.

I shouldn't be thinking of sex on my way to a funeral, I reproached myself as I buckled into the car. *But isn't that just human?* I defended myself. It's life-affirming. It's distracting. It's present.

The church service was carried along by repetitive hymns and familiar-ish readings. It was the rhythm of it, more than the content, that was comforting. The very existence of a set service reminds that death has happened over and over, and grief has been survived. The readings told what the Bible says about what happens to dead people; I worried about what happens to those of us left behind.

I wanted to slip away at the end without having to explain myself to anyone. The priest had positioned himself by the main door, so I used the excuse of looking for the ladies' room to seek a back way out, or at least to wait out the handshaking. I wished that Simon had come with me after all, to deal with the priest, or to hold my handbag if I ever found the toilets. My blouse smelt of his cologne because we'd embraced earlier, or maybe I just imagined that it did, remembering.

So I was reminded of our incongruous groping earlier

when I walked in on Henry Ware and a woman, in a closet I'd mistaken for the ladies' loo.

I recognised him by his sandy hair and the hint of a carefully trimmed beard just above his collar: the grieving husband. The woman was almost fully hidden by his body, her face covered by his. Their clothes were mussed but on, thank goodness. Her arms around his neck were in black sleeves; her legs were in black tights. *Close enough to Hannah-Claire to wear black to the funeral*, I thought.

They were kissing and rubbing in there, a tight, frantic clutching. I gasped like an ingenue. He grunted, either in pleasure because of her or angry because of me.

I slammed the door and ran out of the church.

The route is ingrained. I ended up in front of Christ's College gate.

Christ's had been home to me for six years. Well, I didn't always live in college, but, even when I lived out, college was one of my homes. As I entered, Doran, one of the porters, greeted me by name, even after all these years. They're magical, porters. They know everyone and never forget. The familiarity was enveloping, and warm. I wrapped my arms around my middle in an anxious self-embrace.

There was a bit of time before Clara expected me. I needed to calm down. I didn't want to bring that kind of turmoil to my daughter.

How dare he, was my first thought, as if Henry's actions today could still somehow hurt poor Hannah-Claire. Then, *What if it was a relative, instead of me, who'd walked in on them? What if it had been a child? Irresponsible.*

137

Inappropriate. Self-indulgent. Arrogant! Prioritising his lust, or – best-case – his overwhelming grief, over respect for others and the memory of his supposedly beloved wife . . .

I wondered who the woman was. A close friend, judging by her ostentatiously black outfit, or perhaps just an acquaintance with dramatic flair. Was it an affair? Had they been carrying on for weeks or months? Were they . . . celebrating?

I shuddered, then reminded myself that what they were doing didn't mean that there was an extramarital relationship a week ago. I reminded myself that even if there had been an affair, it didn't mean that either of them killed Hannah.

It was motive.

I argued back: *It's not my business.*

Again, my route was automatic. My footsteps took me to New Court, and to the aptly nicknamed 'Typewriter': stacked concrete boxes on a slope, the ceiling of each student room serving as a front patio for the one above. It's an anomaly when compared with the much older and harmonious architecture of the rest of the college. The Typewriter had gone up in the sixties, as much a victim of fashion as the clothes of the time.

The word 'victim' made my shoulders shimmy in disgust. At the funeral I'd seen people who didn't seem sad or involved, just interested. The possibly criminal nature of her death had attracted gawkers.

A student with a heavy backpack jostled past me on the path. I had lived here when I dated Tom. The memory of our breezy happiness then and later my intense, acerbic grief softened me. Henry could just have been lonely, achingly lonely.

A student came up the path behind me, with what appeared to be her parents in tow. They *oohed* at the lifesized bronze of young Darwin, Christ's most famous alumnus, seated on a bench in a little garden. That was new, from the Darwin bicentennial not long ago.

He looks so young, Darwin. The girl with her parents looked young too. I had felt so adult when I lived here. I was engaged and about to graduate. I'd had no idea how young, desperately young, I was.

I glanced at my watch. Time to visit Clara.

The bag of books banged against my thigh as I walked. I'd chosen Edward Lear nonsense poetry for Clara. Tom used to read her 'The Jumblies' when she was little, and 'The Owl and the Pussycat'. I got it today so she could read it in little spurts between studying, little reliefs.

Next to Lear in the bag was a pair of oversized, colourful Orlando books for Prisha's new niece, about the adventures of a cat family in the 1930s and '40s.

In the shop, on the shelf above the Orlandos, I'd seen the book that Annalise Williams had mentioned: *Small or Tall*. It was just as she had described it, with the skyscraper, moon, and cape. I noted the copyright date: 2009. I had just assumed she'd been remembering a book from her childhood. Evidently not.

But I was forty-two and was shopping in the children's section. Perhaps she babysat or had little siblings, or older siblings who had made her an aunt. I'd tucked it back between its neighbours on the shelf and retreated to the main floor of the shop. In 'True Crime', there she was, Annalise Wood, with her serene smile in the last school photo of her. I'd snatched up both paperbacks with her on the cover and paid for everything before I lost my nerve.

I'd felt furtive carrying those crime books in my bag, guilty even. It's not my place to explore things related to my clients' private lives. At the bookshop till I'd added in a beautiful blank book and boxed pen for Prisha, clearly, I admitted to myself, to compensate for doing what I know she wouldn't approve of. I'd also added a coffee-table book for Blake, photos of the insides of all the Cambridge college chapels.

Clara met me at Jesus College's porters' lodge. She noticed my bag. 'Ooh, a present for me?' she asked automatically. That has always been her question, whether I'm carrying armfuls of groceries or a briefcase full of work. Now she asked it out of sentimental habit, to make me laugh. It worked.

'As a matter of fact, it is. And your gloves and scarf. I'm so glad you asked me to come by today.' We hugged. Her wavy hair tickled my cheek. She's beautiful, more beautiful than I remember being at that age. She was wearing a rugby shirt over leggings, studying attire, but she shone.

'I've got two dresses for the May Ball. You have to help me choose.' She slipped her arm through the crook in mine and led me towards her room.

'Thinking ahead?' I asked. The annual college balls – held in June despite the name – are extravagant and exhausting, and were seven months away. If you build them up too much in your mind, they disappoint, but if you go for just a bit of fun, special moments have half a chance of surprising you. I wanted to tell her that, but she left no gaps, describing hairstyles and fascinators and what her friends might wear.

Passing through the cloister led us out into Chapel Court. A vibrant lawn mown in strict stripes was bordered by a symmetry of red-brick nineteenth-century student rooms. A rare blue sky swelled behind the dozens of chimneys. This has become a home to me, too, via my children.

When Blake had received his offer from the college, I'd been proud of his achievement, of course, and pleased he was able to follow in his father's footsteps, which he had so desperately wanted to do. With those reasons for happiness had been one more: that a university so grounded in continuous history, so full of traditions and . . . and order, I realised, was good for him. I recognised then that he needed order, even if I hadn't yet articulated it that way to myself. His eventual attraction to religion should not have surprised me.

Clara's room is at the top of her staircase. All the rooms had been recently refurbished, with new en suite bathrooms and decorated in the college colours, red and white. The upgrades made the student rooms more viable as conference accommodation out of term, and justified the costs that had been added since I was a student. We were fully subsidised in those days, but with fewer frills. I was tempted to lecture her on how luxurious she had it. I remember wandering the halls of Christ's in my dressing gown with a basket of shampoo and soap, off to the communal showers.

She had a painting up that I hadn't seen before, of a woman in an old-fashioned bathtub.

'Is that you?' I asked. The head was facing away but the hair was similar.

'No! Of course not.' But she cocked her head. 'It does look like me, doesn't it? I know the artist. I bought it for ten pounds. I never sat for it, but maybe he thought of me when he painted.' She struck the pose and laughed.

She hadn't told me about any boyfriends. She talked about the May Ball as if going with a clique of girls. I'd have guessed she was still a virgin but I tried not to think about it. I supposed she felt the same way about my sex life.

I gave her the book, and she cooed over it. She stood it up on her desk so, she said, she'd remember to notice it. She was clearly pleased, but was too excited about other things to linger on the topic.

She pulled out two dresses from her closet: one a long white halter dress that a goddess might wear, the other a princessy affair with net skirts and a ballerina top, both from charity shops. 'I promised Anna that whichever one I don't wear, she can. What do you think?'

She alternated holding them against herself and went on. 'Eleanor said the white one is more flattering, which is fine for everyone who's going to be looking at me, but the pink one is good for twirling and more fun to wear.' She demonstrated.

I was trying to keep track of the important people in her life. 'Eleanor is the one whose mother is a newsreader, right?'

Clara rolled her eyes. 'Yes, Mum. Honestly, we've been friends since last year.'

I held the white one up to the window to check if it got see-through in direct light. Maybe that's what Eleanor had meant by flattering . . .

'And Anna's a *new* friend,' Clara explained. 'She's a graduate student. I'm not supposed to tell you, but she's dating Blake.'

I flinched. 'Blake?'

Blake was so serious. He had friends, but his energy went into his studies and chapel responsibilities. He hadn't yet attended a May Ball.

'If they're still together then. Wolfson doesn't have a May Ball.' Clara pursed her lips at the mirror in annoyance. 'It's so easy for the boys. Blake already has a proper suit, black tie.' She snatched the white dress out of my hand, and squinted at it. 'I'm just being selfish. This one' – the white one – 'would look better on Anna, so I'll wear the other one. Problem solved.'

'Tell me about Anna,' I said.

'She's very nice. She makes Blake blush. She's getting an M.Phil in history. She was at Warwick as an undergrad, like Lindsay is now.'

Lindsay was Clara's best friend when she was ten. My brain plucked that information right out, even though I hardly ever think of her. It plucked a more recent memory too. *Warwick* . . . But a lot of people have gone to Warwick. A lot of people are called Anna. It might be the most common name in the world.

Clara had thrown the rugby shirt across the bed and was pulling the pink dress up over her leggings. 'Ta-da!' she announced, pinching it shut behind her back. She looked like a Degas.

My throat tightened when I asked, 'What's her last name?'

'Who?'

'That girl. With Blake.'

'Williams. Anna Williams.'

She was looking in the mirror, so didn't see my face.

Before she turned around, I forced myself to smile. I forced myself to breathe.

She looked hopefully at me.

'You look perfect,' I told her. 'You chose the right dress.'

She jumped up and kissed my cheek. Her half-dressed state reminded me of the snogging mourners in the church closet. This had been an awful day.

I needed to excuse myself. 'I promised Simon I wouldn't be out all day.'

Clara ducked her head, then turned to slip her shirt back on. 'I know it was really weird when you told us you were getting married, but Simon is really nice. He's really nice. I think you picked the right guy.'

She'd never said that before, not directly. She'd toasted us at our wedding dinner and was as polite as you could ask over Christmas in the new house, but she'd never specifically approved of him before.

'Thank you,' I said, fervently. I apologised for one errant tear and wiped it off my face. 'I went to a funeral today,' I explained, deflecting.

Her eyes widened. 'Oh no – whose?'

'A friend. No one you know,' I quickly clarified, having forgotten how sensitive she still is to ceremonies of death. She'd hated Tom's funeral, every moment.

She hugged me. 'You know what I wish for you, Mum? No more funerals.'

'I'm afraid that as one grows older, there are only more and more.'

It was unfair for me to be honest with her. She would discover it soon enough and didn't need to hear it now. Still, she recovered brightly and plopped down onto her bed. 'And I have to study. Thanks for the gloves.'

I fumbled for my handbag and my books. I said a silent prayer of thanks that I had impulsively bought a present for Blake. It had been so important when they were young to keep everything even and fair that I still tried to balance things out of reflex. 'I have something for Blake. Do you know where he is?' He lives in a terraced house around the corner, or could have been in any of a number of lectures or supervisions.

'Chapel?' she suggested, already working, her eyes flicking across the dense text of a thick book she'd opened to the middle. 'College library?' He has roommates, so takes advantage of the enforced library silence to study there.

'Thanks. I'll check.'

I slipped out of the room and down all those stairs, out into the court. I breathed better out there. I called his phone; he didn't answer.

Annalise Williams was pretty. She was twenty-four; Blake was twenty-one. She had the kind of assertive personality that's needed to get a shy man's attention; anything more subtle, and he'd never guess that she was interested. She was getting an M.Phil. She knew that I'm from near Lilling. She'd been playing with me. She knew who I was.

Blake had been supposed to meet me that day after her first session. *What if he'd been there after all? Had she met him then? Had she already known him then?*

I was in no condition at that moment to have a conversation with him about her. Maybe I should leave the chapel photo book for him, I considered, with a note that we need to make a lunch date? No, what if she read the note? I pictured her laughing at me. Wearing Clara's goddess dress.

Damn. As a therapist, I have to guard the information she's revealed in sessions. As a mother, I have to grant my adult children autonomy, because control backfires, especially romantic control. But as myself, as . . . as a stalking victim, that's what I felt like . . . I had to have some rights. Didn't I?

I couldn't see what she wanted. If she wanted him, she apparently had him. Why tell me? Why deliberately become a client, and give me a front-row seat? She wanted me to figure this out. She wanted to rub it in my face.

I glanced over at the college library. It was new, like the Darwin bronze. If Blake was there, I couldn't do more than slip him the book. No talking, unless I persuaded him to drop what he was doing and come outside with me. To say what? That I heard he has a girlfriend? Clara hadn't been supposed to tell me anyway.

I walked back through the cloister. The chapel was busy; I could hear the choir, and brass. It sounded grand, too big for evensong rehearsal. Must be for a concert. Blake wouldn't be in there. He only assists with services.

I exited past the porters. *Blake might be at home*, I thought.

Then, *She might be with him.*

What had Clara said? 'Wolfson doesn't have a May Ball.' Yes, Annalise Williams had told me that was her college. I turned my back on Blake's front door and headed across town for Wolfson College.

The city's changed in the twenty years since I was at university. I've continued to live here, so the gradual process should have blended together for me; but it hasn't. The changes from the city I was young in to the city it is now are underlined to me. *That patisserie used to be a bicycle shop. Woolworths is gone . . .*

I found Wolfson on the other side of the river, deep in residential territory. It's one of the youngest colleges at less than fifty years old, but that's still older than me, so as far as I'm concerned it's as much a fixture as the colleges that go back centuries. I'd been there before, for a party or two, but the porter here would not recognise me.

'Hi? I'm from Christ's.' Not currently, but declaring my affiliation was bound to be helpful. 'I'm looking for Anna Williams. Have you seen her come through today? Longish brown hair?'

I was fishing. Maybe, maybe, Blake's Anna Williams wasn't my Annalise Williams. I willed for the porter to counter with a description of curly black hair or a bobbed blonde.

The porter looked blank. 'Sorry, who?'

'Oh, I'm sorry. She's an M.Phil student here. History? Anna or Annalise.'

The porter checked a list, probably only to humour me. Porters know their students. 'No, sorry.'

'Look, this is ridiculous. I feel like I've made a silly mistake. Maybe Annie? Hannah?' There are a lot of starts that can end up at the nickname Anna. *Melanie? Diana?* 'Surname Williams,' I repeated.

He typed something into his computer; I released my pent-up breath.

'Sorry,' he said again.

'No Anna?'

'Who did you say you are?'

'Sorry,' I said. He'd apologised half a dozen times; it was my turn. 'I've been such a bother.'

I dashed out of the lodge, feeling light. It wasn't her. However I'd misunderstood Clara's information, whatever Anna herself had claimed to me, Annalise Williams wasn't a student at Cambridge. Whomever Blake was dating was Anna Something-Else, or perhaps Some-Other-First-Name Middle-Name-Anna Williams.

What if this supposed 'Annalise Williams', who lied to me, is with Blake and also lying to him?

I went cold. I wished I could play the recordings for Simon. Would it be enough to explain that she's not really a fellow student of Blake's? That she'd spun a story to finagle herself into our lives? Not just Blake, but me, and Clara . . .

I called Clara. It went to voicemail.

I rang off. My request was too bold to leave as a message. It required tact, and responding to her reactions. Blake would not react well to interference from me. Clara could probe things that I couldn't, and would let him down more easily. She could help him save face. She could say that she came to Wolfson and discovered no Anna Williams there. He'd never have to know that I knew.

When did Blake become so fragile? I marvelled with sadness. He used to be a typical boy: bold and oblivious, easily pleased. I thought about that for a moment, and about how Annalise had manipulated him. Perhaps he hadn't changed after all.

The pedestrian light turned green. I entered the Lammas Land playground, dodged manic children, and eventually came out the other side to the comparative calm of a commuter traffic jam on Fen Causeway. Cambridge has always felt compact to me, but today it felt elongated, stretched, and far too wide for the particular things I'd had to do.

At the end of Lensfield Road, I found myself back at the Catholic Church. Our Lady and the English Martyrs. *Martyrs*. More death. My stomach tightened.

Don't be ridiculous. The funeral was long over. No one would be left, in a closet or otherwise. Indeed, mine was the only vehicle left in the car park.

It was surrounded by police.

My breath caught in my throat. I angled my path, to get nearer to the cluster of confusion and uniforms while obscuring that that was my destination.

I saw the shoe before I saw the leg. I recognised it: black suede and a bow. I'd seen it that morning in the supply closet, on a foot rubbing up against Henry Ware's ankle.

An official-looking man was talking into a phone or radio, something chunky and rectangular in his hand. 'Sandra Williams,' he said into it, followed by numbers and jargon. *Sandy. Hannah's cousin?*

I recalled once watching a television programme about famous artists, which showed the way that figures can be reduced to an assortment of shapes: oval head, conical hat, triangular torso. That's what I saw then: shapes. The leg was a sausage-like tube. The curve of the foot was a Roman arch.

I turned away. I wanted to cross the road. Traffic was tight. The man behind me with the rectangle recited into it what I assumed was a driving licence number, presumably the victim's. Also, my number plate. I wanted to get across the road more than anything.

A gap appeared. I slithered through, and, on the other side, phoned Simon. 'Please come pick me up,' I said, breathless. 'Come now.' I walked purposefully in the opposite direction of the church, back towards the city centre.

'Why? Are you all right? Did you have a breakdown?'

He meant the car. I answered 'yes', meaning me. 'Yes. Yes. Please, Simon. I need you to come get me now.'

I heard him shutting down his computer. I heard his keys and his breathing. I wanted him to get out of the house before the policeman phoned our number from my vehicle registration. Simon would tell me to go back to them. I couldn't, though. I just couldn't.

'Where do you want me to find you?' he asked.

I considered. 'Silver Street.' The bollards there block through-traffic except for buses and taxis, so there would be room to pull over. More importantly, it was far from here. Back I went through the city that wasn't quite right any more: the post office had moved across the street; the Grand Arcade had sprung up out of nowhere.

All of these thoughts about the city were denial and self-defence; I recognised that. My mind was taking a roundabout journey away from my car as much as my body was. She . . . the body . . . was tucked between my front bumper and a brick wall. That probably meant that she was – I groped for unvivid words – put there when my car was the only one left behind, after everyone else had gone.

Everyone but two: her, and someone with her.

I had to tell the police what I'd seen. I had to tell them that she and Henry . . . And they'd want to know how I knew Hannah. I needed to get my head straight. There

150

were things I should say and things that I shouldn't.

The tube-leg. The arch-foot. The oval-face, tilted away from me, towards the wall. Thank God for that, I thought. Thank God.

I crossed the bridge at Silver Street. Recent studies have shown that doorways have a physical effect on the brain, causing that common experience of going to get something and forgetting it when you cross a threshold. I concentrated on the bridge underneath me, begging it to make me forget.

On the other side, nothing had changed: there was still a body in the church car park. The police would still follow up on my car and call me at home.

I hadn't seen the face, so my mind gave me Hannah-Claire Finney's. But the body wasn't like hers; it was younger; so I picture Annalise Wood instead, as on the covers of those true crime paperbacks. They're not that different, except that Hannah had become older than Annalise ever got the chance to be.

Is this how memory works? I wondered. Would my mind ever see any other face on that body now, even later when I'd know who it was? Would I recognise her; had I seen her at the funeral? But I'd stayed in the back and kept my head down, not wanting to invade the family's privacy.

It suddenly felt important to know, desperately important, and selfish. I couldn't bear having Hannah or Annalise dead under my bumper, even just in my mind. It needed to be a stranger. I turned around, bumped into a child who'd been following too close behind me, returned the mother's glare. 'Excuse me,' I mouthed without sound, and pushed myself back towards the church.

151

I phoned Simon as I walked, but he didn't pick up. He must have already been driving.

Medical people were putting the body on a rolling bed, so she must not have been dead. I still couldn't see the face; I saw only a paramedic's back.

He moved. Cousin Sandy's head lolled in my direction. It was Annalise, but not the book-cover one, not the one who'd gone missing in Lilling forty years ago.

It was Annalise Williams, my client. She was dressed in black, bloody, and barely alive.

CHAPTER TEN

Chloe Frohmann

Dan had called my bluff. I should have guessed he'd do something like that.

'It was your idea,' he claimed, bouncing our daughter. 'You suggested it.'

I bit my lip. He kept a straight face. He'd called her after Stephen Fry. Well, he'd called her Stephanie. Stephanie Robin.

I'd have to make up a story if people asked how we'd come by the name. I could make up an obscure but beloved relative. I could say it meant 'diligent' or 'happy' in . . . French? Swedish? (Maybe it did, for all I knew.) I didn't want to admit that I'd left it entirely up to Dan. I didn't want to admit that we'd named her after a comedian, for Christ's sake.

'You love it,' Dan said, lifting our happy (and possibly diligent) daughter up to my face. 'Ste-pha-nie,' he said, tapping my nose with her reaching fingertip.

'It's going to take some getting used to,' I said, because if

I said that I loved it, or, worse, said the name itself, I would cry. It's bad enough that my chest leaked; I had to get that from my eyes too.

Dan looked worried. 'It's all right, isn't it?'

'It is,' I said. 'It's a good name.' I took her in a cuddle. 'I'll feed her now,' I told him, settling in on the couch. 'You can use a bottle later if I'm gone long.'

Dan puttered, clearing the coffee table. 'Who are you seeing today?'

'That's a sensitive subject.'

'Sorry,' he said, quickly. There are sometimes things I really can't share.

'No, not like that. I need to talk to Spencer.'

'What about?'

'Morris.'

'Oh,' said Dan, meaning 'Oh, shit.'

'And "oh" about me assisting on a case off the books. I'm not sure how he'll react to that.'

'Why talk to him at all?'

I repositioned the – *no, not 'the baby' any more; Stephanie* – and spilled all. 'Our old case has collided with a current case. Maybe.' After all, someone being delusional about their relationship with a famous crime doesn't mean that they're actually connected to it. Except, when the delusional person ends up suddenly dead just around the time we're looking into it, maybe it does . . .

I explained about Charlie's DNA and the clothes on the body, and what they meant for the date the body had gone into the ground. More importantly, for where the body – dead or alive – had been before it got those clothes on and went into the ground.

154

I told him what Morris had learnt from the previous investigators about how sure they were – or weren't – that the body was Annalise. It had the right hair, though not grown significantly longer over the three or more years between disappearance and burial. It had matching teeth, but only in that the teeth had had no work done, which could match many, many people. It was the right stage of development for a sixteen-year-old, or thereabouts. It was in Annalise's clothes, but those clothes were identified only by initials, not the full name, so it's possible, somehow, that they'd been chosen without awareness of whose they'd been years before. After all, even if it was Annalise, why would the killer, or the girl herself, prioritise finding a fresh iteration of her old clothes to wear? Unless it wasn't Annalise and the killer wanted us to think that it was . . .

Dan pointed out, 'That would only be if he expected the body to be found, which doesn't seem to be the case. And if it had been found any earlier, the face could have been recognisable as not-Annalise. If he was waiting for a storm to blow over a tree and a man to walk a dog, well, he was playing a long con . . .'

'What if he wasn't just waiting? What if . . . ?' I grabbed the paperback shoved between the couch cushions. I'd been reading and highlighting while nursing. 'The dog walker, Clemmy Osborne. Clemmy? Well, thank you, Dan, for not calling our daughter that . . .'

'Named after his mother, Clementine, perhaps?' He sat too and read over my shoulder. Mr Osborne had lived in the area all his life. He'd been rather thoroughly interrogated by the police in 1992. The afternoon that Annalise went missing, on her way home from school, he had a perfect alibi with many witnesses at a gathering of model railway enthusiasts.

'So not him,' I conceded, meaning all the usual caveats: *not him that day, not him alone*. An alibi for one part doesn't necessarily mean he wasn't involved at all. 'But what if that was the reason? What if someone wanted to create the illusion that Annalise's body had been found, even if they knew they had to wait years for the decomposition to make it believable?'

'To comfort her family?' Dan suggested. 'For a certain definition of comfort, I suppose . . .'

'They were dead by 1992. In fact, it was their deaths that got the clothes and Annalise's other belongings out of the house, so someone with access to the clothes would have already known they were dead. Unless they took the clothes directly from the house before then . . .'

'You have to chase those clothes. Find out where they ended up.'

'I do.' I felt a tug and springy lift. She – *Stephanie*, I reminded myself – had fallen asleep and let me go. And I'd forgot to switch her halfway through. My left breast, still full, ached.

'Damn.' I tried jiggling her a little as I turned her around to my other side. I mashed her mouth up against my nipple, but she was utterly asleep. I leant my head on Dan's shoulder beside me and closed my eyes too, but I wasn't dreaming. I was thinking. 'Morris is revisiting homes around Lilling, following the trail of interviews from years before. If Annalise had been kept before she was killed, there could be some evidence of . . . a secret room? A converted shed? The original investigators weren't looking for anything like that.'

'And you?'

'There's one house that piques my interest. It was a private home when Annalise went missing, and it's a law office now. But in between it was a boarding house. I don't think that makes it a candidate for hiding the girl. After all, a boarding house is by definition shared by too many people for secret-keeping to be easy. But I'd wondered why the killer had chosen that burial spot by the tracks. It seems a risky and exposed place. But could it have been worth it if he'd been able to look at his work every day? The boarding house had a tower room that frames that view exactly. Morris even found that noted in an old interview, but the assumption then was that the body had been buried shortly after disappearance. In 1976, it had been a little girls' room. That line of enquiry had been dropped.'

'Can you find out who rented that room?'

'Trying to. I'm hoping the law office receptionist will come through. Or her estate-agent cousin.'

'Gossip at its most useful.'

Just then, wriggles in my arms. Stephanie was rooting in her sleep. I rolled her towards me and she latched on.

'So how does this involve Spencer?' Dan asked, again. Somehow with all of my words I hadn't answered that.

'There was a woman who thought she was Annalise Wood's secret daughter. Or, was worried that she was. She wanted to check. Morris heard about this from both of the old investigators he spoke to. She'd been hoping to do some kind of DNA comparison. But the body was cremated.'

Stephanie fell off again, still sleeping. I shimmied myself into a more comfortable position. It felt ridiculous to have such a businesslike conversation with my shirt hiked up to

157

my neck. Dan pulled it down and tucked a throw blanket around my shoulders. 'The only chance Annalise could have had a baby was the year before, when she was in France. Well, supposedly in France, if you think she instead went somewhere to have a baby . . . I interviewed someone who went to France with her, who said that Annalise was there. She could be lying, I suppose, but there was a whole theory about Annalise getting together with a French boyfriend in 1975 and running off with him in 1976. Not a police theory, but gossip. The point is, people talked about it. Surely if she hadn't really gone to France it would have come up. Surely her parents would have told the police. The father of her child would have been a suspect. So why this woman thought she could have been Annalise's daughter . . .'

'You're speaking of her in the past tense,' he observed.

I sighed. 'She died. She fell into the river in Cambridge.'

'"Fell"?'

'That's Spencer's job to figure out.'

Dan recapped: 'So, the clothes, the boarding house, and the woman who fell in the river.'

I agreed, adding: 'And Morris is reinterviewing Lilling locals, with the new idea in mind that Annalise might have been kept somewhere for a while. Without letting on that that's what he's after, of course.'

'So today?'

I cuddled in the blanket around my shoulders and Stephanie sighed in my lap. Her having a name felt different. It felt weird. It marked her as a specific person, already narrowing the infinite possibilities of her life into finite actuals. It felt vulnerable, and limiting, and necessary, grounding, and real.

My work is also real. 'I'm going to prod my sources regarding the boarding house, see if I can get a lead on how Annalise's belongings were disposed of – those are phone calls and emails – and ask Spencer what he thinks happened to Hannah-Claire Finney. That'll be in person.'

'Where?'

'He's taking a part-time course in "Applied Criminology and Police Management" at a manor house near Cambridge, ambitious boy. This weekend it includes taking tea between lectures. I may even get a scone.'

'You really think there's a connection?'

'Not likely. We just have to be sure. Just wondering where her delusion came from at the same time that we're looking into the case. And what if someone who believed in her story took action?'

Dan nodded, thinking. 'What if someone who mistakenly thought she had Annalise's DNA in her didn't want it to be compared to the body from the train tracks? Someone who didn't know it had been cremated, or who worried that the police had samples?'

'Someone who wanted us to keep believing that body is Annalise. Holy shit.'

'I should've been a cop.'

'I should have designed buildings. Can you take her now?' I said, rolling Stephanie towards the best man in the world. 'I have to put on a new shirt, one that doesn't have easy access.'

At the doorway, I turned and looked at how easily he held her, and how happy she was to sprawl across his chest. 'Can you imagine feeling so unconnected that you fantasise your mother was a famous murder victim? As if that's some kind of improvement on your life?'

'It's the Disney thing. Your mum's a dead royal. Makes you both a princess and completely free. Makes you a heroine.'

He had a point. 'Like how people are proud to have been beheaded aristocrats in a past life.'

'Don't laugh. I was Julius Caesar,' Dan joked.

'No wonder you look so good when you wear nothing but a sheet.' I leant over to kiss him goodbye.

I almost asked him then. I almost felt that, having given the baby a name, I had gained standing to request something that I knew would be hard for him, for us. But he spoke before I spoke, and my daring was lost.

'Maybe later you could wear something with easy access again.'

We tried to kiss again but ended up giggling into each other's faces.

Madingley Hall dominates the village to the west of Cambridge from which it gets its name. The University reaches even here, running its continuing education school from the grand house and manicured gardens.

The inside is a combination of tatty-yet-impressive country-house glamour, and conference facility practicality. I was taken to a great room on the upper floor and left to gaze out at the lawns from a dignified stuffed chair. Spencer's group would be released here between lectures. Two young women were setting up industrial amounts of coffee, tea, and biscuits.

I'd texted him that I was coming, so he wasn't surprised. He was curious, though. I hadn't told him what I was there for.

'I'd thought you might have brought the baby,' he said, peeling off from the crowd when he caught sight of me. He hasn't met her yet.

'Soon. She has a name now!'

'Do I get to know it?'

I realised that I hadn't even told it to my mother yet. *More to add to the endless mental list.* 'Stephanie,' I said out loud, for the first time.

'That's a pretty name. Tea?'

'Coffee.'

He fetched some for both of us, and two little packets of shortbread.

'Good lecture?' I asked him.

'That's not why you're here.'

'But I'm polite.'

'Since fucking when?'

I laughed. I liked him. We had got along on the one case we'd worked together, up until things went to shit with Morris, and I ended up on emergency bed rest.

'I need to ask you about a case.'

He squinted at me with suspicion. 'That's a surprise. Did you cut your leave short?' He sat next to me, in a matching stuffed chair, so we each had to turn to face the other.

'No. Still on maternity leave. In fact, I'm at home right now. You can't even see me.'

'Can't I?'

'Look. Morris Keene is back on the job. You know that, right?'

'I'd heard.'

'It's cold cases. Nothing to do with us. But, well, maybe to do with us just this one time.'

161

'He asked you to come to me? That's bullshit. That's cowardly bullshit.'

'No! No. He hasn't asked me to do anything. It came up; he and I are friends; I wondered if you could help. I wondered if I could see if there's a connection.'

He clattered his cup and saucer onto the little table between us. 'What case?' he asked, but he was frowning.

'Hannah-Claire Finney.'

'Fell in the Cam.'

That's all: just four words and a stone face.

'An accident isn't a case,' I observed.

'Maybe an accident. Maybe a suicide. Maybe pushed,' he acknowledged. 'But there's nothing we can do about it. I don't like her brand-new husband; it's been claimed by his sister that he was at the least verbally abusive, possibly physically. But there are no witnesses from the night in question, and no injuries related to her death that can't be otherwise explained. It doesn't smell right, but it's a prosecutorial dead end.'

I sipped at my coffee, too milky and now cool.

'Well?' he asked. 'Are you going to tell why you're interested?'

I wanted to. But the buzz of the crowd around us . . . The name Annalise would whip round the department before I got home.

I shook my head. 'It's probably nothing. Just . . .' I breathed in, considering my words. 'If it wasn't the husband. If it was a stranger to her. Does that ring any bells for you?'

'Is this an old serial killer thing? Because I don't recall any cases of serial river pushers.'

'Not a serial killer, no . . .' I put down my drink, right next to his. *Still a team*, I was trying to communicate. 'We have reason to believe that Hannah-Claire was herself pursuing an old case. It may have got her into trouble.'

He opened his hands wide. 'Are you serious? We're going to play a game where I give you information, and you withhold it?'

'No, no. Just . . . not here.'

'We could have had this meeting tonight. We could have had this meeting in my car. You chose here.'

I didn't have an answer for that.

'If Morris Keene has questions for me, he can ask them himself, after he tells me exactly why he wants to know, naming names.'

'And here I thought you were going to say that he could go fuck himself. You're more civil than I expected.'

He smiled, but it didn't turn into even a chortle.

'I'm sure he'll come to you,' I said, in as appeasing a voice as I could manage. 'I'm sure he will, if it turns out that there's a good reason to. I was only trying to see if that reason exists.'

Spencer's crossed leg bounced in annoyance. 'There was broken glass near where she went in. But, there's broken glass in various places around Cambridge every night, as I'm sure you know.'

'Bottle glass,' I suggested. Sloppy drunks.

'Usually. We got the analysis back yesterday. This was from a picture frame. There was even some adhesive on the corner where there had been a price sticker.'

'Just the glass?' I asked.

'Just bits of the glass. No frame. No picture. Probably nothing to do with Hannah-Claire.'

'And her injuries?'

'A healing bruise on her upper thigh and bottom. Her husband said she's an avid cyclist. Could have got it falling off. Also old marks on her upper arms, the kind you might get if someone squeezes; not as easily explained. As for her death, it was cold that night, and the water colder; when she hit it she had a heart attack. Then she drowned.'

I leant back. There wasn't a lot to do with that. Without a witness, someone could get away with this. I asked, 'Do you have reason to believe she was depressed, that she might do this to herself?'

'She'd lost both her parents not that long ago. A co-worker told us she was having panic attacks.'

I thought, *Maybe that explains her pursuit of an alternate parent, though why she'd want a dead one is one for the psychologists.*

People had started to drift towards the door. It must have been time for another talk. One of the young women in staff uniform took our cups and eyed our unopened biscuit packets disapprovingly.

Spencer said, 'I have to go back in. I'll tell you whatever you need but bloody hell, do the same for me.'

'I will,' I said. 'Morris will. It's a touchy case.'

Just then Spencer's mobile rang. He answered it, turned his back the way people do, as if that creates privacy. 'I'm on my way . . . I will . . . Okay. Text me the number.'

He rang off and muttered, 'I'll probably have to write an extra paper to make up for missing this lecture.'

'What's happened?'

He looked me right in the eye, considering before he went on. 'Hannah-Claire's cousin was attacked after the funeral today.'

'Attacked?' I asked, stunned.

'Beaten, apparently. She's being taken to Addenbrooke's. I'm on my way to the scene.'

I stepped in front of him.

'Can I come?'

He shook his head, but it wasn't a no. I think he was marvelling at my nerve.

'Fine,' he said. 'Follow me there.'

He walked ahead, down the staircase and out through reception. As he walked he phoned someone else. 'Hello, this is Detective Sergeant Spencer from the Cambridgeshire Police. Is Cathy Rigg there?'

I stopped in surprise, then scrambled to catch up with him and keep listening.

'I'm sorry, but this is an emergency. She would want to be interrupted.'

I could hear unintelligible jabbering from the other end, presumably Rosalie explaining why Cathy was unavailable. His mouth hung open. 'I'm sorry, who?' he asked. 'You've been dealing with DI Chloe Frohmann?'

Spencer and I locked eyes. I lifted my shoulders. I had not expected any of this.

'I'm afraid I really can only speak to Mrs Rigg. Could you give me her mobile number, please? It's about her daughter.'

I frowned. *Daughter?*

Spencer got the number and called it, while glaring at me suspiciously. He wasn't happy to learn I'd spoken with Rosalie.

'Mrs Rigg, this is Detective Sergeant Angus Spencer of the Cambridgeshire Police,' he said smoothly. 'I'm very sorry to tell you that your daughter Sandra has been taken to Addenbrooke's Hospital. I've been asked to tell you. I'm on my way to the scene and I hope to meet you at the hospital later.'

The panicked, high-pitched voice at the other end pelted Spencer with questions, but left him no room to answer. When the call finally ended, I clarified: 'The beaten woman is Hannah-Claire's cousin and Cathy Rigg's daughter. Cathy Rigg, ex-wife of Charlie Bennet now married to Nigel Rigg, is Hannah-Claire's aunt. Is that so?'

'Sounds like you have a lot to tell me,' he said. He was right.

CHAPTER ELEVEN

Laurie Ambrose

'Simon,' I said into the phone, even though he hadn't picked up. He must have still been driving. The ringer at the other end pulsed. *Brrrt. Brrrt. Brrrt . . .*

The policeman had asked me to wait. Someone was going to come and ask me questions, like why the near-dead woman they'd just taken to hospital was between my car's front bumper and a brick wall.

The uniformed officer kept looking over at me. I dialled another number, but didn't hit the green button. Instead I talked to the empty space of the incomplete connection. 'Tom?' I said, holding the phone to my head so no one would think I was crazy.

'Tom, it's Laurie. I've found a bit of trouble. I don't know what to do. Simon is coming, but he's not here yet, not even headed here yet because I asked him to pick me up at Silver Street. I didn't tell him what was happening because I didn't want to say it. I don't want it to be true. I'm worried about Blake. What has he tangled himself up in? I'm sad over Hannah-Claire. I'm horrified about Anna. I'm scared for me. I don't want to be involved. I'm already involved. I don't know what I'll say when I'm asked. I can't tell them everything because even dead clients have privacy rights. And Prisha's not here to advise me because of her sister's baby. Everyone's life is just moving forward at such a pace and I can't ask for help from anyone, not even from Simon, because he's driving responsibly and not answering his phone.' I wiped my forehead and realised that I was sweating ridiculously. It was so bad I'd thought I was crying, but I wasn't. Not yet.

'Tom,' I repeated, just for the indulgence of saying it. 'Tom, I miss you. I miss how things were. I miss my mum being well; I miss our kids being safe, indulged children at home; I miss our home, a house attached to our past by memories in every corner. I miss being a student myself, I miss feeling ambitious, I miss planning my future. I'm living my future, living plans we made years ago. It's lovely, Tom, we made some good choices, but making those choices feels so long ago. I didn't know that it was making the choices that was the exciting part . . .'

Tears now. Apparently a bloody, beaten client is what it takes to shake loose my general existential dread/midlife crisis.

'I love Simon. I chose him. You'd like him. What am I saying? You did like him. But it's different getting married in middle age. It's . . .' *BZZZT!* My phone rang, right in my ear. I answered it, and turned away from the officer, who must have noticed that I'd just been talking to a non-existent connection.

'Laurie? You phoned?'

'Simon! Are you at Silver Street?'

'Nearly. I'm stuck in traffic on Queens Road. Felt safe to call you back since I'm not moving.'

'Come to the Catholic church. That's where my car is. The police want to talk to me.'

'The police—?'

I didn't let him finish asking. 'It's awful. I'll tell you afterwards. Just please come here. Just . . . just be here so that when they're done I can jump into the car with you and we'll drive far away.'

'What about your car?' Ever practical.

'I don't know if they'll let me take it.'

His voice got panicked. 'Did you hit someone? Sorry, traffic's moving, I'll be there as soon as I can.' He rang off.

I kept the phone to my ear. I nodded as if I was listening to good advice. I imagined Prisha telling me to be calm, a solicitor telling me to tell the police nothing. I put on a show of careful composure for the officer, who may or may not have still been looking at me.

'Ma'am?'

The man who came up behind me was not in a uniform but was clearly one of them. He wore a suit and flashed me his warrant card: Detective Sergeant Spencer.

'Thank you,' I said into the phone. 'Goodbye. No, I'll call you back, there's someone here . . .' Anything to keep the upcoming real-life conversation at bay.

DS Spencer waited pleasantly, expectantly. Eventually I pressed my thumb to the screen as if to hang up and slid the phone into my pocket.

'You're Laurie Ambrose?' he asked, having presumably been briefed by Officer Watchy-watchy.

169

'Dr Laurie Ambrose,' I corrected, which I don't usually do, but I wanted to spell the names, give him my middle one, recite personal statistics rather than answer anything about my car and whatever happened here.

'Doctor. Thank you.' He made a note. 'Dr Ambrose, do you know Sandra Williams?'

Annalise Williams. Hannah-Claire's cousin Sandy. It was a stretch to turn 'Sandra' into 'Anna', but I'd seen stranger nicknames than that . . . I could imagine her arguing that it's a form of 'Sandra', but really she just wanted to be like Annalise. Both of them had been obsessed with her. The relationship made sense. After all, what were the odds that two unrelated clients would bring up Annalise Wood to me?

'She's the woman who . . .' I waved my hand at the car.

'Exactly how did you know Ms Williams?'

This was tricky. This was where I could use Prisha at my side. I'm not supposed to violate client confidentiality even by admitting that they were my clients at all. I settled on, 'Through work.'

'And your work is . . . ?'

'I'm a psychologist.' Next he was going to ask if she was a colleague or a client, and if I said I couldn't say, he would know I meant client, which is the same as just saying it. 'Look, I'm uncomfortable with this. I know you need to investigate, but I need to be mindful of the obligations of my profession.' That was as good as telling him flat out, but it clarified my position for further questions.

'Ah.'

I read it all on his face: now he wondered what was wrong with her, as if asking for help is a moral failing.

170

'I understand that there was a funeral here today. Did you accompany Ms Williams?'

I wanted to say yes, which would get this section of the questioning done, but that would be lying, which could come back to bite me. 'No.'

'Why did you come, then? Did you know the deceased?'

'Yes.'

'How did you know her?'

'Through work.'

'I see.'

And I'd done it. I'd lowered both victims in his eyes. Hannah-Claire was possibly a victim too, if her death wasn't an accident, and now I was attached to both of them.

'This is your car?' He gestured to it. It was no longer alone in the lot. Police cars and what I assumed was his sedate-looking sedan now kept it company.

Denial clamoured in my mind. 'Yes.' I had bought that car when Blake started university. Emptying nest; fresh life.

'Do you know how Ms Williams ended up between it and the brick wall?'

I shook my head before I found my voice. 'No. Absolutely not. I was with my daughter, at Jesus. Jesus College,' I clarified. It's normal for University people to just say 'at Jesus' but I know it can sound strange to outsiders.

'I know, Doctor.'

Had I insulted him? Maybe he went to Cambridge. Maybe he went to Jesus. Maybe he knew everything, like that mysterious policeman in *An Inspector Calls*. Clara had studied that play in school. I was fainting.

He reached out to steady me. There was no place to sit out there, and the church was locked. We ended up in his car, with the doors open so that I felt less trapped. Well, that was the reason my side was open. His could have been open for any reason at all. Maybe his legs were too long. Maybe sitting in his car was like sitting in an aeroplane seat. Tom had always felt cramped in aeroplanes.

'Dr Ambrose?'

'Sorry, yes, I'm here, I'm fine. I'm not going to faint.'

'You can faint if you like. I just don't want you to hit hard ground if you do.'

I managed a smile. 'Thank you. No, I'm fine. I mean, I'm not fine with what happened here but I don't know anything about it. Honestly. I knew them separately. I hadn't expected to see . . . Ms Williams here.'

He noticed my pause. I'm sure he did. But he didn't ask.

I continued, 'I hardly knew either of them. When I left the service, lots of people were still here. I know it was naughty of me, but I had an errand and so left my car . . .'

'Naughty'? What is it about being questioned by police that makes one feel ten years old?

He closed his notebook. 'And it was the only hiding place left in the lot when someone needed it. Thank you.'

I blinked quickly. 'Is that it?'

'Is there anything else you think you ought to tell me?' He asked as if he already knew that there was.

I rifled through my mental files. I couldn't tell him that they had both mentioned Annalise Wood. I couldn't tell him that Anna – Sandy – had made me uncomfortable, that she called herself Annalise, that she was evidently the one who'd told Hannah-Claire that Hannah was Annalise Wood's daughter. I couldn't tell him that Hannah-Claire was deeply hopeful of her relationship with Henry Ware,

172

but that she hardly knew him at all. Hopefully there would be family and friends to tell them that. I didn't trust Henry Ware. I didn't . . . 'Yes!' I blurted, realising what I could say, what I must say. What I saw that day had nothing to do with our therapeutic relationship.

He leant in over the gearbox.

'After the church service, I was a bit lost. I was looking for the loo. I opened the wrong door, and the husband – Henry – he was . . . Sorry, this is embarrassing.' I took a deep breath. 'He was with Ms Williams' – I couldn't call her Sandy – 'and they were kissing.'

'Let me clarify: Henry Ware was behind closed doors—'

'It was more of a closet.'

'He was in a closet, at his wife's funeral, snogging his wife's cousin. Do I understand you correctly?'

'Yes, I . . . Yes. At least . . .' I was second-guessing myself. 'He was snogging a woman. She was in black, like family at a funeral wears black, and I recognised the shoes. To be honest, I recognised the shoes on the legs under my bumper as belonging to the woman from the closet before I recognised her face as Ms Williams.'

'So perhaps it wasn't Ms Williams with Henry. Perhaps it was someone else in similar clothing.'

'Yes, it's possible.'

'But you know Ms Williams.'

'I know her, yes, but I didn't realise that she knew Hannah-Claire, so I didn't think she would be here and it didn't register when I saw them. I closed the door rather quickly. And he was . . . his face was covering hers.'

'I see.' He was scribbling in his notebook again. 'Did he see you?'

'I don't think so.' I hesitated. 'I don't know.'

'I have your contact information. I'll be in touch. You may go.'

I suddenly didn't want to. 'What if he did see me?'

'Does he know you?'

'No.'

He went back to scribbling. I took back what I'd thought about him going to Cambridge. He wouldn't have got far on his A-levels with a scrawl like that.

'May I take my car?'

'What? Of course. We've already taken photos and samples.' *So that's what was going on while I was talking to Tom.*

'I only thought . . .'

'Her injuries were not compatible with having been driven into.'

'The crime scene tape . . .'

He put his notebook in his pocket with a great heaving sigh and exited the car himself as an example to me. I followed him.

I got out my keys and stood near my driver's-side door while DS Spencer unstuck the yellow tape blocking the drive. At the same time, he held up a hand to prevent someone from driving in. *Simon.*

I rushed forward. 'He's for me,' I explained, but DS Spencer was unmoved.

'He can park on the street,' he said to me, while waving Simon away. As if this weren't Cambridge on a Saturday, full to bursting with shoppers. Simon obediently backed up. He looked terrified at the crime scene tape, but relieved to see me upright, arguing with the sergeant.

I phoned Simon. He pulled into the Scott Polar Institute. He couldn't leave his car there, but he could stop.

'Simon. I have to take my car. They're making me, I . . .'

'If you don't feel able to drive, don't.'

'No, I'm fine, I . . . I'm fine. But the blood . . .' A smear on my bumper. Little dots on my hood.

He soothed me while he walked around the corner. He glared at DS Spencer, whose head was bent towards a woman who also looked official. Her car had joined the party. I wanted to get my car out of there, out of this threatening place.

Simon handed me his keys. 'You drive my car. I'll drive this one.'

'Yes.' I couldn't manage much else.

'Unless you're not safe to . . . ?'

'No. I can drive. I want to get home.'

'Good.' He looked at the marks on the hood. He swallowed. 'Are you sure we're supposed to . . . ?'

'I didn't hit anyone. Someone was . . . dumped here.'

He went pale.

I explained, 'She's alive. She's at the hospital. It wasn't all that much blood.' I tried to sound devil-may-care and above-it-all but I think I sounded deranged.

'I'm calling Clara. She can put my car into a car park for the night. I'll drive us home in this one. We'll stop at a car wash on the way.'

I nodded. I didn't say anything. *Thank you* seemed inadequate.

Spencer glared at us. I think he wanted to put the crime scene tape back up.

I opened the passenger door. Simon had walked a bit

175

away to talk to Clara. I got into the car and closed the door. I held my phone up to my ear. 'Tom,' I said. 'Simon's good. I'm fine. Everything's going to be all right. You don't need to worry.'

'Who were you talking to?' Simon asked as he slid in under the wheel.

'Just leaving a message. Prisha. Confidentiality things.'

He thought he understood. He thought this was just about Hannah-Claire having been a client.

He started the car.

He didn't know I was sad. He didn't know I missed Tom. No, that's not true. He knew. He had to. Missing Tom and loving Simon weren't opposite things. That Simon understood that was one of the things I loved about him.

As we pulled out of the church car park, the woman who'd been talking to Spencer waved to Simon and he rolled down the window.

'Dr Ambrose, I'm Detective Inspector Frohmann. DS Spencer tells me that we have your information. I just wanted to let you know that I'm looking forward to speaking with you again once we've had a chance to interview the family.'

I nodded. Simon started us rolling forward but the DI put her hand on his window.

'And you are?' she asked him.

'Simon Towey-Jones,' he told her. 'Laurie's husband.'

'Mr Towey-Jones,' she said, writing it down, while she still leant in so we couldn't drive away. 'Or is it "Doctor"?'

'No, just one doctor in the family.'

'Just one DI in mine,' she answered, winking as she pulled back.

'Drive,' I said, my throat dry.

'Thank you, Dr Ambrose!' she called after us, waving.

'She winked,' I said, not meaning to.

'I don't think she did.'

'It was awful.'

'She's a police detective.'

'She has eyes.'

Simon paid attention to the road.

'Simon, I don't care if a woman winks at you. I do care if police officers investigating serious crimes crack jokes. A woman was beaten and left for dead here. Hannah-Claire may have been murdered.'

'Maybe that's how she copes. Like you. You don't let your clients get to you. You can't.'

I didn't tell him that I apparently did let my clients get to me.

Then I remembered: 'Oh, Clara will need your keys!'

'Clara has her own keys to my car. She used it over the summer, remember?' He smoothly joined the roundabout.

That's right; we're a family now. I'd almost forgotten.

CHAPTER TWELVE

Anna Williams

I wanted to open my eyes, but it hurt to try it, and the sliver of light that got in hurt too.

I squeezed my eyes instead. Sparks burst in my vision. I lolled my head. I was on a pillow. I was on a bed.

Someone leant over me and I flinched, which hurt more. A hand dabbed at the top of my cheek, and the pressure felt like fireworks inside my face.

'She's awake,' said a woman's voice.

I sensed people gathering around the bed. I forced my eyes open; the right one opened wider than the left. They were two nurses and a doctor. I tried to ask questions, but my mouth only breathed, without sound.

One of them felt the pulse in my wrist, then pressed a stethoscope just above my left breast. I was wearing black, I noticed. I'd been to a funeral.

Hannah-Claire's funeral.

I pushed to sit up and four hands pressed me gently back down.

A fifth hand, the doctor's hand, pressed down on the bed as he leant over me. I tilted toward him a little. He said things I couldn't quite turn into meaning, but the voice itself was comforting. I let people take care of me.

I woke up again.

This time was abrupt, and absolute. Sounds at full volume all at once: chatter, ticking, footsteps . . . even scraping, sliding, grinding. It was all magnified.

I could sense light even through my closed eyes. It was too bright already. I lifted my hand towards my face to shield myself, and the pain in my shoulder made me gasp sharply. No one rushed to me. No one was fascinated by my wakefulness this time. The sleeve of my blouse felt like it was cutting into my arm when I bent at the elbow so I dropped my arm back to the bed, sliding against the rounded metal rail that was keeping me from rolling out. I tried to roll in the other direction, to sit myself up, but bending at the middle made me gasp again.

Breathing hurt. Everything hurt. I made croaking noises. A nurse noticed.

'What . . . happened?' I pushed out of my throat.

A police detective told me.

He said that I had been discovered in the church car park after the funeral, badly hurt.

A doctor explained my injuries: I had been beaten in the face, shoulder, and abdomen. I had been unconscious.

I was helped to the toilet by a nurse. I was swollen around one eye. My whole left side was a dark bruise, multi-coloured the way that oil stains are, all swirly. My right shoulder was useless.

This all took time, possibly hours. Maybe days or years; maybe I was old now. The medicine made me slow.

The detective asked me questions. He had ginger hair. He told me his name but I couldn't hold on to things like that. He wanted to know who had hurt me. He wanted to know who to phone for me. He probably asked those things separately, but they came at me as if they were on two sheets of tracing paper, one on top of the other.

I tried to think of people I wanted. I'd already told Blake not to see me any more. The policeman asked if I wanted my mother and I sort of yelped and that hurt, like punching my stomach from the inside.

He didn't even ask if I wanted my father. It's as if he knew that was ridiculous.

I could have wanted to see my sister. She was here for the funeral, from her normal home now up north. We're a small family. We have to make a show even for cousins. Hannah was just a cousin. She hadn't even grown up in England. She came from Canada after her parents died, and suddenly we were supposed to be family, a real family with her at the middle of it, all grieving and needing attention.

If she had stayed in Canada, she wouldn't be dead.

The meds kicked in. Breathing didn't hurt any more. I found a position I could rest in and stayed in it. Someone brought some disgusting food and left it next to me where I had to smell it. The police detective came back and wanted to talk to me again. This time I was ready.

'What's the last thing you remember, Sandra?'

I shook my head. 'Anna,' I corrected him. Everyone at uni called me that, because it's a perfectly good nickname for Sandra and I prefer it, but I've had to correct my family for years. I still do.

'Anna . . . Williams?' he asked, maybe wondering if he had the wrong girl.

'Yes,' I said. My head rolled onto my other cheek. This was tiring. 'My mother named me Sandra.'

'She's been here,' he told me. 'You were asleep.'

Tears. It wasn't fair. None of this was fair. *Look what she made me do.*

'Would you like me to call her?'

'No.'

He had a phone in his hand, and he kept glancing at it. I don't know if he had notes there, or Facebook, or what.

'Do you know what day it is?'

The doctor had already asked me something like that, except he'd wanted to know the year. I'd got it right. I'm not as fucked up as I might have been.

'It's Saturday,' I said, and then I wondered how long I'd been here. 'Isn't it?'

'It is. Do you remember what you were doing today?'

'Hannah-Claire's dead.'

He nodded.

'Today was her funeral,' I elaborated. 'I'm wearing black,' I pointed out.

'Were you and your cousin close?' he asked, I suppose leaping from black clothes to being best, best friends.

'She was my cousin,' I said, because it was none of his business how I felt about her.

181

'Do you remember the funeral?'

Do I? I had to think about that. I remembered the church. I remembered the coffin. Henry had insisted on burying the body instead of cremation, but it hadn't been open, thank God. As I understand it, drowned people look terrifying. I breathed harder.

'Yes.' I swallowed. Swallowing hurt. I wondered if I'd been punched in the throat too.

'Do you remember after the funeral?'

My heart was beating faster. I said, 'No,' because I wanted to not remember.

'Are you sure?'

I shut my eyes. Squeezing hurt the eye that was swollen, but I squeezed anyway.

'Henry,' I said.

'What about Henry?' the detective asked.

I kept my eyes closed. 'I talked to him.'

'About what?'

'About Hannah-Claire.'

When Hannah had moved in with Henry, she'd let me take her Cambridge flat. She was quitting her museum job to marry him and be free to travel on his business trips, so she didn't need to be there any more. And my parents had found out that I'd fucked up uni, instead of graduating like I'd told them I had, so I couldn't really stay at home any more. Hannah would have never said no to me asking. She wanted us all to like her, including me, so she had said yes.

She hadn't moved everything out yet, so of course I used her desktop computer. It was just there, like a piece of furniture. I just used it for normal computer things. Her bookmarks were news sites and art history for work and one tame erotica site that she'd kept tucked away at the end of the list. And she had left her passwords in there, so sometimes I read her emails. It was funny to do that, that's all. She sometimes emailed her work friend at the museum about Henry, which is how the police knew what we already knew: that Henry wasn't always nice.

She never said he hit her, but he made her feel terrible, like she maybe deserved to be hit. Once he pushed her. I bet that was why he was arrested about her death, but they'd had to let him go again. Of course they had. Pushing her in general doesn't mean that he'd pushed her into the river. They'd had no evidence. There was nothing they could have done, not without actual proof of serious violence.

I'd been sure that I could get him to do what I needed him to.

The detective starting talking again. I'd been quiet too long. 'A witness says they saw you and Henry together.'

My throat tensed up. *What had they seen?* 'I was crying. He gave me a hug.'

That was true. I'd followed him into the back part of the church after he'd been outside for a smoke. I'd touched his arm as if I was lonely and sad and he'd touched me back.

'A hug,' the detective repeated.

'We really needed each other,' I said, and tears popped out as if I really was grieving, as if I really was lonely. 'We needed something,' I amended. 'Have you ever just needed to touch another person as proof that you exist?'

The detective wrote something down. Maybe exactly what I was saying.

I chose my words very, very carefully: 'I just wanted to . . . to kiss and be close . . . but he was . . . he was forceful. He pushed me into this small room . . . storage, really . . . and I liked kissing him but after a while he, then he . . . And then he . . . hit me.'

'Where?' he asked.

I looked at the detective's face. He was indignant for me. I felt my face get warm. I pointed to my cheek. 'He slapped me. I slapped him back. That's the last thing I remember.'

It genuinely was.

'Will you be willing to testify in court?'

'Yes,' I said. 'He's very strong,' I added. 'Hannah-Claire was afraid of him.'

He looked up. 'She told you that?'

'She didn't . . .' I covered my mouth.

'What exactly did she say?'

I thought carefully. 'She loved him more than he loved her. She always tried not to do anything wrong.'

He wrote that down.

'Would you allow the nurse to take scrapings from under your fingernails, please?'

I nodded.

'Do you think we should do a rape kit?'

I shook my head. 'He didn't . . .'

'Good.' He looked down at his phone. 'Your mother wants to know if you're awake.'

My mother thinks she wants to know things but she never really does. She wants to know only the right things, right to her. She cares about appearances more than about people. Which is why I hadn't been able to tell her about uni, that I was losing my mind near the end, that I couldn't face the last exams. I tried to write my thesis, I honestly tried, and in my head I did, I wrote so much. But on the page there was just nothing. I ended up trashing my computer – which is why I had to use Hannah-Claire's in her flat; it's not as if I snooped just to snoop – and I'd told my advisor that I'd lost everything. Saying I was too stupid to have made a backup felt better than admitting that there hadn't been anything to back up in the first place. I told my friends that I couldn't face starting it over. Then I just stopped. I didn't go to lectures any more. I stayed on a friend's couch for a few months. I came home when the term was done and told my mother that I just didn't want to go to graduation. She was busy with work and her husband and relieved not to have to spend a weekend taking pictures of me with all of those people she didn't know. She'd already done that with Sadie. Dad came to that and Mum hated having him around. Of course, if he hadn't come she would have complained that he just didn't care.

She found out that I hadn't actually finished when a friend's mother bumped into her in London. Small damn world. By then I was living back at home. Well, with her, but it was the law office house, not the home I'd grown up in. And I knew her husband didn't like having me there. They argued a lot, though I can't actually say that it was because of me, can I? *Maybe they argue anyway. Maybe they argue every single night after they work together all day downstairs, even with me not there any more.*

She always sounds the same when she argues, with me, with him, with Dad.

With nurses.

'My daughter is here and I'm not leaving until I see her!'

'She's with the police right now . . .'

'I am unnerved that no one phoned to tell me that she's awake.'

'She's over eighteen, ma'am, and . . .'

'What is your name?'

It went on like that. The detective and I held our positions, not speaking, with only a flimsy curtain between us and her.

A visibly shaken young nurse literally said 'knock-knock' before tugging the curtain aside. 'Excuse me, Detective Sergeant. Miss Williams, your mother is here.'

'Thank you, Milly,' Mum said icily, pulling the curtain wider. 'DS Spencer,' she added, nodding to the detective. *Ah, his name was Spencer. That's right.*

He nodded back. 'Mrs Williams.'

I stiffened. I knew she wasn't going to let that blow over.

'Mrs Rigg,' she corrected him. I think she was prouder of that surname than anything else about her. I honestly don't know if she was upset that I hadn't taken it too, or if she'd been relieved to keep it to herself, just her and him. I'd already changed my name once for her, from my Dad's name, Bennet, to her maiden name, Williams, when I was a kid. I hadn't wanted to change it again when I was at university. And when I get married someday, I won't change it then either, unless it's to something that the two of us pick together.

'Thank you, Miss Williams. I'll be in touch.' Detective Spencer left. The nurse was already gone. I was alone with her.

'Are you staying here tonight?' she asked me.

I honestly didn't know. The doctor hadn't told me yet.

'Sadie has offered to stay with you at Hannah's flat, if that's required. Concussion, you know.'

'It's my flat now, Mum.'

'It's her name on the lease, so if the landlord puts two and two together you can't really act surprised, now can you? You'll always have a place with us if you need it, but you have to show you're actually trying, do you understand? And if you want to finish your degree I'll see what I can do but I can't promise that Nigel—'

'I don't want to finish. I'm working. It's fine.' *It's a phone job. It sucks. But it's fine.*

'Well. That's good to hear.' She didn't ask for details.

She didn't ask for details about what happened after the funeral either. Maybe she was being considerate of my feelings and readiness. *Ha, no* . . . Maybe she's so wrapped up in her own secrets that she automatically assumes no one else wants to share theirs.

Milly the nurse came back, with trepidation. 'The detective asked me to scrape under your fingernails.'

'What on earth for?' my mother demanded at the same time that I said, 'That's fine.'

'It's for the investigation,' I said, while Milly took my hands. 'They think that Henry did it.'

'Henry?' She seemed genuinely shocked.

'It was Henry, Mum.' It was suddenly difficult to speak. I felt squeezed inside.

'He hit you? He hurt you?' Her hands traced my injuries in the air, just inches away from my body.

'He did it all, Mum. Hannah-Claire too. He did everything and the police are going to make him pay for it.'

That's when I cried, great big gushes of tears, pumped out by deep breaths and heaves that hurt my abdomen. But I didn't close my eyes. I watched Mum's face. I wanted to see that spark of recognition. I wanted to see that she understood.

But she closed her own eyes, and covered her closed eyes with her hands after that. I kept looking and looking, as if my stare could pry open her fingers and eyelids, and as if there'd be something important to see once I did.

I did stay in the hospital that night.

It was easy to fall asleep but I kept waking up.

And each time I thought I was hearing my mother arguing with a nurse about visiting me, but she wasn't there. I was just remembering.

It was Hannah-Claire's fault. She had caused all of this, all of it, by trying to make us into a family for her after her parents died. It's because of her that my mother had to argue with my dad, who wasn't even supposed to be in the house. Mum's husband doesn't like him, obviously. But Mr Rigg was away and it was a weekend and Mum didn't know I'd come back from the shops. I had, though, and there was Dad's car, and I could hear them through the kitchen windows. I had stayed outside. Mum still doesn't know I heard what she asked him to do.

It had been warm then. It was spring, with me home for Easter break. Hannah-Claire had already been in England since a month after her father's funeral. Mum was the one to fly out for it, because Hannah's adoptive parents were her aunt and uncle. Mum came home quiet, which is normal when family members die, but this quiet had gone on and on. By the time she got my dad in the house, all of the saved-up loudness and sharpness were bursting out of her. She'd asked him for one thing, '*One thing, Charlie!*' and he'd said no.

I remember that I was on the gravel driveway when I started listening, not on the soft lawn, because as I realised what I was hearing I had to be super careful to not stir up any gravel in a way that they could hear. I worried that even the sun glinting off my bicycle frame might signal them to look in my direction. I held very still.

Everything made sense, suddenly, but it was an ugly sort of sense. Sadie is my older sister, and I always felt like I never lived up to her. But, more than that, there was always the feeling of something else that neither of us was living up to. I used to look in my mirror figuring out which parts of me look like my dad, and maybe that's what she sees when she looks at me. But it wasn't only that. It turns out that there was someone before both of us, someone before me and before Sadie. I've been jealous of Hannah-Claire all my life; even without really knowing her I'd been jealous of her, and it turns out that I was right to be. It turns out that Hannah-Claire was Mum's first. Before me, before Sadie, even before Dad.

Oh, Mum and Dad had known each other then. (Of course I later looked up Hannah-Claire's birth date and matched her life with Mum's school years to see how they fit together.) But Mum and Dad weren't together yet then. That's what Mum was asking him to lie about. She wanted to tell Hannah-Claire the truth when she came to England. But Mr Rigg is rather strict about some things. Mum adjusted for him; that's a nicer way of saying 'changed'. She dressed more conservatively now, with higher necklines and longer hems. She stopped swearing. He didn't like her past with Dad, but he'd accepted it; further reconciling himself to a past before that, a past with some random boy who wasn't even a serious boyfriend, and with whom she'd had a secret child, well, she didn't think he would accept that. So she asked Dad to say that Hannah was his.

'Charlie,' she'd said, in a sweet, wheedling tone. 'Nigel already hates you. It'll be nothing different for you. But this way he won't hate me.'

I held my breath waiting for his answer. Birds kept tweeting and a squirrel made some kind of thud on the ridiculous, elaborate bird feeder the receptionist had set up on the lawn, but I was silent. The kitchen was silent. Then Dad's voice burst out.

'I can't.'

'You have to!'

'No, I can't. I won't. I don't want another child.'

'She's not a child! She's a grown woman! You won't have to do anything, anything at all.'

'Is that what she'll say, you think? Or will she want some kind of "father figure" in her life?'

'Well, Sadie and Sandra would appreciate a father figure but you've never felt compelled to do much for them!'

Silence in the kitchen again. The squirrel scrabbling on the round top of the feeder.

'That's exactly my point. Exactly.' I heard a chair scraping against the stone tiles. He was about to exit the house.

I pushed through the gravel to the grass and walked

quickly around the other side of the house, keeping my head down as if that would help. I heard the front door open and footsteps on the porch.

Mum begged him, 'Please. She's my child. I want to be able to tell her that.'

'Tell her then,' Dad said. 'But leave me out of it.'

He drove away. I waited around the back of the house for fifteen minutes before circling around to the front and pretending to arrive then. I went straight upstairs to my room. I slept in the tower when I was home. I knew that Hannah-Claire's therapist thought it was fucked up to keep thinking and thinking about a dead girl who you didn't even know, but the room I slept in faced the spot where she'd been eventually dug up, so how was I supposed to help it?

Mum didn't tell her. I felt like I held my breath at every enforced family gathering in the first few months that she was here, but nothing blew up. Mum was happy to have become Mrs Rigg, as far away from Mrs Bennet as she could get. And better than Ms Williams. We'd had some difficult years after the divorce. She didn't want to risk losing what she'd finally attained.

It was summer, when Mum and Dad still thought I'd graduated, when Hannah-Claire had cosied up to *share some feelings* with me. She told me that she had been going through her parents' papers and had found her birth mother's medical records. She'd always known she was adopted; she'd been adopted by her grandparents from their daughter who had died. That's what she had always been told. But the blood type wasn't right. She asked me to look at some papers she had.

'I'm type O,' she'd said. 'I'm a universal donor. That's why I give blood whenever I can.'

I internally rolled my eyes.

'But see? It says here that she was blood type AB. And my mother' – by this she meant her adoptive mother, who she thought was her biological grandmother – 'well, she was too. See?' She pulled out another piece of paper. Then she pulled out a chart. 'But look. An AB parent can't make a type O child. They just can't. See?'

I could feel myself getting cold. I had to make her stop going after this.

So I told her. I knew that Mum had her in 1975, during the time that she was supposed to have been in France for school. I knew that Annalise had gone to France then. There had been rumours that she had run away the next year with a French boyfriend. And every night on my school break I had to look out of that tower window, sleeping on a daybed surrounded by boxes of files, staring at those poplar trees, the only two left after that storm in 1992 had pushed the others down and their roots upended the body enough for a dog on a walk to notice.

This is what really killed me. She cried. She cried like it was a terrible thing, instead of an honour. I wish, I *wish* that someone would tell me something like that. Tell me I'm special. But it hurt her. I shrugged. There was nothing I could do about that.

I woke up again. This time someone was crying. I thought, for just a moment, that it was Hannah-Claire wishing that Annalise wasn't her mother. But it was just the stranger in the next bed.

* * *

In the morning I was free to go. Sadie, my sister, was coming to take me back to my flat. Then I was going to ask her to leave, but I needed her with me for the hospital to let me out.

First, the detective was there again. *Sergeant Spencer.* I was alert enough to know his name now and really pay attention.

'We've arrested Henry Ware,' he told me.

I tried to lean forward. I was on enough painkillers that I could sit myself up now, but bending any farther than that wasn't possible.

'He denies what you've described, but we have a witness who backs you up.'

I blinked twice, quickly. 'Who?' I asked.

'An acquaintance of Hannah-Claire's. Laurie Ambrose. Do you know her?'

My thoughts became jagged and jumbled. I didn't know what he meant. *How was it that Dr Ambrose could have seen anything? Why had she been at the church? Had she and Hannah-Claire become secret friends? Did they meet over coffee and chat and compare notes? What did she know?*

'Hannah introduced us,' I said, vaguely. It was true in its own way. I had found Dr Ambrose's information in Hannah-Claire's email history. 'I didn't see Laurie Ambrose at the funeral.'

Sergeant Spencer tilted his head. 'I see. Do you think she could be lying?'

He had his phone out to type into again. He was going to write down my answer.

'I don't know. She could have been there. People were

there. I was in the front because I'm family.' I didn't want tears right now. I didn't want my voice to shake. Actually being a victim of something is nothing like pretending to be one, but I knew that going in. I didn't do what I did for sympathy. If Dr Ambrose suggests that this is something I made happen because I like people to feel sorry for me, she's a worse psychologist than I thought . . .

'Are you all right? Would you like a nurse?' the sergeant asked kindly.

I left my cheeks wet, and smiled in between them. 'I'm fine, really. It's just a lot to take in.'

'Is it your version of events that no one saw you and Henry Ware together after the church service?'

I looked at the wall over his shoulder to give myself a break from his eyes. 'When we were in the closet, the door opened for a second. I thought he'd pushed it open by accident, and shut it again. That's what I assumed.' I'm glad I hadn't known it was someone else. I would have worried that it had been my mother.

'That all fits together then. Thank you.' He put his phone away.

'Sergeant? Did Dr Ambrose see Henry attack me?' I genuinely didn't remember beyond the slaps. The doctor had told me that losing the memories immediately around a concussion of this severity was normal.

'No,' he said.

I thought ahead to a trial. Someone official would describe it, wouldn't they? The doctor would have worked it backwards from my injuries, and they would have figured out exactly what he did to me. I wanted to know.

'Thank you,' I said, smiling bravely again.

I figured the sergeant would have a nice smile. He has a boyish face, so you'd assume they would go together. But he didn't show me one. His phone must have vibrated in his pocket; I didn't even hear it ring. He just nodded at me and pulled it out and started talking to someone else.

CHAPTER THIRTEEN

Morris Keene

No one knows at exactly what point on Annalise's half-hour route home things went wrong, but there aren't that many options.

The road connecting her school in Bishop's Stortford and her home in Lilling is well-travelled, and was back then too. Not jammed at commuter time, but busy enough that there should have been a witness to something.

Some regular commuters thought they might have seen her; they had seen cyclists in general that afternoon, a couple of teenage girls with long hair billowing out behind them; no helmets back then. But no one had been certain. None of her school friends admitted to travelling even part of the way with her that day, but several had been confident of the time: at twenty minutes past four p.m., Annalise had left a French club meeting to go home.

The burial place along the railroad tracks was less than a mile from the road, at about the midpoint between the school and the village, but if what we'd learnt from the skirt was true, that didn't really matter. She had presumably been lured or forced off into one of the several sidetracks, or got into someone's car, and then been kept somewhere. Her purple bicycle was never found, despite a wide search for it. That made my job easier; every garage, shed, and barn that had been already looked into was not likely to have been her prison. That meant I needed to use the list to find the garages, sheds, and barns that hadn't been voluntarily opened up to the police.

I printed out a map, so I could write on it. *Well, 'write' is a fancy word for it* . . . I scrawled a blue highlighter over the railway line, awkwardly with my left hand, and then a yellow highlighter along the road. I usually wrote only by tapping on a touchscreen, or, in this case, making some awkward left-handed marks. Still, the act of dragging the pen around the paper helped me to think.

'Dad? Do you need help?'

It had been almost a year since the injury. Even just six months earlier, an offer like that would have been a flick against my cheek, reminding me of my uselessness. Today it was a hug around the neck, like she used to give when she was a kid, jumping from the stairs onto my back. She's fifteen now, well past that sort of gesture, but the kindness in her voice knocked the breath out of me today the same as her old jump-hugs used to. 'Thanks, Dora. I'm just figuring out where I need to drive today.'

'Work?' She leant against the table edge. I realised that her noticing my weakness didn't hurt me today because her offer to help meant that she's feeling stronger. All I want in this world is for her to get past the events of this recent fucked-up summer. If she surpasses me in conquering trauma, so much the better. That's what a parent wants: better for their kids.

'I'm working on a case from before you were born,' I told her.

'How much before?'

'*I* was just born.'

She thought for a moment. 'Okay. The seventies.' She leant over the table to better see the map. 'Oh, Lilling! That girl. Her name began with *A*?'

I nodded. 'Yes, that girl. You've got to keep this utterly to yourself, understand? Nothing to any friends, even if they've never heard of the case before. I don't want to trigger the press.'

'Won't whatever you're about to do in Lilling trigger the press?'

I rubbed my forehead. *Yes, probably. Maybe already has.* I just wanted to find something good to give them before they found out about it.

'Don't you know who killed her?'

'No. It was never solved.'

'So he could still be alive?'

'I hope so. I'd like to lock him up.'

'Or he's in jail already. That's why it hasn't happened again.'

Is that certain? Was it a one-off, or the start of a later pattern we've failed to recognise?

'What's the blue line?' she asked.

'Railway line. Her body was found here.' I pointed. I didn't elaborate on my questions about the certainty of the body's identification.

'And the yellow?'

198

'Her route home from school. She rode a bike. Should have taken twenty-five minutes.'

'With friends?'

'Not that day.'

'Why not?'

Annalise was a popular girl. The photographs showed that. The breathless media had proclaimed it. But if it were true, why hadn't she been in the centre of a group that afternoon, or even just one of a pair? It might be in the old notes somewhere, but I didn't recall seeing it. Was it usual for Annalise to cycle home alone?

'Did she make it home?'

'No,' I said, though technically she could have gone home and then gone out again. The parents had insisted to the original investigators that there was nothing to indicate she'd made it into the house. No glass in the kitchen drunk out of, no fresh slice missing from the cake on the counter. No handbag or school bag dropped by the front door (it was later established that she left her books in her school locker and carried with her only her small personal bag). She hadn't changed out of her uniform; her mother had claimed to know her wardrobe with an uncanny degree of precision.

Dora grabbed her bicycle helmet off the newel post at the bottom of the stair bannister. 'Well, I'll be back later.'

We'd chosen this house in Cambourne in part so Dora would be able to cycle to school. But, 'I'll drive you,' I said.

'Dad. I'm not going to get . . . whatever happened to her.'

'I'm not thinking that.' Of course, though, I was. I improvised: 'A car is safer in case of an accident than a bicycle. I'll drive you. I'm going now.' I gathered up my papers and phone and keys. My supposed safety concern wasn't unfounded; death by road accident is twenty times more likely than death by murder. In the seventies, before seat belts and bike helmets, roads were infinitely more dangerous than back alleys. When you look at the statistics, it's astonishing that anyone managed to unexpectedly die by anything else. Annalise had defied the odds.

Yet she'd been on a bicycle. On a road . . .

Dora broke into my thoughts. 'I need my bike. I have to be able to get home again.'

'I'll—' But I couldn't know if I'd be back in time to pick her up. And it was futile, anyway. I knew that. It was bailing out the ocean with a bucket. I gave in.

My wandering thoughts also gave up on their tangent. *If Annalise had been in an accident on Bishop's Road, that would have been discovered quickly, if not witnessed.* No, what had happened to her was not an accident; it was 'a deliberate', as Dora used to say when she was small.

'Dad, I'll be fine.' She slipped her backpack easily over one shoulder. Her school had switched to ebooks for most of their texts. No more back-breaking lifting.

She could manage it if it were full of books, I said to myself, full of parental admiration. I kept these words in my head; she wouldn't have wanted them said out loud. But I appreciated her strength. She'd never had to spend a night in jail but the arrest itself, and all that led up to it, had been traumatic enough. That she was back at school at all made me proud of her.

Dora stopped with her hand on the doorknob. 'What did happen to her?' she asked.

200

'She disappeared,' I said, because every other more concrete answer, I was realising, wasn't necessarily true.

Dora shrugged. The light backpack lifted up and dropped down jauntily. 'Maybe she just left.'

She shut the door behind her. The door thudded within the frame; the latch clicked into place.

If Annalise Wood had 'just left', she'd have been either escaping something bad, or running away towards something good. The obvious people with enough power to make a child run away are abusive parents; but the original investigators couldn't find anything that pointed to them, and besides, if Annalise had been afraid, she could have returned after they died. She could have been running to a boyfriend, but surely with all of the media attention she would have been shamed into returning home once she realised how much she was missed. Even if she'd wanted to stay away, she would have been a virtual prisoner because of all of the publicity. No, if Annalise had been alive beyond the afternoon she disappeared, I was confident that she'd been held prisoner against her will.

I examined Google Earth for outbuildings and isolated houses within a four-mile-diameter circle centred between her school and home, and dabbed an orange highlighter to mark the locations of the more significant-seeming ones that didn't have a record of being searched for her bicycle. *Start with the obvious, only widen the search if you have to.*

Chloe was working this from the other end. Spencer was allowing her access to Hannah-Claire Finney's phone, to see if any of the calls she'd made recently related to people involved in the Annalise case beyond the two ex-police porters we already knew about, and her Aunt Cathy and Uncle Charlie, who seem too much of a coincidence for this to be just a random case of obsession on Hannah-Claire's part. Then again, if my aunt and uncle's friend had been famously murdered, I might end up strangely obsessed, no further association with the actual case required.

My only request to Chloe was to keep me well out of that end of the case. I didn't trust myself to be in the same room with DS Spencer. I didn't have enough of an answer to Annalise yet; I didn't want to face him ignorant.

And Chloe had handed over to me the trails she'd been following with regard to the disposal of Annalise's clothes after her parents died, and the residents of the boarding-house-now-law-office in the eighties. Which, it turned out, had dovetailed. Her talkative contacts, Marnie and Rosalie, had decided to shut their mouths after Cathy's daughter had been attacked at Hannah-Claire's funeral. But Marnie had given Chloe one last piece of information: the name of the charity to which the clothes had been given. The local representative of that charity in the early eighties had been Amanda Collingwood, now deceased, then an older woman living at the same address as Cathy's husband's law office. She was one of the boarders, and the clothes had been brought into that house. Apparently, at least one set of them had not made it to their intended charitable destination.

The boarding house, and the possible year of burial arguably falling in the eighties rather than the seventies, gave me a good cover for my interviews today. I didn't want to tell them yet that this was about Annalise. Besides, asking for a glass of water or a chance to sit can get one inside better than a request to search the property.

It worked for the most part. I knocked on the doors of seven houses, and, of them, four had people home. All of those invited me in. Three of them were older women alone.

My first try went like this: 'Excuse me, Mrs Brent.' (I had the names from the years-ago interviews and current real estate records. This woman had lived there since 1985 and had been interviewed by Peter Gage in 1992.) 'I'm very sorry to disturb you. I'm with the police' – shows identification – 'and I'm trying to get some help with an investigation. I need some guidance on local history and I'm hoping you might be able to help me.'

From her I got tea, stale but earnestly offered biscuits from a Marks & Spencer Christmas tin (not from this year's holiday season), and lots of fascinated questions about drug dealing. I didn't quite agree that drugs were what had brought me there, but didn't deny it either. She was intrigued, and keen to speculate, but had no first-hand knowledge herself about anyone who had lived in the boarding house.

At the next house, I embraced the implication of drugs, which continued to spark speculation. There was always an assumption that the person we were looking for at the boarding house was a 'young man', which worked in my favour. I wanted to find out if these homes I was in had any men between the ages of about seventeen and forty living in them at that time, and I got to that by asking if anyone living there then might have been friends with anyone staying at the boarding house. The woman in the second house had a brother in that range, but he, she said, hadn't had many friends.

Ah, a loner . . . Well, that could be who I was looking for.

'I bet *you* were popular,' I said with a smile, to not seem too interested in the brother just yet.

Lucy – her name was Lucy Minton, née Burke, fifty-something years old with tightly pulled hair and a stern frown – did not appreciate it. 'Don't flirt. It isn't work-appropriate.'

I apologised. I asked for a glass of water. (She'd allowed me in but had not offered tea.)

She took her time considering this request. 'No, sorry. I feel that you were trying to take advantage of my age with false charm. I may not be married any more but that doesn't mean I can be taken in by a little flattery. I'm well aware that I'm past being fawned over honestly.'

'I apologise, ma'am. I so much appreciate being flattered myself that it just pops out of me sometimes.' I got all of that out with an entirely straight face.

'If my brother were here, you'd be better behaved.'

'Is he coming back soon? I'd like to speak with him.'

'He lives with a woman in St Albans.' She stood, so I did too.

'Well, thank you, very much. You wouldn't have your brother's phone number, would you?'

'It's *her* phone number. He doesn't pay for anything. Her last name is Smith. Good luck.'

Back in my car, I was able to find his name in the 1992 interview records: Joshua Burke. *All right, living with a woman named Smith in St Albans* . . . Not impossible to find. Just a pain in the arse. But this property had a derelict-looking barn behind the house. He was on the list.

Actually, he was the entirety of the list so far.

The next house, occupied by a young couple in the

middle of renovations who I don't think had even been alive in the eighties, I didn't add to the list. Their barn, however . . . A couple of compliments was all it took to get into their soon-to-be art studio. The leftover rubbish they were attempting to conquer seemed to lean more towards storage room than prison, but a lot of years had passed. Given a couple of decades, normality can swallow up deviant history the way that jungle vines obscure ancient cities.

After lemonade with the renovators, I genuinely needed the toilet at the fourth occupied house. There was a woman in the front garden who looked about seventy, pushing a mower. I took a chance based on the file. 'Miss Russell?'

She stopped the mower's engine and pulled a pair of pink earmuffs off her head. 'Yes?' she shouted far louder than necessary, and shook out her bobbed white hair. Whatever noise-dampening had been attempted with the earmuffs, it didn't seem effective.

'Miss Russell, I was just with your neighbours. I'm sorry to have to ask this, but could I please use your toilet?' I raised my voice so there would be no repetition required; I was in a hurry.

She squinted. I smiled. At last she wafted her hand not in the direction of the house, but towards a cluster of outbuildings. The door to the shed was open; presumably that's where the mower had come from. Next to that was an outhouse.

I hesitated for only a moment.

When I was finished, I glanced into the shed. Storage. *Well, storage now.* In any case, much smaller than the barn that was becoming an art studio. Not really room for even a bed. But there was a garage-like building on the other side of the house. And, of course, in each of these cases there was the house itself.

If you're willing to hide someone completely, you don't actually need much room.

'Thank you, Miss Russell,' I said as I rejoined her. She was looking in my car. She jumped when I came up from behind.

'You're not a carpenter?' she asked anxiously. I realised that in my haste I hadn't identified myself and she'd assumed I was a contractor working on the barn conversion. I showed her my ID.

'Police?' she said, so aghast that I wondered if she might have shoplifted something on a recent outing.

'I'm with the police, yes. I'm investigating something that happened at the old boarding house at the edge of Lilling back in the eighties.'

She breathed in deep and then laughed it all out as she gestured towards my car. 'When you first drove up, I thought I'd forgotten which day it was. My friend Pamela takes me shopping on Thursdays.'

'And what an enormous disappointment to see me emerge instead.'

She blushed. *Ah, flattery would work this time.*

'Miss Russell. Ginny. May I call you Ginny? I'm Morris.'

We shook hands. Hers were tougher from yard work. She didn't seem to notice the faintness of my grasp, which I covered as best I could with a strong thumb. 'Of course,' she said.

'Ginny, I know from the property records that you've lived

here since before the eighties' – I avoided even using the word 'seventies' – 'with your father, John Russell, is that correct?'

She nodded, and her eyes slid towards the house.

I followed her gaze. 'Is he still alive?' I asked, sounding more shocked than was polite. It was actually impressive that she would have a living parent at her age, but it would be rude to show the degree of incredulity I felt, implying as it would that she was herself terrifically old (she was) and/or that her father had, well, fathered her when he was very young (possibly, and not my business). Then I noticed a ramp coming down the side of the steps, presumably for a wheelchair, and a garden table with two empty, used teacups.

'You look after him,' I said, my tone acknowledging what a workload that must be. Peter Gage's old interview notes had indicated that they had been living like that even in 1992, just the two of them, the mother long gone. 'That's very admirable,' I added, inwardly shuddering at what might be ahead as my own parents and in-laws got older. 'Did either you or he know anyone who lived at the boarding house?'

She lifted her chin sceptically. 'Are you really asking? Don't you know?'

'I know extremely little, Ginny. Why they let me keep my job I've no idea.' *Smiling, smiling, meaning both I'm-harmless and I-need-your-help . . .*

She liked that. She relaxed her shoulders. 'I used to work there. I cleaned once a week.'

'Really? Can you remember any names?'

'All of them! I'm very good at that. Can I send you a list?' Her eyes slid towards the house again.

'You can, but I'm happy to wait right here, or to come back later . . .'

'Please, I'd rather post it. Do you have a card?'

'I do.' As I fished one out of my inner jacket pocket, a tinny jingle came from inside the house. Her father was ringing a bell for her.

'I'm sorry, I'm so sorry . . .' she said, gathering up the loose hem of her denim shirt in an anxious fist as she took my card with her other hand. 'You have to go.'

I pulled my car out of sight of the property, in case her anxiety about her father's potential reaction to my presence was correct. I didn't want to make trouble for her.

I parked in what was probably the start of someone's driveway or a farmer's tractor path, and added notes on my tablet. I put John Russell on the list. Why not? If he was, say, ninety now, then in 1976 he would have been in his fifties. No reason he couldn't have taken Annalise.

He and any of the other hundreds of men within spitting distance of Lilling. And it didn't even have to be someone around here. People have cars. She was taken from a road. *Shit.* This was hopeless in 1976, never mind now.

All of the new leads depended on one thing: Annalise being the girl in that grave by the tracks, her burial now time-shifted by at least three years. But I was feeling it deep in my body that she wasn't Annalise, and I finally figured out why.

If that body was Annalise, there would have been no need to re-dress her in something identical to what she was already wearing the day she disappeared. Even if the original uniform was old or torn by then, it was just going into the ground. I couldn't come up with a scenario that made sense.

It was at first equally baffling to wonder: *Why would someone dress another young woman in clothes from Annalise's wardrobe?* But did they even know? The initials on the name tape wouldn't have stuck out to someone not specifically looking for them. It was just a school uniform, in a donation box. We know that this young woman didn't go to Annalise's school, because Annalise is the school's only question mark over several decades; so it wasn't someone needing a uniform for actual school.

It was a sex thing, I said in my mind. Then I typed it into my notes on my tablet: *schoolgirl sex thing*. Maybe she was a prostitute. Maybe she was a runaway. Someone – likely someone at that boarding house – had given it to her to wear while she was still alive.

Usually when a theory comes together, it feels like slipping into your own car after driving someone else's: suddenly everything fits, there's room for your legs, everything necessary's within perfect reach, and the radio is set to the good stuff. This didn't feel like that.

This felt clammy, because I was sweating. This felt stifling, even though I was panting.

I rested my head on the steering wheel.

I wasn't going to solve Annalise, I realised. At best, we were going to identify some poor girl who wasn't as famous, maybe not as wanted and missed as Annalise. At best, we would comfort a grieving parent or two, if they were still alive. *That should be enough*, I reminded myself. *Truth should be enough.*

But the truth is that I was going to become the detective who un-solved Annalise Wood, and made us know less of what happened than we thought we did before.

All of this 'kept in a shed' business would come to nothing. We'd only thought of it to make sense of Charlie's DNA getting on her three years later. But if the girl in the grave by the tracks had nothing to do with Annalise except the clothes, then what happened to Annalise herself wasn't time-shifted by Charlie's DNA. It was probably the same as we always assumed; she was just in a different and unfindable shallow grave.

That's when I stopped knocking on doors, and drove back to the road between Bishop's Stortford and Lilling. There was nothing to see on it, and hadn't been for years; only for a brief moment in 1976, when no one was looking.

CHAPTER FOURTEEN

Laurie Ambrose

Thank God for work.

I rescheduled the next day's clients. I didn't stay at home, though. I went into the office. Habit was going to keep me upright.

I played at working: fully dressed, sitting straight, doing desk things. My office is an odd combination of cosy and impersonal. I want clients to feel 'at home' here, so there's a soft, bright-blue pillow on one of the chairs, a craftsman-style desk lamp, and a beautifully carved wooden clock on the wall; but I need the focus off me, so there are no family photos or evidence of my hobbies. Today, that personal neutrality was comforting. Dealing with the details of my actual life would have been overwhelming. Instead, my office felt like a kind of waiting room. It was a place to gather my strength before re-entering the specifics of my life.

I thought about Hannah-Claire. I thought about the clients I had just cancelled. *How would I feel if one of them died before I could see them next? Would it be in part my fault? Was Hannah in part my fault?*

I didn't know if anything I knew mattered. The professional guidelines regarding client privacy leave it to me to decide what's important enough to share with police. Hannah-Claire and Anna being related was a shock for me, but would it be meaningful to anyone else? That Anna made Hannah-Claire believe that she was Annalise's daughter, playing with Hannah-Claire's grief and linking her to something vividly terrible, adding to Hannah-Claire's roster of dead parents . . . It was cruel, but not criminal. Did it have anything to do with her death? If her death was a suicide, possibly, but not prosecutably. It was a vicious lie, but lying isn't criminal.

Assuming it was a lie.

It must be, surely. If Annalise Wood had had a child, that would have come out by now.

And if it were true, how would Anna – Sandra – know it? And why would she have kept it to herself except for this one slip? I don't believe that for a moment. If she knew something this explosive, she would have exploited it just to insert herself into the case. It had to have been something Anna created to hold some kind of power over Hannah-Claire.

But even if it were true, I reminded myself, this had nothing to do with Hannah-Claire dying and Anna being attacked.

Unless someone else believed it was true. Unless someone believed that Hannah-Claire and Anna 'knowing' this thing – whether Anna actually believed it or if it was true at all – was a threat to them.

And me knowing it too could be a threat to me.

That thought felt like a voice outside myself, a voice I didn't recognise. Since when had I become a coward?

I fished for my phone in my bag, wondering where I had tucked the business card from that detective sergeant I'd had to interact with yesterday. *Had I thrown it away?* Part of me hoped that I had, so the decision would be out of my hands. But something knocked against my window: three raps. I flinched and dropped the bag, spilling my wallet and phone onto the carpet.

My window has blinds over it, which I'd tilted but not pulled up. I saw a striped version of outside, distorted by the missing parts. In strips: the street, cars coming off the roundabout, and a hand, and a head. I jumped back, and my chair rolled against my rubbish basket.

She stepped back. I stood and pushed apart two slats of blinds with my fingers, and saw her in full. Anna Williams was outside my office. She had on sunglasses. She had a cane in one hand. She mimed hugging herself, as if she were cold and pointed to the front door.

She smiled, and nodded, as if we were friends.

I walked back from the window, until she couldn't see me. She would think I was going through the door of this room, to open for her the door to this building. *Should I do that?* I wondered. I didn't want to. But if she left I wouldn't know what she'd come for. I didn't want that either.

I opened my office door. There was no one in the entry lobby, nor anyone on the worn wooden stairs. This had once been a house. It felt like Anna Williams was outside the door to my home.

The buzzer went off, a razzing, vicious sound. She'd rung the main bell.

I was too slow. My colleague Justine appeared at the top of the stairs. I waved her off and forced myself to the front door, and opened it.

Anna stood there, leaning on her cane, looking cross. I could see bruising around where her sunglasses covered. 'It's really hard to walk up stairs,' she said accusingly.

I had the nasty thought of inviting her to one of the offices on the next floor. But I stepped aside so she could limp towards my room, and followed her in.

She chose the chair with the pillow, just as she had last time.

I pulled a mini-recorder out of my desk and set it down where she could see it. I'd recorded her previous sessions, with her permission, but I did it this time as a challenge, not just as a matter of course.

'You may not want this recorded,' she said. She tried to look confident, but she couldn't cross her legs or get comfortable.

'Who did this to you?' I asked.

'Your son.'

I froze. The wooden clock made an audible tick as it hit the hour. I was tempted to turn the recorder off. I turned my head away. I wanted to run.

'Let it record,' she said. 'You can always erase it at the end.'

My bag was still on the floor, its contents spread around. I nudged them to the side with my feet rather than perform the indignity of bending over in front of her. The recorder faintly whirred.

'You lie about a lot of things, Sandra,' I said.

She took off her sunglasses and held them in her lap. A dark bruise covered over a third of her face.

'Everyone calls me Anna. Except for my family. That's not a lie. It's been my nickname since I went away to university.' She shifted to lean her weight to one side. Apparently the chair wasn't a good fit for her injuries, and I leant back in mine, ostentatiously stretching.

'You're not at Wolfson,' I said, boldly, considering that I hadn't checked the name Sandra. But I felt confident at this point that she simply wasn't a student.

'No, but I had to say that I was with the university in order to be able to talk to you. If you didn't have rules like that, I wouldn't have had to lie.'

I didn't argue; there wasn't any point with someone like her.

She continued: 'And once I did it, I liked it. I was allowed to say anything I wanted, to describe things however I felt like saying they were. There's something about being a student that makes your whole life feel like a fresh start. That's what it was like with Blake. And Clara, too. She's so friendly! You must have been a very good mother.'

I went onto autopilot. I pretended these weren't my children she was naming. 'How did you meet Blake?' Inside I was screaming.

'Here! Well, just outside of here. It was after my first session with you. He and I literally bumped into each other. *Literally.*' She laughed.

Blake and I were supposed to meet for dinner that

215

evening. When he'd phoned to apologise later, I'd heard a woman's voice in the background.

Blake is a sweet boy. Blake lacks confidence. Blake has good friends, but doesn't always trust that he does. Maybe he should have gone to Oxford instead, or Edinburgh, or Durham. Has he stayed too close, and has it made him more vulnerable, less resilient? If his father were alive would he be more confident? I wanted to imagine a Blake who would have walked away from Anna, not one who would be flattered.

'He was a perfect gentleman,' Anna said. 'You know how he is.'

'Why did you want to talk to me?' I asked. I meant both then, and now.

She answered about then, with a shrug. 'Because you'd helped Hannah-Claire. She acted like she was better than me. She said that I needed "help". I think she meant it flippantly, but I figured she had a point.'

I didn't say anything. This is the point where a client often reveals their assumptions of what I 'must' be thinking.

'Look at this!' She pointed to her face, then swivelled and pulled up her sweater. 'These are real. This really happened to me. I didn't make this up.' She started to cry, in big, vocal sobs.

'Do you need a doctor?' I asked, as if she were a normal client. She sounded as if she were in physical pain.

'It's another hour before I can take more meds.' She wiped her nose and took a deep, shuddering breath.

'Does it feel good?' I asked.

She widened her eyes. 'Does what feel good?'

'You wanted to be a victim. You wanted to be like

Annalise. Does it feel good to have a real story to tell?'

She flung her arms out wide. 'Fuck off.'

I waited.

'No, seriously. I mean it. Fuck off.'

I said nothing.

'Let me explain something to you,' she said, and her voice cracked. She seemed exhausted. 'My cousin *died*. Do you get that? It's really fucking terrible . . .'

She cried for a little while. I watched the smallest hand on the clock lurch from one second to the next.

'If this is what you came here for . . .' I began, tired of her manipulations.

'I know what Hannah-Claire told you, and it's not any of your business. And it's not the police's business. I think we can help each other.'

I stood. 'You should leave.'

'No. No! You want to know how this happened?' She gestured to her whole body. 'The police wanted to arrest Henry for Hannah-Claire's death, but they couldn't. There wasn't enough evidence. But I knew he has a temper. I knew what he's capable of. So I gave the police a reason to get him. They've already put him in jail.'

'This has nothing to do with me.'

'It does. Because I needed Blake's help. I knew I could get Henry's DNA under my fingernails, and I knew I could make him angry, but there wasn't a guarantee I could get him to hurt me badly, enough to get him punished for what he'd done to Hannah-Claire. I needed Blake to finish the job.'

My mind was blank. I stuttered but ultimately had no words.

'Henry hit me, but it wasn't enough. I needed Blake to do the rest. For Hannah-Claire.'

'You're lying.'

She stood, leaning hard on her cane, that arm quivering from the pressure. 'I'm not. Blake is a good man, and that's why he did it. To help. And it worked! Henry's in jail, and he'll go to court, and he'll go to prison. So, I won't talk to the police about Blake, and you won't talk to them about Hannah-Claire, either. Understand? We both know things that don't need to be shared.'

'Blake could never . . .'

I didn't finish the sentence. He could never hurt someone out of sadism, or even anger. But to help someone? *Could he do that?* I didn't know.

Looking at her, I overlaid the image of her, bloody under my bumper, yesterday. *No, Blake could not do that.* He would have stopped himself. He could never do *that much.* He couldn't make her unconscious. He couldn't make her bleed.

I shook my head. 'No. That didn't happen.'

'If you say so. I just wanted to let you know.'

She started hobbling towards the door.

'Sandra!' I said.

She turned around. 'My mother calls me that all the time. You can't rattle me with that.'

I didn't help her with the office door. I didn't help her with the heavy front door, or the steps. I just held still, holding my breath until she was gone.

I locked my office and first thought to walk to the college. Blake could be in his house. He could be in the library. I could look up his lecture schedule and wait for him outside the hall doors.

But I know my son.

I went home. Not our home now, which is a drive away, but our home before, when Tom was still alive. We had a lovely house not far from the city centre, on Adams Road, abutting the secret bird sanctuary.

It's not a secret-secret, but it's unlabelled. There is no sign or name, just a lock on a gate, to which only the members know the code. There's no website; membership is run by paper mail, so that the code number, which changes every year or so, comes on a little slip that I had to pin to the refrigerator with a magnet or I'd never find it again.

This number I remembered, because it was the year of the Battle of Trafalgar. The last one had been the year of the Battle of Thermopylae, with a zero on the front. I hadn't recognised the history references, but Blake had. It's lovely when children become old enough to know more than you do.

I twisted the reluctant gears in the lock. Trafalgar was still good; it clicked open. I entered and locked it behind me.

This neighbourhood, Newnham, had been colonised in the 1800s when college fellows were at last allowed to marry. They moved out of their college rooms and into newly built semi-grand houses. The largest ones have now been chopped up into rooms for rent and graduate student accommodation, and some are still family homes, all of them crammed up next to each other. In front of these houses is an unbroken chain of parked cars, bumper to bumper, belonging to people who got into the city early enough to get free spaces here and not have to resort to the expensive multistoreys closer in. In short, Adams Road feels full, and busy, but behind this gate there is suddenly an acre of nothing.

I hold on to that word: 'nothing'. I mean that there are no houses in here, no cars, no people. No jostling, no shopping, no advertising. The trees and pond and trail and overwhelmingly prolific growing things everywhere are not *actually* nothing, but they're nothing in the way that a blank piece of paper is nothing. A piece of paper is, if you must be literal, a thing, but it's empty as yet of intrusion and claimed identity. It's the base state of the world before it's been parcelled out to owners and made use of.

Bird chatter fiddled in the background.

Tom used to bring the children here all the time, when they were very little and it felt like an adventure. As they got older they realised that it's actually quite small. Blake started coming again after Tom died. I wouldn't follow him in; he needed his space. But I always tried to remember the number, in case I needed it.

I followed the path around the pond, carefully stomping down on slippery, wet leaves, pushing pliable, reaching branches out of my way, and brushing up against thorniness, leafiness, and green everywhere. At the far side of the pond are two hides for birdwatchers. Blake was in one of them, at the top of the ladder, facing backwards towards me instead of looking through the view slits in the front. He had to have seen me coming. He didn't move.

I waved from below. He shook his head.

'Blake,' I called. 'Please.'

He descended the ladder with the physical nonchalance of the young. They won't know that this is their prime until they're past it.

I learnt years ago not to hug him in public, only at home. I wasn't sure which this was. I touched his jacket. 'We need to talk,' I said.

We walked to the nearby benches. His left hand brushed against my right. It felt rough. I looked. His knuckles were scratched, and the back of his hand bruised.

I sucked in a breath.

'What?' he asked, honest-sounding, innocent-seeming.

He's taller than me, so unless I tilt my head deliberately up he can't see my expression.

We took the bench, which faces the pond in hope of entertainment from ducks, and geese. I looked there, not directly at him. 'One of my clients says she knows you.'

'What do you mean?' He sounded innocent still, innocent in the literal sense of not knowing what I was talking about.

'Her name is Anna.'

Ah. That hit home. He leant forward, elbows on knees.

'How did you meet her?' I asked.

'It's really not your business.' He ran his hands over his hair.

'I think she's telling lies about you.'

He flinched. 'I don't want to know.'

'You need to know.'

'No!' He sat upright. He faced me. 'No! I don't need to do anything. I don't need to attend my lectures. I don't need to meet my deadlines. I don't need to go home. Just stop. Everything needs to just stop.'

I reached towards his shoulder but held just short of touching it. 'She was in the hospital yesterday.'

'Is she all right?' He asked this breathlessly, and his mouth hung a little bit open while he waited for my answer. There was genuine caring in his eyes. *Is he worried only for her, or also for the consequences of his own actions?*

'She's out now. She told me that you hit her. She told me that she asked you to.'

He leant away from me and shook his head. 'I've never hit anyone.'

'She says you did.'

'I didn't. I wouldn't do that. *Fuck*.' He pounded his right hand against his knee for emphasis.

'What happened to your hands?' I asked.

'Not that. Not that.'

'What?' I used my gentle mum-voice, the soothing one.

'I hit the wall, then hit the glass table in our house. It's a piece of shit and actually broke. I hit things, not a person. Never a person.'

'What were you angry about?'

'I am not a fucking client! Stop! Stop.'

I stopped. I held still. He didn't leave. That became my overwhelming goal: *Please don't leave.*

Once everything had kept still long enough, I said, 'She came to me, Blake. I didn't come to her. She's lying about you.'

'Stop. It doesn't matter. Nothing matters.'

'*You* stop! You! This does matter. It all matters.' He's been this way on and off since he was little, these futile surrenders. 'She's done something terrible and she's

222

covering it up. She's using you. She's using me. We've got to do something.'

He didn't leave, but neither did he answer. A pair of Canadian geese landed on the water and held his attention.

I choked out, 'I think she killed somebody.'

It had come together suddenly for me. Why would she care if the police knew she lied to her cousin about being the daughter of Annalise Wood? And if she really believed that Henry Ware had something to do with Hannah's death, why would she risk the perfect setup she'd created to jail him, to put the blame on Blake instead? That would only make sense if she knew that Henry actually didn't do it. She wasn't avenging Hannah; she must have been protecting herself . . .

'That's insane,' Blake said, then stopped short, because I'd spent years correcting him and Clara when they used words like that casually.

'She's a very disturbed person,' I said carefully.

The geese on the water squabbled and flapped at each other. I waited.

Blake kept looking straight out, not facing me, but he talked. 'I've only known her a few weeks. We bumped into each other around the corner from your office. Literally bumped. She was on the phone and not paying attention, I guess. I knocked her phone onto the pavement. I didn't mean to, and even though it was fine I felt terrible, and to be honest I already felt terrible because I knew what you were going to ask over dinner: am I making friends? Am I happy? My friends' parents ask about supervisions and studying, and they hate that. You're supposed to be so different, caring about me *as a person* instead of about

223

grades, but you don't understand what the problem with *all* of those questions is. They're not actually different questions. They're all actually asking, Are you still a failure? No one wants to answer that. No one. So by the time I bumped into Anna, I already wanted an excuse to get out of dinner. Apologising to her seemed like a good one.'

I didn't comment. I held my expression still. But even that stillness was a reaction he could read, and a stereotypical therapist one at that.

'She said that she was new to Cambridge,' he went on. 'She seemed like she needed a friend. She's at Wolfson and Cambridge is overwhelming, she said. I understand that. So we talked for hours. She thought it was funny when I admitted I'd skipped dinner with my mother to go to a cafe with her. She made a joke about mental health. Holy shit, had she just come from being with you?'

'Yes.' I was frantically trying to figure out how she could have known Blake is my son. *Is my Facebook page insecure? I hardly use it. Blake was mentioned in Tom's obituary, but there was no photo of him . . .*

'I told her what it is that you do, and she laughed. It seemed strange at the time but I . . .'

That made me feel hopeful that she had been surprised by the connection. It was still something put into motion by me, by my appointment with Blake and my appointment with her skimming against each other at the end of that day, but at least I hadn't helped her plan something using information I'd been careless with.

'Then she asked me a lot of questions,' he said. 'She thinks that having a psychologist for a parent must make me feel . . . manipulated sometimes.'

224

I looked away. He's allowed to feel that way, even if I deeply hope he doesn't.

'We went out a few times after that. It's not important.'

I didn't bring up that she'd met Clara. I didn't bring up that she'd been talking about May Ball dresses, months and months away. I did say, 'She's charming and needy, and she's involved with a police situation. It's very important that you stay out of it.'

'She was hurt? She said that I hit her?' he asked, quietly.

'She said that to me. Only to me.'

'I swear I did not.'

'I know.' I believed him, but an accusation could still be devastating.

'Is she all right?'

He still cared. It broke my heart. 'She was well enough to be discharged. She'll heal.' While I mouthed vague comfort, I strategised: Blake's broken glass table and any mark on the wall would have to be photographed, to protect him, just in case.

I asked him, 'Where were you yesterday afternoon?'

He shook his head. 'I stayed in bed most of the day.'

'Were your housemates in?'

'Is that when it happened?'

I nodded.

'Matt was home part of the time. I heard him. He was upset when he saw the table. But he wouldn't have known I was there. He banged on my bedroom door and I ignored him.'

My mind weighed possibilities. *Good: a witness to the shattered table. Bad: supposed proof of Blake having a temper . . .*

225

Does this mean that Blake has a temper? What would I think if someone Clara was close to reacted in anger like that? Would I trust him to be with her?

'Why were you angry?' I asked him.

'She broke up with me.'

He wasn't finished, he was still explaining that with all that had happened to her cousin she had to focus on other things, how it was yesterday morning and she was already dressed for the funeral and how that made her seem distant and costumed to Blake, not real, but in my mind I paused to correct him. I wanted him to say 'didn't want to see me any more' not 'break up with' because the latter implies a more serious relationship. In my mind I was grooming him for explaining to police if he had to, for explaining in court if he had to. It was difficult to breathe. I gulped in big, fresh gulps of air, but none of them felt like enough.

'Mum, are you okay?'

I forced my chin up. 'You can't see her. And you can't hide. Go to your lectures and supervisions. Act normal. I'll take care of this.'

'I don't feel normal. I don't want to pretend.'

'I don't care!' I waved my two fists in front of me like spinning gears. I suddenly understood, profoundly, how one could want to hit a table and a wall and to break something.

He stood up. The geese took off. 'I don't want you to fix it for me, *Mum*. Anna can say whatever she wants. I didn't do it. I'll say so, and it's the truth.'

I shook my head, half in 'no' and half as simple quivering. *No, he mustn't risk it.* 'She's not worth it, Blake.'

226

'What do you know about anything? What do you think *I'm* worth? I was messed up after Dad died. Him being dead was in my mind literally all the time, and I was pretty sure that on top of losing him I was about to lose literally everyone else, because who would want to be around me when I was like that? With Anna, I was different, because *she* was the hurt one. That made me the strong person, or the kind person, instead of the fucked-up kid whose dad died. That felt good.'

I had to tell him. 'She's dangerous,' I said. 'I think she killed her cousin.'

His mouth opened but he said nothing at first, just let his jaw hang there, accusing me of a step too far.

'You think she pushed Hannah-Claire into the river?'

'It's the only thing that makes sense! She told me that if I revealed to the police what she and Hannah-Claire had talked to me about in sessions, that she would put her accusation of Henry onto you. If she really believed Henry had done it, why would she be willing to take the pressure off him? It must be that she set Henry up in this way to protect herself from being found guilty of Hannah's death herself . . .'

Blake laughed. At first it blended in with the chatter of birds, but then it got louder, like a flapping of huge wings.

He said, 'You're *crazy*.' He emphasised the word deliberately, no shame, no apology.

'I know it's difficult to contemplate about someone you care about but—'

'No. Stop. No.'

'Blake, she's not who you think she is.' In my mind, I amended it to 'who you wish she was', because really he hardly knew her at all. He was infatuated, clearly, and feeling hurt and wanted to be a white knight for her, but . . .

'Stop *analysing* me. God. Really? I don't just "think" she didn't kill Hannah-Claire. I know she didn't. I was with her that night. I was with her all night. Hannah-Claire had just left when I arrived. I saw her. I saw her just before she died.' He started to shake.

I stood but he held up his hand before I could take a step.

'No. I don't trust you right now.' He walked away. His footsteps crunched on and shuffled through the leaves on the path.

I forced myself to not chase him. It wouldn't help. I knew it wouldn't help. I forced myself back onto the bench. I literally sat on my hands.

I pushed my thoughts down a logical track, an analytical track, to keep myself from feeling sick over her and Blake . . .

Anna had been attacked, horrifically. Someone had done this to her. The police believed that Henry was the one, which is what Anna said she'd wanted. She'd told me that she egged him on to get him to reveal his true violent self, and then had Blake finish the job. If I believed Blake, and I did, she was making that part up. It really had been Henry, whom she'd triggered at great cost to herself. How could she be willing to let him get away with this? What was more important than seeing him punished for his violence?

A question rose like a soap bubble, and just as fragile: *I've studied the effects of concussion and trauma. Memory loss surrounding such an incident is a real thing. Does she even know for sure who hurt her?*

She seemed to be choosing from among several possible realities as they suited different situations: to the police, she accused Henry; to me, she accused Blake. She was controlling us. Henry had been arrested. I was keeping my mouth shut.

I am. I'm doing that. Then, *Should I?*

I needed to protect Blake, from even accusation. But if we accomplished that with silence, it would always be hanging over his head.

What was Anna trying to hide? If she truly believed that Henry was responsible for Hannah-Claire's death, she wouldn't let him get away with it. But if she's not protecting herself, who is she protecting?

The key had to be in what Hannah-Claire had told me. *Or in what Anna thought Hannah-Claire had told me.*

If I could figure that out, then we'd have something to use against her.

'Tom,' I said. There was no answer, of course. Just wind pushing through leaves, ducks squabbling, songbirds jabbering. Whether you believe in life after death or not, the person is *not here* any more. Their at least being somewhere else is supposed to be a comfort, but from my selfish point of view it's not very different from not existing at all.

If Tom was ever going to give a sign, it would be now, for Blake. Or maybe he already comforts Blake directly. What do I know? Tom was never interested in religion, but perhaps Blake found him in that chapel, or some promise of him.

I said, 'Tom' again. Again, Tom said nothing back.

Maybe he was on the other side, wishing to be able to answer, but we weren't in the same place any more. Maybe he knew that I missed him; maybe he didn't. But I didn't know anything. I wasn't reachable.

Just then my phone rang. I snatched it up, as if it might be him.

CHAPTER FIFTEEN

Chloe Frohmann

I got Dr Laurie Ambrose on the phone. She sounded anxious and breathy when she picked up. There was an improbable goose honk in the background.

I'd just spent an odd half hour chatting with Clemmy, the Dog Man, as I'd come to think of him. He was the one who had found the body by the tracks. Hannah-Claire had phoned him a week before her death. He confirmed to me that she had come to see him, hoping he might know more about the body than the police let out. Maybe she hoped he'd taken a secret souvenir, some kind of token she could use to prove or disprove her parentage. It was grisly to think about; had she been hoping for something like a finger bone with some marrow still inside? *Eugh*. I wrinkled my nose. The man denied knowing anything, and assured me that he'd told Hannah-Claire the same. We both had to repeat ourselves several times, because of all the barking on his end. Clearly the dog he'd been walking in 1992 wouldn't still be alive, but it would seem that in his old age he'd acquired several rambunctious replacements.

When Laurie Ambrose picked up my call, I was looking forward to some peace and quiet. But, *bloody geese.* I couldn't wait for Stephanie to wake up with her customary wail and join the fun.

'Dr Ambrose, I'm Detective Inspector Chloe Frohmann. We met briefly at Our Lady and the English Martyrs.'

'I'm sorry, what?'

'The Catholic church.' It's the most prominent one in Cambridge, at arguably the worst junction in Cambridge, and a landmark on its own, no full name necessary.

'Oh, yes. Yes. I remember you.' She sounded icy. Admittedly, I had possibly been insufficiently serious back then in the church car park. *All right, I'd been giddy to be on the job again.* I resolved to treat her more carefully.

'Dr Ambrose, we're very worried about what was done to Ms Finney and Ms Williams. I understand from Detective Sergeant Spencer that you were their therapist? Were they in some kind of family therapy together?'

'I can't talk to you.'

'As I understand it, Dr Ambrose, in the case of criminal activity and for the sake of Ms Williams' safety, you *can* talk to us. You should.' I'd looked up the rules. They're guidelines at best, not like what priests in the confessional get.

'It's precisely because of Ms Williams' privacy that I won't. It's up to her if she wishes me to share what we discussed in our sessions. If she doesn't wish it, then neither do I.'

She was going to be a tough one. I pulled my feet down off the couch where I'd been sprawled and sat up straight. 'Is that what Ms Williams asked? You discussed this with her?'

Hesitation. Then, 'I'm not going to tell you *anything* we've discussed.'

'Dr Ambrose . . .'

'Inspector, the guidelines make it clear that it's up to my good judgement to decide what to tell police, if anything. I've exercised my judgement, and I'm tired.'

I imagined 'judgement' to be a pet golden retriever, ready to flop after a vigorous walk. 'Of course, Dr Ambrose. I apologise.'

She rang off before I could give it another go from a different angle, but it turned out that my first try had been enough.

At eleven o'clock that night, Dan and I were in that deep blackout between baby feedings. My phone buzzed, making the side table vibrate, and I tried to snatch it up before it woke Stephanie in the crib in the next room. Parenthood had made us near-superstitious; any sound that we could perceive, no matter how distant from the baby, could wake her. She was the princess; my phone had become the pea.

'Damn!' I said, louder than the phone itself, which I'd knocked onto the floor. I finally retrieved it, saw the number, and called Dr Ambrose back.

'Inspector?' she said. Her voice was a sharp yelp, as if I'd stepped on her tail. *On her judgement's tail*, I added.

'Yes, is something wrong?'

'It's the news. I saw something in the news.'

Shit, shit, shit. I padded my slippered feet into the lounge and closed the door. I opened my laptop. *Was Anna dead? Had someone finished the job?*

'Inspector? Are you there?'

'I am. Sorry, I'm waking up.' Connecting to Wi-Fi. New browser tab. 'What news?' I asked. Then I saw it.

Our reinvestigation of the Annalise Wood case had gone public. 'New DNA evidence'. No mention of Charlie specifically, thank God. No details except Morris's name (*he won't like that*). *Shit*. Not as bad as another death, obviously, but this was our other nightmare: the press taking the story out of our hands.

'Inspector?'

'Yes, sorry. What about the news story you saw?' I was wondering if it was Marnie or Rosalie who'd leaked it. Or someone else? Not Cathy or Charlie, surely . . .

'I said it's about Annalise Wood.' She must have said the name as I'd read it in the headline and I'd thought I was just hearing it in my head.

'What about her?' I asked, playing ignorant.

'Both Anna – Sandra – Williams and Hannah-Claire Finney had come to me, separately, about Annalise Wood.'

She told me everything. The words tumbled out of her, chasing each other. There was no holding back.

'When Anna – Sandra – when she threatened me, I was only thinking about Blake, but then later I started thinking about Anna again. What exactly was she afraid of? What power did she think I had? Did I – do I – have some power here? Well, I'd better because when she sees that in the news she's going to think that I had something to do with it and she's going to call Sergeant Spencer and tell him that Blake . . .' She sobbed like, well, like Stephanie when she's so upset from hunger that she's not able to swallow and it just gets worse and worse.

234

'Dr Ambrose, you did the right thing to tell me. I'll talk to DS Spencer.'

'Thank you.'

'You're welcome. Listen, I'm going to want to see the transcripts.'

'I know.'

'Can you get them to me?'

'I can, but . . . I think I've found what she was worried about. I think I found it.'

It turned out that after Hannah-Claire emailed Dr Ambrose goodbye, quit her job, and moved in with Henry, she'd continued to email, but this time from her personal email address instead of the university one she'd used at the museum. Unlike that email, these new ones had all gone into Dr Ambrose's spam folder.

'I was using my phone, not my laptop. On my laptop, I have all these folders but on my phone it's just easier to search. I searched by her name, not her email address, to find her goodbye note, and up popped all of these extra emails. I'd never seen them before. Never. I wish I had . . .'

She forwarded them to me. We stayed on the phone while I read them.

From: Hannah-Claire Finney
To: Laurie Ambrose

Dear Dr Ambrose,

I know I'm not supposed to write to you. You didn't answer me before, when I said goodbye, and that's fine. But I've quit my job at the Fitzwilliam, and without a University association I'm not allowed to make a proper appointment. Besides, the time we did meet I did all of the talking, didn't I :-) So here I am again, talking, and I can imagine you approving. That is what I imagined, you know. Maybe you thought I was ridiculous and romantic and stupid. Maybe you weren't even listening. But I imagined that you understood me, and that was comforting.

I quit my job because I've moved in with Henry(!!!), and the commute is too far. It's not because I can't cope. I could have coped, but now I don't have to. Maybe that's a lie, but that's what I choose to think about the situation. I could have kept on at my job and the panic attacks were slowing down anyway.

I'm going to meet the rest of his family at Christmas, which is a relief because I don't want to spend it with the remnants of mine. I had hoped that my cousins would be more like sisters once I closed the physical distance between us, but that is really, really not the case. Sadie is an island. She shows up for milestone events as required but is otherwise a work machine, and she lives in York. Sandra (who insists on being called Anna, which is why I push so hard at my double-name, so we · don't get mixed up) asked me for help. I thought we were friends as well as family, so I let her move into my apartment near the Fitz. She's at a bit of a loose end. She should finish her degree, but you can't tell her anything.

So I get to start life with a new family at Christmas. I'm pleased about that. I've been praying. I don't usually tell people that, but I'm imagining that you think that it's good of me instead of thinking that it's deluded. I pray that I'll fit in with his family and that we'll make a beautiful home together. He's made room for me in his place, but it's not the same as starting from scratch somewhere that's fresh for both of us. I've brought up that idea but he's not able to consider it at the moment, with the way that work is. I didn't bring a lot with me when I moved to this country, anyway.

The most important thing is that there's room for ****me**** in his home. I feel like he really wants me here. That feels good.

From: Hannah-Claire Finney
To: Laurie Ambrose

Dear Dr Ambrose,
I'm frustrated, and I don't want to say it to Henry, because he's distracted with a big client and is on the edge right now. If they shut down, that's a big loss for us.

I've tried making friends with the neighbours, but hardly anyone else is home during the day. I haven't had any luck finding a good job fit out here, so I've started writing a book. It's a children's book. It's based on still-life paintings, or, as my young student said, the 'still alives', like the Dutch paintings at the Fitzwilliam. Except they don't keep still like they should. That's the joke. They're not still; they're just 'life'. I mean it to be like those museum movies where things come alive at night, but unlike dinosaur bones and Egyptian mummies, which make for exciting adventures, the flowers and fruit just end up wasting themselves. They have adventures (well, as much adventure as sentient objects can get up to), but as they do, petals fall off and apples brown. They're all withered by morning and when they jump back into position they don't look right, they can't really go back to how they were, no matter how hard they try. It's not a cheery book.

This morning I got the bill for the storage place I'm using back home. It's past due, because it had to cross the ocean, and then it had to get forwarded from my Cambridge apartment. I need to phone them once it's morning there, to make sure they don't get rid of everything. I hear that some places do that: you miss one payment, and they take those big metal clippers to your lock. So I'm waiting for it to be nine a.m. over there, and I'm looking up how to phone Canada from England, and I'm actually considering letting them take it all. Why not? When am I ever going to want it? Everything about my parents that matters is what we did together. I remember that. It's not in the storage facility.

The only thing I would have to worry about are the papers with account numbers and things like that. Someone could use those for identity theft. But then what would it matter? I took my paperwork out. They're dead. They won't care.

And, see, part of the reason I think I won't call the

storage place is because maybe all of that *should* be thrown out. Maybe it's time. Do you think it's time? And even if you were in the room you wouldn't answer me; you'd ask me if ***I*** think it's time. Well, I do. I do.

Remember I told you that my cousin told me that I'm not really adopted from my parents' daughter? (Ha, that's a sentence not many people get to write!!) That I'm really the daughter of a **completely different** dead teenager?? And you're probably wondering why I believed it, and you probably think I'm like those people who are so ready to believe that they're the reincarnation of Marie Antoinette. But it's not just vanity. It's not just gullibility. Those records showed me that I can't be Jenny's child. The blood type isn't right. So those records can just go fuck themselves. Maybe they'll make some kind of bonfire. It'll be so warm I'll feel it from here.

That's why I had to ask Anna. That's why I trusted her answer. Because I know there is an answer other than the one I've been told my whole life.

I haven't told Henry. I haven't wanted to be a bother. There's nothing he can do about it, anyway. **I'm** going to do something. I'm reading the books about Annalise, and I'm trying to track down someone who worked on the autopsy. Maybe Annalise Wood did have a baby. It would make sense. It would explain why we moved so far away, and stayed so far away. And there's France.

My cousin made me swear I wouldn't ask Aunt

Cathy and Uncle Charlie about it. She said that she tried to ask them about Annalise once and that they went ballistic and it ruined Christmas. According to the books, Annalise went to France the year before she died. That would have been the only time to have a baby. I don't mean in France; I mean while she was supposed to be in France. So it could be real. It doesn't have to be untrue just because my cousin is awful.

She really is awful. I don't like her. But what if my birth mother isn't Annalise? Somebody has to be. What if the last lead I have left is a lie too?

Henry's home. I'm hitting send. He doesn't like when I 'waste time on the computer all day'.

From: Hannah-Claire Finney
To: Laurie Ambrose

I feel embarrassed about the last message I sent you. I was blue. Isn't that a lovely word for an ugly thing? I was BLUE. I can't believe I told you about those silly ideas I sketched and called them a 'children's book'. Maybe for VERY DEPRESSED CHILDREN, ha ha. Anyway, I'm feeling much better. I am no longer blue. Today I am . . . yellow, I think!

Henry has a grandmother who won't want us to share a room at Christmas (reminds me of Aunt Cathy's obnoxious lawyer husband but NEVER MIND!) because we're not married, so we've decided to elope!! We could have played French farce the whole time, sneaking about in dark hallways to visit

each other, but this is much more romantic <3 <3 <3
Besides, this will placate my uncle too. Anna told me
he doesn't approve that I've moved in with Henry. I
wish she wouldn't tell me these things. I would like
my illusions, please!!

I'm getting married today!! That's what I wanted
to tell you.

From: Hannah-Claire Finney
To: Laurie Ambrose

Being married is lovely, Dr Ambrose. Have you done
it? You should. I feel different now. I'm seriously
considering changing my name. The problem is the
rhyme: Hannah-Claire Ware. Ugh. But I want this,
I want him and me to be a little family together.
I think I'll surprise him with the name change for
Christmas.

By the way, I did call the storage place. My things
are fine. I had prepaid the whole first year, which
means they gave me some leeway for the transition
to monthly bills. Now I've put it on automatic
payments with my bank here, though I'll have to
watch that too because I'm not adding new money
now that I'm not working. Henry and I still have to
work out money things. We talked about adding me
to his accounts, so I'll have to remember to move
my bills over.

But the reason I called the place is that I forgot
about the photo. I'd brought my parents' albums with
me, of course. That's the kind of stuff you'd pull out

of a fire. But there was one picture I'd left behind. It was with the medical records and blood type and all of that stuff that I had no desire to deal with when I found it. It was of me as a baby. The reason it wasn't in the albums, I suppose, is because in it my mother was holding me. You can't see her face, just her neck and a young, skinny arm. Obviously a teenager. That it was filed away should have told me as clear as the blood type that I wasn't their daughter's. If I had been, this photo would have been framed. I realised I needed that photo, Dr Ambrose.

The other day I went to my (MY!!) apartment to get some things I'd left behind (there are a lot of things Henry already had), and Anna had added her things in there. Which, of course she had, of course she had; she's living there. Clothes in the closet, obviously, and food in the fridge, but also her own framed photos, and teddy bears; personal things. They felt invasive.

And I suddenly felt embarrassed about the things I'd left on the shelves. I've saved some children's books from when I was little, which is normal; lots of people do that. They're in storage back home. But I'd also bought a new one, which was in the apartment, in fact now out on the coffee table, which means Anna has read it. It's a board book – the kind that babies can chew on – called *Tall or Small*. It's about how things get defined by what they're compared to. If your siblings are stupid, for example, you may get to be 'the smart one', but that doesn't mean you're actually smart, necessarily. Or if your siblings happen to be geniuses, you may be 'the stupid one' even if you're quite clever. (The book doesn't use that example. That would be cruel. That example is mine.) Anyway, I came across it while buying a gift for a friend, and I bought it for myself, because I realised that I'm like that. I don't feel like I have an inherent identity that transcends situation; instead, I feel defined by what I'm compared to, and by what I'm next to. I feel like my relationships make me 'a loved person' or 'not a loved person' and therefore 'a loveable person' or 'not a loveable person'. I'm deserving or pathetic depending on what the people around me do, not on what I do, which is an untethered feeling, Dr Ambrose. It's something I can't control. I feel lucky to have Henry, but what if I didn't? What if I were the exact same person but without him; would I, the very same I, therefore be awful instead of wonderful? It makes me feel afraid of him stopping loving me, which makes me needy and maybe manipulative, which I don't want to be. All of that is wrapped up in that little book, and I saw it out and I felt like Anna now knew all of that about me.

I suddenly hated her sitting on my couch. I suddenly hated her fingers on my keyboard. And I realised that I really need to get it all out, all of my stuff, or give it to her officially, and just live my life moving forward. I think you would approve of that, Dr Ambrose. It sounds like something a professional would call a breakthrough.

It's made me realise that I don't need to 'make nice' just because they're all the family I have left. I have Henry now, and his family, and his doting mother and judgemental grandmother and his sister who sells candles. That has given me courage.

I'm going to take back that baby book, *Tall or Small*, to throw it away. I just don't want Anna to have access to that part of me. And there are some things about her and our family that her belongings have given me access to as well. There are some things that need dealing with.

We're going to talk some things through tonight, me and my family.

I'll write again if I fuck everything up.

Must go! I need to tidy before Henry gets back. He still isn't used to this being 'our' home. I think I'll ask again about us getting a new place together. Maybe that can be his Christmas present to me.

'The last one is from the day Hannah-Claire died,' Laurie said.

'You're her doctor. What do you think it means?'

'I was only her therapist for one hour! One hour! That doesn't make me "her doctor".'

I backed off. 'All right. I'll have a go. Sounds like she was rather up and down. Emotional. Someone in a state like that might take risks, or make a statement.'

'She said she was going to talk things through with her family. She was with someone from her family. The way she used that word makes it clear that she meant her old family, not the new one.'

'Yes, and after that conversation she could have been even more upset, and done something dramatic. I'm not saying that I think she did, but if you're trying to prove that she was murdered rather than suicidal or drunk and clumsy, we're going to need more. As for Henry, look, she loves him, but it comes off as a bit desperate, in my opinion. He seems . . . tightly wound, at least from the way she reacts to his imminent arrivals.'

'So you agree with the sergeant, Henry did it?'

'She was in the middle of Cambridge near her old flat, her old job, her old life. Maybe Henry didn't like that.'

'Maybe,' Laurie hesitantly acknowledged. 'But, Inspector, Anna was scared by me having these emails. I'm sure of it. Hannah-Claire says in them that she had left lots of things in her flat, including her "keyboard". If she'd left her desktop computer, and Anna had been using it, she could have found these in the sent folder. If she deleted them from there, the only copies left would be the ones in my spam folder. Anna had to have assumed I'd received and read them. There's something in here that she doesn't want us to know.'

I nodded, pacing. This was what it had come to: our attempt to solve what happened to Annalise was going nowhere, and now the press knew it – but we were going to figure out what had happened to Hannah-Claire. 'The obvious thing would be that Anna was hiding her own meeting with Hannah-Claire. But you say that Blake gives her an alibi?' For the duration of this conversation, I'd decided to take Blake's claims at his word.

'Yes. Hannah-Claire was there, Blake said, but she left alive. Anna must be protecting someone, someone in their family.'

The dates clicked into place. That was the afternoon I'd been at the office of Rigg and Loft, and Rosalie had answered a phone call from Cathy's niece. It had been a confirmation of the niece meeting Cathy later that day.

That had been Hannah-Claire, and Anna must be protecting her mother.

CHAPTER SIXTEEN

Morris Keene

I pressed the nipple-bell at Chloe's door. A ringing; a baby wail. Familiar now. But instead of Dan answering, it was Chloe. She was already dressed, even though it was ridiculously early. The baby must have been with Dan, because it wasn't on her. She said, 'I've seen the news.'

That pulled me up. I hadn't seen the news.

'What's in the news?' I asked, already wincing. We'd been waiting for it. The word 'Annalise' coming out of a policeman's mouth made it inevitable. Someone had talked.

'Is that not why you're here?'

'Coffee, please. *Please*,' I said, making it clear with the second 'please' that this wasn't an 'ordering her around' request but a desperate one.

She led me to her kitchen table, which was overfull with mail and catalogues. 'Did you know that they just send those?' Chloe asked, as she fitted a cafetière together and boiled water.

I nudged the thick booklets with the back of my hand. Babies in very expensive clothes and beside very expensive toys smiled manically at me. When Chloe handed me a mug, I used a baby's grin as a coaster.

'TV or paper news?' I asked.

'Online.'

Right. Shows I am getting old, that that wasn't my first guess. 'What was the headline?' I asked.

'New DNA Evidence in the Case of Murdered Teen Annalise Wood.'

I sipped. 'That's actually restrained.'

'I know! I was expecting "raped teen beauty" or something like that.'

No doubt that would come. 'Named sources?'

She shook her head. 'But—' She hesitated.

'What?' My coffee cup had made a ring around the catalogue-baby's head, halo-like.

'Your name.'

I nodded. The press would soon come looking to me for quotes. The press would come looking to me for a *solution*.

'And Hannah-Claire Finney.'

I sat up from my fatalistic slouch. 'Really?' I tapped the table. 'That narrows it down,' I said, meaning that only a few of the people I'd spoken to knew also that Hannah-Claire Finney had been thinking that she could be Annalise's child.

'It does more than that,' Chloe said. She told me about Hannah-Claire's cousin, and the cousin's threats to their shared therapist, while popping toast emphasised random points.

'So, this woman, Sandra—' I began.

'She calls herself Anna. She's a little *into* Annalise.'

'All right, Anna. She believes that Henry Ware killed Hannah-Claire, and set out to provoke more violence from him, of which she was certain he was capable, in order that he would go to prison for something, if not the murder itself. Is that right?'

She nodded, while buttering. She had four slices piled up in front of her.

'But to stop the therapist from revealing . . . something . . . Anna threatened that she would lie and claim that her boyfriend – do I have this right, the therapist's son? – was actually the one to do it, at her request, in order to *frame* Henry, who in this version hadn't done it. That's what's happening.'

'And that doesn't make any sense, because it would undermine the whole point of her injuries, which are, truly, awful. This was no light thing. She put herself at significant risk. If her point was to sacrifice herself to put Henry in jail, well . . . But that couldn't have been her point if she's so willing to change her story to keep the therapist's mouth shut.'

'You're grinning. You know something.' I know that look. She likes to get one over on other cops.

'I think her point wasn't blaming Henry so much as it was protecting someone.'

'Herself?' But Chloe wouldn't have phrased it the way she had if that's what she was leading up to.

'No. Alibi with the boyfriend. So who would she care about?'

'You trust the boyfriend?' It's not like Chloe to trust anyone in a case.

249

'They'd broken up. I think he's telling the truth, and so does his therapist mother. Which leaves us . . .'

'Family.'

'And who is her family?' in that voice in which parents ask children what colour grass is.

Chloe had told me yesterday. 'Charlie. And Cathy.'

'And her sister, Sadie, and her stepfather, Nigel Rigg. But, yes, mostly Charlie and Cathy. I think Cathy.'

'You think what about Cathy, exactly?'

'I think she killed Hannah-Claire Finney.'

Chloe explained about Hannah-Claire's lost emails to Laurie Ambrose, and the plan they revealed for Hannah to meet 'family' the night of her death, which was what Anna had most likely been trying to keep quiet. What Anna didn't know was that Chloe had witnessed a phone call from Hannah-Claire to the Rigg law office confirming her plans with Cathy that day. And a mother is an obvious person for someone to want to protect.

I took the role of damp to her enthusiasm. 'We don't even know that Hannah-Claire was killed. We can't know. It could have been an accident. We can't prove otherwise.'

'But I think we do a good job of proving – well, implying strongly – that Anna *believes* that Cathy killed Hannah-Claire. Or at least fears it. Otherwise why should she go to all the trouble? All of this specific, horrific trouble?'

'Which means that Anna presumably knows something we don't yet know, something that maybe could prove that Hannah-Claire was killed, if we can get it out of her . . .' By now the catalogue's perfect cover-baby was marred by Chloe's crumbs, a smear of butter, and a splash of my coffee.

Chloe laughed. 'Who would pay a hundred and ten pounds for a cardigan for a baby? A white one, no less!'

'Speaking of which, where's the real baby?' I hadn't heard a sound since that initial waking burst.

She leant over the table to confide: 'Bottles. Amazing.' Presumably, Dan was also involved, not just bottles on their own.

'I should take a turn,' she said, I assumed meaning with feeding. 'Then go back to bed. Laurie Ambrose and her revelations kept me up last night.' She stood, then remembered back to the start of our conversation. 'Wait. You said you didn't know the Annalise investigation had hit the press. Why are you here?'

I shook my head. I brought the now-empty mug to my lips to stall.

Chloe sat down again. 'Morris?'

I'm not sure exactly when it happened, but Chloe and I call each other by first names, instead of the more professional use of surnames. We're friends. I can trust her. That's why I'm here.

'The Review Team does more than cold cases,' I reminded her. 'We also review current cases under very specific circumstances.' I locked eyes with another cover-baby, this one disconcertingly riding a cartoon tiger.

'Meaning what?' she asked, leaning over her plate.

'Bob Cameron told me to leave off with the Annalise investigation yesterday. He looked at what we have, which to be honest isn't likely to add up to much, and decided that it would be better not to "upset the apple cart" by pursuing the theory that the body by the tracks is someone else. He's one for clichés, our Superintendent Cameron. He thinks it's unlikely we'll be able to identify who the body – which, to be fair, we don't actually have any more, thanks to cremation – actually was. He thinks it would "undermine public confidence" to try to do so. He is also one for arse-covering. I wonder if he's got a Google alert about the news story.'

'It'll be in the *Daily Mail* by tomorrow, with full-colour photos from 1976.'

'It probably will.'

'But that could be good for us, good for the case. Cameron might have to let you go on with it, if the cat's already out of the bag.'

No doubt using that exact phrase.

Chloe tried to comfort me. 'I know you didn't want it out, I know you don't like your name attached to such a well-known case without a proper resolution, but this could work for good. It already has with Laurie Ambrose. She wouldn't have told us anything if the news mention hadn't pushed her.'

'It may be pushing Anna Williams, if she thinks Dr Ambrose told the police what Anna didn't want her to. Spencer should keep an eye on both of them.'

'I already tipped him off to that.'

I raised my eyebrows. She'd called him last night, or this morning, but not called me.

She saw my face. 'It wasn't urgent for you. He needed to do something about Laurie Ambrose's information.'

'So do I.' I sucked in a breath and pushed it out slowly.

'Hannah-Claire's death was an incident of potential domestic violence that was under police investigation. Anna's attack is an escalation of that incident and has been deemed in need of Review Team oversight.'

Chloe pushed her chair back. 'You? They gave it to you?'

'My two colleagues are deep in another case. I've been asked to use my suddenly free time to "assist" Detective Sergeant Spencer. That's why I came to see you.'

She nodded, but then tilted her head. 'For what? What do you want me to do?'

'I just wanted you to know. I – I think I came here to put it off, to be honest.' I held my hands in my lap, the left one squeezing my right, hard. For some reason that helps me to stop unreasonable panic from escalating.

The noise was unsettling. At first I thought it was the baby, because I couldn't imagine Chloe would make that sound at me. She was laughing. I pushed back from the table.

She covered her mouth. 'No! Morris! Don't you get it? Don't you?'

'Apparently not.' Apparently I was stupid as well as everything else.

'Please.' She put her hand on my arm. 'You idiot. Do you not understand that Spencer feels embarrassed by what he did? He feels foolish for having been so tough with Dora. He has to take it from your old mates who tease him. He's the one going to be humiliated by you coming to look over his shoulder, not the other way round.'

'I know he won't like it. I know that. But that's exactly

what'll make him want to humiliate me first. And if he tries, what do I have to fling back at him? What do we have?'

She smiled. 'You said "we".'

'You've been a help.'

'I can still be a help.'

I squinted at her. 'What do you mean?'

'You and Spencer go after Cathy and Anna. Cathy wouldn't appreciate seeing me again anyway. I'll keep following what we've got about Annalise.'

'We don't have anything much about Annalise. What we have are clues about the body by the tracks, which I'm increasingly persuaded isn't Annalise at all.'

'Tell me.'

So I did. I told her my theory that the school uniform, which had come with the other donated clothes into the boarding house, may have been voluntarily worn, possibly as sexual role playing, and possibly without anyone knowing it was Annalise's specifically; just random discarded clothes costuming a schoolgirl fantasy. The vantage point from the tower possibly indicated that the person who did the killing – or, at least, the burying – was the one who lived in the boarding house, rather than the girl being the one who lived there (though, of course, they could have both lived there). I hoped that Ginny Russell, the dutiful daughter who had looked after her father literally all of her life, would get back to me with her memories of the boarding house's residents. *Perhaps she's dutiful in all things.* I could only hope.

'That's settled, then,' Chloe announced, all efficiency. 'I'll go and see Ms Russell. See if I can get that list of names of people who lived in the boarding house. You go and see Spencer.'

'That's the plan,' I agreed.

I was grateful. I knew it would be easier facing Spencer if I had the possibility of an eventual solution to hold on to. Any solution. Maybe if we can't name the girl, we can still name the man.

'Chloe,' I said. 'I hate today. I hate it. I don't want to walk into Spencer's case. I don't want to make him feel small. I don't want to fight. But he has to respect me. Whatever happens or doesn't happen with Annalise and this thing we started with Charlie's DNA, he needs to respect me.'

She leant on her arm, clearly exhausted. I knew I should go but I stayed because I needed something. 'You can't control what other people do, Morris. You can only control whether you deserve respect, not whether he gives it to you.'

'You sound like you're speaking from experience.' She has not always had it easy in Major Crimes.

'Look, I watched a lot of telly when I was on bed rest. I mean, enormous amounts of it. *Huge.* And there was a multipart dramatisation about the discovery of King Tut's tomb that was somehow framed as a doomed romance. You can look it up if you must. Anyway, I found myself getting angry as I watched it, and it took me almost the whole way through to figure out why.' She carried her plate and my mug to the counter. 'The whole premise was that Howard Carter – he's the man who discovered the tomb, in case you didn't study history properly when you were at school – found it because he was tenacious.

Because he was determined. Those were presented as his unique virtues. Only he deserved the tomb because only he persevered.'

'Isn't that fair?' I asked. 'If everyone else gave up . . .' I wanted to help with the dishes, but the counter was covered in many more than I could make a start on without making more of a mess first.

'It was only virtuous of him to continue after everyone else moved on to other things because we know now that the tomb was there, full of treasure. What if it hadn't been? Then he would have been stubborn and stupid instead of determined and brilliant. My point is that whether he was stupid or brilliant wasn't defined by his actions. It was defined by the tomb. If the tomb was there, he's a hero. If it wasn't, if the valley had been emptied by all the previous expeditions, he's a fool. And I was frustrated with the TV programme because that's our job. That's our job! We don't know if there are findable answers. We don't know. There might not be any. We just have to do the work, and whether we're ultimately heroes or time-wasters isn't on us. Even if we do everything right, there might not be something to find.'

'Is this intended to cheer me up?'

She threw up her hands. 'You don't need cheering up. You need shoring up. What's the worst that can happen? Spencer embarrasses you? He's rude to you? He's not going to apologise, if that's what you're after.'

'I'm not after anything,' I managed to squeeze in.

'You should be. You should be after finding out what Anna knows about Cathy, and who killed Hannah-Claire,

256

and who attacked Anna. That's what there is to want. Everything else is just . . .' She shrugged.

Dan walked into the kitchen holding the baby, doing that bounce that everyone handed a baby automatically does. 'Are you talking about King Tut again?'

'I am,' Chloe said, accepting their reaching daughter. She seemed to have grown in just this short time since I met her.

Dan asked by way of welcome, 'Did she tell you the name?'

'Name?' It took me a moment to mentally get from ancient Egypt to baby names. Besides, I'd got used to thinking of her as 'the baby' the way that some people end up with a pet still called 'kitty' years in.

Chloe said, 'Stephanie. After Stephen Fry.' Her voice had the cadence of citing a beloved grandmother or admired heroine as inspiration.

I raised an eyebrow.

'That is actually true,' Dan admitted. 'But the name belongs to her now, and it's lovely.'

'It is lovely,' I agreed.

Chloe snuggled. Stephanie had been fed, so she wasn't rooting; instead she was playing a rudimentary game of peekaboo then mashing her face blissfully into Chloe's shoulder.

'I'm going back early,' Chloe said. 'Not immediately, but sooner than planned. I'm ready.'

Dan kissed her on the top of her head. 'It only took her months to tell me the truth.'

'No!' Chloe protested, but she was beaming. 'It took me months to admit the truth to myself. You see, Morris,

257

it wasn't just mummies and attractive archaeologists that kept me from madness while on bed rest. I watched a lot else, including a documentary about seahorses. Did you know that the males look after the babies? I normally don't care much about sea life apart from what's on my plate, but I was entranced. It seemed magical. You're not allowed to think I'm awful! I love Dan's work. I love what he creates. But I finally got up the nerve last night to ask him to stick with part-time freelancing, instead of joining a firm. This job I have – this job we have, Morris – you understand. You asked it of Gwen. It's not something I can do from the house if Stephanie has a cold and can't go to nursery. It's not something that promises I can be home at the same time each day. It's not something that can be picked up and laid down as needed. It just helps if one of us can do that.'

Dan didn't look like he minded. He looked relieved, actually. Maybe he wanted to stay home; maybe he wanted to be able to be more picky about the jobs he would take on. Maybe he had been worried that suggesting it would make him look weak, or would constrict their finances too much; just as she had been worried that suggesting it would make her seem uncaring.

'Have you told Spencer yet?' I asked Chloe. I don't know why that popped out of my mouth.

Chloe held back her answer for a few seconds, looking at me quizzically. 'Is this a test of friendship? Of partnership?'

'Curiosity,' I muttered.

'No, I haven't. You're the first. Well, technically, I told Stephanie first, last night, after getting off the phone with

Laurie Ambrose. You got told at earliest convenience. It is just eight o'clock in the morning, after all.'

Eight already. I stood. 'I have to go.'

She stood too, hoisting Stephanie, and having caught a rocking version of the contagious bouncing from Dan. 'Spencer's not stupid. I know he's done . . . non-optimal things. One specific non-optimal thing. But he's not stupid. That's a good feature in a cop.'

'And what do you tell him about me?' Again, my mouth was just powering ahead without my dignity.

'You think we gossip about you? What else do you think we get up to, painting each other's nails and plaiting each other's hair?'

'Never mind,' I said, grabbing my coat from the back of my chair. My hands were under control. *Good.* I was determined to not drop or fumble anything in Spencer's presence, and that determination made it about a thousand times more likely that I would.

At the door, Chloe whispered, 'I tell him you're the best I ever had,' while giggling.

'Fuck off.' We never have, never would. She was having a laugh.

'I tell him,' she said in a normal voice, 'that I trust you. And he should too.'

I nodded, grateful. That's what I'd come for.

It won't be so bad, I told myself in the car. *It'll be over in an hour*, I figured, at least the awkward-direct-conversation-with-Spencer part. Hopefully we could split up with specific tasks.

I thought of Annalise, and whether there would be anything left for Chloe to find, under all of that metaphorical desert. She was right: all the searching in the world couldn't find what isn't there.

Maybe Spencer and I shouldn't split up . . . I considered. An idea was coming together. Maybe there was something we could do as a team.

CHAPTER SEVENTEEN

Anna Williams

I hate this house.

Mum was so proud of it when they got married and it became hers too. Never mind that half of it is for the office, and we were put upstairs, like tenants. She acted like she was the lady of the manor.

It turned out that she was right about Hannah-Claire's landlord not wanting to let me keep the lease after he found out that she had died. Sadie was relieved not to have to babysit me any more; she headed back to York immediately. Nigel had to let me come back here. He always hated me here no matter what, but he hated this more because I needed a ground-floor room for a month at least, and that meant I'd be taking up a small conference room, instead of one of the actual guest rooms.

This looked like it had been a bedroom once before, when this place was a boarding house. Marks on the floor implied that there was once a heavy wardrobe against one of the walls. And it felt like a bedroom, even with chairs shoved into the corner to make room for me to sleep on an actually really comfortable sofa that they moved from the lobby. It had a watercolour of flowers on the wall, which was six hundred times better than the portraits in the big room. I've looked it up, and old paintings like that look like they'd cost a lot, but unless they're painted of or by someone famous, no one really cares. They'd been screwed to the wall in case of attempted robbery, not because they're actually valuable, but because they're the sort of thing chance thieves might imagine are valuable.

I stretched, and rolled up the sheets and blankets under the sofa. I had to get dressed but that involved bending and pulling in ways that hurt. *Maybe I'll sit in this T-shirt and socks for ever and just get colder and colder until I die.*

The portraits made me think of Annalise again. The newspaper photos were her 'portraits'. I wonder if the people who sat for these paintings felt flattered by them, if they recognised themselves, if the results matched the way they saw themselves.

Hannah-Claire's picture had been in the news after she died. It was from her registry-office wedding. She'd had her hair blow-dried that day and it looked really good.

I knew what picture I'd give if anyone wanted it. Detective Spencer told me that journalists shouldn't be allowed to bother me, and I could tell them to leave me alone if anyone tried. No one had asked me yet, but I had a picture ready if they did.

I looked at it on my phone. It was a really good picture. It was better to look at than a mirror. A third of my actual face had become bruise-brown in a kind of weird continent shape, but in the picture, no one had hit me yet.

I knew about the news almost right away, because I kept track of what people said about what was done to us, me and Hannah-Claire. That's how I found out that Dr Ambrose called my bluff. The article mentioned new DNA evidence in the Annalise case and that Hannah-Claire had been looking and looking to prove – well, disprove – the Annalise connection, as if possibility plus imagination weren't completely, utterly sufficient. *Did they mean Hannah-Claire was the new link? Was it her DNA the police were investigating?*

There was nothing mentioned about Hannah-Claire's death except just that it happened. They made it sound like an accident. So Dr Ambrose hadn't told them the most damning bits. Or she'd told the police, and the police had leaked out only a little.

I would find out soon. Sergeant Spencer had said he was coming to see me.

I had to get clothes on.

I had to figure out what I would do. I'd only threatened Dr Ambrose with blaming Blake because I thought that would mean something to her. I didn't want to actually do it. *But now she may have told the police even that. She may have told them anything.* I didn't know what to do. I didn't know.

Well, I decided, starting with yoga pants. I could pull those up without overstretching too much of myself. *I can just tell Sergeant Spencer that she's obsessed with me. That she makes things up. That she doesn't like me dating her son.*

That's something else I gave up. I told Blake to fuck off. I hope that's appreciated. I made a lot of sacrifices.

I pulled on a long jumper and popped earrings in and brushed my hair. Every time I lifted my arm my side sparked with pain.

I didn't use make-up. Nothing short of theatre stuff would make any difference. The colours and lumps of the bruising would come through anyway, like if you try to frost a really crumbly cake.

I could hear the doorbell. Rosalie would answer it. I leant towards the window to see if I could tell by the car, but it was just a blue car. Could be a law client. Could be the detective. *Hell, could be an Amazon delivery.* You just didn't know any more. *You just don't know anything, Anna. Not a thing.*

There were two of them.

I knew that there could be, but I had expected the second one to be a woman detective. A few days before the funeral, I heard Rosalie on the phone with her sister or cousin or whoever she is, saying how Nigel – *excuse me, 'Mr Rigg'* – had been pretty upset that a policewoman had come and spoken to Mum, and that Rosalie wasn't allowed to say anything to them any more and was almost in trouble. I didn't think Nigel would ever let her go; I suspect she may be running the office, actually. But *she* believed that he might and that had been enough to make her quiet. To the woman detective, I mean. She kept blathering to her relative. That's when I realised I had to do something. That's how I knew that Mum needed help. Nigel telling the detective to stay away wasn't going to stop anything.

She's lucky to have me, I reminded myself. *And, look,*

now there are two *detectives.* Two men. Nigel would have a more difficult time warding them off.

Mum was with me. Sergeant Spencer explained that she didn't have to be, because I'm an adult, but that in consideration of my fragile state I should have support. We sat at the big conference table in the once-a-dining-room. The portraits made the room feel crowded, almost party-like. Rosalie brought us coffee. I decided to act like a hostess. I asked our guests about milk and sugar while Rosalie first poured and then tactfully withdrew.

The sergeant sat at the head of the table, with a coffee so overfull with milk and sugars that I thought it would spill when he lifted it. He was a baby-faced ginger oozing sympathy while the other man, with dark hair and no expression, seemed to blend in among the dour paintings.

'Ms Williams, Mrs Rigg, I can't thank you enough for your time.' That was the sergeant. You can tell by the deference. He must be the designated good cop. That made me worry about the other one.

He continued: 'We're obviously deeply concerned about what happened to Hannah-Claire, and to you, Ms Williams. That's why I felt I had to deliver this news personally.' He looked down. He cleared his throat. He glanced at the other man, who was leaning back in his chair feigning a lack of interest. 'Mr Keene here has been brought in to review our work on your cousin's case.' I liked that he used the word 'cousin'. That meant he was talking more to me than to Mum. 'We're concerned that if the two incidents, her death and your attack, are linked, then our own possible failures must be examined. If Henry Ware had abused his wife and then another family member, well, that would warrant

265

some serious self-examination on our part for having failed to prevent what was done to you, Ms Williams. I take that very seriously.'

I was blushing. I could feel it in my cheeks.

'Ms Williams,' he said again, as if he just liked saying my name, 'we had to let Henry Ware go this morning. Please,' he requested, 'please don't be alarmed. He's been instructed to keep his distance from you and we're confident' – here he exchanged a look with the other police person, this 'Mr Keene', who nodded – 'very confident that he means you no harm.'

Mum did what she was supposed to do, which genuinely surprised me. 'How dare you!' she said, standing up, the wheels of her chair squeaking as it rolled a bit away behind her.

'Mrs Rigg,' said Mr Keene, who didn't bother standing to match her. He just sat up straight, as if that small effort were sufficient. 'Sit down.'

She did.

'I think you'll be relieved when you hear the explanation!' the sergeant said, jollying his story along. I glanced around, but the portrait faces outnumbered friendly ones. 'Mr Ware has been released because we now know who attacked you and I assure you he's in custody.'

I swallowed, and somehow even swallowing hurt. Maybe because of the medicines I've been taking. 'I don't know what you mean.'

'I understand that your memories of the attack itself are hazy at best, once we're past the incident in the closet, as witnessed by Dr Ambrose.'

'You can't trust her!' I interjected, quickly, while she was still supposedly on my side in his version of events. They wouldn't believe me if I waited until I was told she'd said something against me.

The sergeant smiled and said in a gentle, hand-patting tone, 'We do trust her corroboration of your story, Ms Williams. Should we not?'

'She doesn't like that I was dating her son. She might . . . she might tell you things . . . to make me look . . .'

'You agree that you were kissing your cousin's widower at the funeral, do you not? That's the story you told us.'

I nodded. I could hear Mum breathing heavily. She sounded like she was pinching her nose but I didn't dare look her way to see for sure. I kept my eyes squeezed shut.

'Did you ask Dr Ambrose to tell us that, Ms Williams?'

'No.'

'Did you plan with her to tell us a coordinated lie?'

'No!'

'So you both, individually, told us the truth about that. That's what I believe.'

I nodded, and rubbed my cheek and eye that weren't bruised. *If this is good cop . . .*

'I'm very sorry to have to tell you this, Ms Williams, but the person who hurt you is someone closer to you than Mr Ware. Blake Ambrose has voluntarily confessed to us—'

'What?' I blurted.

'He has voluntarily confessed to us that after the funeral and your, hm, *interaction* with Mr Ware, that he, Blake, attacked you and left you in the car park. Now, I believe him to that point but this, this is where I diverge with Mr Ambrose's version of events. He claims that he did this at your request. He tells us that you were so convinced of

Henry Ware's temper and his culpability in your cousin's death that you wished to provoke him to reveal himself, so to speak, to reveal the darkness behind what you believe he'd done to your cousin, and by taking it on yourself, you could become the evidence that we lacked. He told us that you begged, even insisted, that he do it for you, when he saw that Henry had stopped himself at a mere slap and walked away.'

'No. No. That's not how it was. I never. I would never. Blake . . . If he—' *It's a lie*, I reminded myself. *It's a lie that I threatened Dr Ambrose with. Now she's just told it herself. But it isn't true. It can't be.* But then I remembered my fingernails, the scrapings under my fingernails in the hospital. Had they found Blake's DNA there? And a corresponding scratch on him? Was this true? I didn't know; I didn't know.

Of course not. Of course not. I hadn't asked him for that. He wasn't even there. He wasn't at the funeral. He'd wanted to come with me and I hadn't let him.

But what if he had followed me? What if he saw me with Henry? What if he was jealous then, and angry, and making this all up now?

I grabbed the possibility. 'No. He – he – he must have seen me with Henry, and been jealous. Blake hurt me because he was jealous. I would never ask for this. I would never ask for this!' I covered both halves of my face with both my hands, which hurt my black eye, and my sobbing hurt my abdomen, and it was another two hours before I could take more medicine.

Mum stood again. I know because I could hear her voice coming from well on top of me. 'Don't say another word.

I'll get Nigel.' Because he's a solicitor. But, *He's not that kind of solicitor, Mum. Shit.* She exited the room.

The sergeant switched seats to sit in the chair next to me. 'That's what I think. You're a beautiful woman. Blake being jealous of Henry makes much more sense to me.'

He was close to me. This is what a man is supposed to say. This is what people would have said to Annalise if she had survived: *You're beautiful. That explains everything.*

The other man cleared his throat. 'If Blake Ambrose acted out of self-interest, and his attack on Ms Williams had nothing to do with the death of Hannah-Claire Finney, then the police did nothing wrong in their handling of Hannah-Claire Finney's death. I can see why that version of events appeals to Detective Sergeant Spencer.'

The sergeant seemed to shrink. 'It's the most straightforward reading of events.'

I found myself nodding, furiously. I wanted to grab the ginger detective's arm but I forced myself to keep within the padded arms of my chair. I swivelled gently, too anxious to keep entirely still. *Where is Nigel?* I was screaming in my head. I suddenly wanted him. He suddenly seemed bigger than both of these men, more imperious, more powerful. I hoped.

Both doors of the room sprang open. Mum was pulling on Nigel's hand, but he stopped in the doorway. His glare wafted past Sergeant Spencer and fell on Mr Keene as the more significant adversary. I didn't disagree.

Mum let go of Nigel and put her hands to use shutting the double doors.

Introductions again. News again. Henry out. Blake confessed. The police under pressure for having allowed my attack while I was linked to an active case of possible domestic violence.

'Are you accusing Sandra of something?' Nigel asked, and I rolled my eyes.

Mr Keene took that question. 'Blake Ambrose is. He's accusing her of having arranged her own beating at his hands, and lying to the police about it, in order to frame Henry Ware. I can find half a dozen crimes in there. Can you?'

Nigel waved a hand. 'A spurned lover. What of it? A boy like that will say anything.'

The word 'lover' made me laugh-snort. We'd only kissed and hugged and talked, even the night that he stayed. *Next they'll be calling him a 'suitor'.*

Mr Keene leant forward, his left hand oddly wrapped around his right. 'Blake says he's figured you out.' He was addressing me, not Nigel, and neither of us liked that. 'He says that you told him the beating and the framing were to make sure that Henry paid for his real crime against Hannah-Claire. But now he's thought a little farther ahead, and sees things differently. He thinks that you had something to do with Hannah-Claire's death, and were framing Henry to cover that up.'

'No. That's stupid. That's stupid. I wouldn't do that. I wouldn't do anything to her, but even if I did, it would be safer to leave it alone than to try to frame someone and get the police looking. It was an accident. It was just an accident. She fell in all on her own . . .'

'Were you there, Ms Williams?' Mr Keene drawled.

'No. Of course not. But just from the evidence . . . Look, I was at home. I was with Blake Ambrose! All night. He knows that. He knows. Ask him that!'

270

'So you trust him to be truthful. So do I,' agreed Mr Keene, and his agreement just made me worry that I'd said something very, very wrong. 'My colleague, Detective Inspector Frohmann, has been here, asking questions, phoning with follow-ups. As it turns out, her questions had nothing to do with Hannah-Claire, but you didn't know that, did you?'

I think that was sweat on my head. Either that or I was bleeding. I remembered in the hospital, or maybe at the church, having blood in my eyes.

'So I could see,' Mr Keene concluded, 'how you might feel the need to see someone else pinned with the crime.'

I was shaking. I was thinking *no,* so maybe I was just acting out that word by wagging my head, but really maybe I was just shaking. 'Blake can't think that. He can't. His mother made him say it.'

'Be realistic, Ms Williams. Dr Ambrose is a respected professional.' That was still Keene, not Spencer-who-thought-I-was-beautiful. I didn't have to lift my head to know the difference.

'No, he knows that's a lie. He was with me. He saw Hannah-Claire leave my flat, and he stayed with me. He knows!'

Nigel was coughing into his hand. *Hypocritical bastard.* Mum moved in here before they were married. Besides, we just stayed up all night, talking. Talking about everything. Blake was sad about his dead dad, and I was sad about my own things. We took care of each other.

And then I had to throw that connection away. For her. To protect us all from Laurie Ambrose and what Hannah-Claire had told her. And she wasn't even grateful.

She wasn't even saying anything. I looked at her but she wasn't even facing me. She was looking at Nigel. It wasn't fair. It wasn't right.

Mr Keene said, 'Blake says you asked him to say that he was with you that night, but that he actually wasn't. He says that you were alone.'

'Is that true, Ms Williams?' asked the sergeant, in a hopeful voice. He wanted me to say no. He wanted me to keep fighting.

Mum wasn't saying anything.

'Where were you that night?' I asked her, asked Mum.

'What do you mean?' she said.

That was her chance to do right. She didn't take it.

Nigel stood up and ordered the police out of the building. Spencer said that the alternative to this conversation was to arrest me and I begged them to stay. 'Listen!' I said. 'Listen.' *They've set me up. Dr Ambrose has already given them the emails. They know. I know they know.* 'Mum met Hannah-Claire that night. Hannah took a photo to show her. It was one of mine that I'd put up on Hannah's bookshelves, and she just took it. I told her to give it back and she just walked out, just like that. Then she died.'

'What was the photograph of?'

I honestly don't know which detective asked me that. They were both the same now. They had always been the same, just playing at taking sides.

Mum interrupted, 'I wasn't there. I don't know what you're talking about.'

Mr Keene reached for the door. 'Shall we bring Rosalie in? I believe she took the phone call from Hannah-Claire confirming your meeting.'

Mum just opened and closed her mouth, with no sound. He called for Rosalie to join us.

She stood in the doorway, no farther in than that. 'Yes?'

'Did Hannah-Claire Finney have plans with Cathy Rigg on the night of her death?' Mr Keene asked.

'Yes. I mean no. I mean yes and no together. They had plans, but then she cancelled.'

In the silence, just breathing, breathing and a little bit of squeaking from the conference room chairs, which roll and turn and bend at the slightest nudge. None of us were moving per se but we were all pulsing, and vibrating, and the chairs magnified it.

The sergeant clarified, 'Hannah-Claire called you back later that day to cancel the plans?'

'Yes!' Rosalie agreed. 'I mean, no. I mean, she phoned once to confirm, when Ms Frohmann was here, and then called again later, to cancel.'

The sergeant repeated, 'Cancel?'

I felt the air squeeze out of me. *Had she cancelled? Did I have this wrong? I'd spoken to Hannah that evening, and she'd said she was meeting 'family'. I'd thought I knew who that meant. But now . . . Who is 'family' anyway?*

Silence stretched out like an expanding balloon.

Mr Keene made a pin of his voice: 'It's very loyal of you to cover for Mrs Rigg, Rosalie, but—'

'I'm not covering any—'

Mum said firmly, 'Hannah did cancel, Mr Keene.'

The sergeant blustered: 'We'll see if the phone records match and—'

'Well, you'll find that they will.' Rosalie was immovable. I admired that.

The sergeant rallied. 'I don't suppose you have an alibi for the evening, Mrs Rigg?'

'Of course not. I was here at home. You don't think to get yourself a witness for an ordinary evening at home.'

Mr Rigg put his hand on Mum's shoulder. 'I assure you all that Cathy was here with me. She was home the entire evening and night. She never left the house.'

For a moment, we were all safe. Everyone in the room, even the one who didn't deserve to be. The two police exchanged looks.

Then, 'You wouldn't know,' Mum said to Nigel. She turned her head sideways, her mouth almost touching his hand, which had started to squeeze.

I felt dizzy. *Is that a side effect? I should read the little inserts that came with the medicines. I should lie down. Maybe I'm supposed to feel this way . . .*

'You're misremembering,' Nigel said, but she shimmied him off and stood up.

'I wanted us to go out to dinner,' Mum said. 'But you said you had to meet a client.'

'That's not true. You can check my appointment book. I had no clients that evening.'

'You went out. You told me you were meeting a client.'

'That was the next evening, remember? I did work the evening we're talking about, but I worked at my desk. You can ask Rosalie.'

'I went home at six o'clock, Mr Rigg.'

Silence again, that silence made of breathing and squeaking.

Mum looked between the two police and chose Mr Keene. 'Hannah did phone a second time, Mr Keene. I was out, and Rosalie answered for me, as she does. She passed the call on to Nigel, and he's the one who then told us that Hannah had cancelled our plans. Rosalie, did Hannah-Claire tell you that?'

Rosalie closed her eyes, to act out a drama of remembering. 'No. No, she didn't. Only Mr Rigg said that, after he spoke to her.' Her eyes popped open and her hand clapped over her mouth.

We all looked at Nigel.

'This is getting out of hand,' Nigel said, stepping back. 'It's time that the police put their efforts towards gathering enough evidence to put Henry Ware back behind bars. I think we can all agree that he wasn't the man Hannah-Claire deserved! His behaviour with Sandra at the funeral made that clear. Disgusting.' He shuddered theatrically.

My voice felt cold in my throat. 'Do you mean kissing me, or beating me?'

'I mean both, young lady! And you're no better, rubbing yourself up against a fresh widower.' His chest rose and fell as if he'd just run a mile.

'I didn't want to!' It felt very important to make all of them understand. 'All it took was to say "I'm lonely; are you?" and he did the rest. I *let* him do it, but I didn't *make* him do it.'

'That's not what it looked like,' Nigel sneered.

Rosalie gasped.

Mr Keene spoke quietly, making us strain to hear. 'Mr Rigg, you were there?'

Everyone spoke at once. Defending, accusing, distracting, asking. I had to shout: 'I did what I did at the funeral because of you, Mum. I did it for you.'

Everyone looked. Everyone: Mum, Nigel, Rosalie, the police. It felt like Dr Ambrose was there too, and Blake, because they would know soon enough. Once I said it here it would get told over and over.

'I thought you'd killed Hannah-Claire, Mum,' I said. 'Hannah-Claire had figured it out,' I explained. 'She'd figured out that you'd had a baby. That you'd had her.'

Mum was hugging herself, but not denying it.

'I knew already, because I heard you and Dad fight about it. I knew. And she was poking around, so I had to give her something. I gave her a version that she should have been proud of, but instead she just wanted more and more and *more* . . . She just kept looking and asking, trying to *prove* it, and it wasn't working. She knew that I knew something more and she tried to get it out of me but I didn't crack, I didn't. Then she saw, over my shoulder, she saw a picture of you as a kid, on the shelf. It's that one with your two friends with the braided hair, and your hair is loose. She saw it and she figured it out. I don't know what in that picture did it to her but she suddenly knew. She knew and she took it and I couldn't stop her.'

They were all standing. This was important.

'She said she was going to show you,' I continued. 'And then she died. She died. And no one said a word about her being your daughter. About her being my sister.' I'd never phrased it like that before, even in my mind. 'So I knew you'd taken care of it. And I thought, you chose me and Sadie. You chose us over her. So I protected you, by making sure the police thought Henry had done it. When I found out from Rosalie that the police had come round asking you questions, that's when I knew I had to do something.

Henry hadn't been very nice to Hannah-Claire anyway, and thin-skinned besides. It didn't take much to provoke him.' Just a few exaggerations of personal criticisms that Hannah-Claire had actually told me, whispered to him in that church closet.

They're going to arrest me, I thought. *For framing Henry. For lying to them and misusing public resources or some such. I'm going to be in jail with my face like this and limping. I'm going to have to beg for my medicines. Maybe if it gets worse I could get put in a hospital instead . . .*

'I wasn't there,' Mum said. 'And I would never do that to her. I couldn't tell her, not without upending my life, but if *she* knew, if *she* told *me* . . .' She closed her eyes and the sigh that came out of her had such love in it . . . She hadn't chosen me and Sadie after all. She hadn't pushed Hannah-Claire away. It was Nigel who'd done it. It was Nigel who'd done it, not Mum. Apparently Mum would never have got rid of her. I'd been right in the first place. I'd been right to have been jealous.

Mr Keene said to Nigel, 'You don't seem surprised to hear all of this about Hannah and your wife.'

'I already knew, of course.'

Mum was shaking her head and mouthing 'no'.

Nigel seemed to be sorting through options. 'It was obvious. I hadn't had to be told. But that doesn't mean I took the ridiculous actions you're implying I did.'

'It was obvious in what way, Mr Rigg?'

'It wasn't!' Mum interrupted. 'I know that it wasn't because I made sure that it wasn't. When Charlie refused to be my cover, when he refused to pretend to be her father, I buried it. I took her in like a niece and nothing more. If

277

you knew, you knew because *she* told you. She confronted you on that bridge and—' She clapped her hand over her mouth. She couldn't even say it.

'I did nothing of the kind,' Nigel said smoothly. 'This is all easily explained. I had you researched when we first started seeing each other. Your past wasn't ideal, but the fact that the child had been put up for adoption seemed sufficient. When Hannah-Claire moved here, I didn't know for sure, but I could see how she was already insinuating herself into our life. She phoned that day to change the place of meeting, and I told her you weren't feeling well and wouldn't be able to come along. Then I told you and Rosalie that Hannah-Claire had cancelled. It was easy. I don't need to resort to the crassness of murder to solve my problems.'

Mum was fierce. 'Is that what Hannah-Claire was to you? A "problem"?'

'Isn't that what she was to you?' Nigel retorted. 'You got rid of her too.'

Mum was crying now, and bent over, and I was sitting because I couldn't stand any more. The detectives had moved closer to the doors, so none of us could run out, I suppose. Rosalie stood between them, her fingers twitching, unconsciously knitting air.

The sergeant said, 'Mr Rigg . . .'

'I understand perfectly, young man. I'm happy to be officially interviewed so long as I can be accompanied by my own solicitor. Rosalie . . .' He rattled off a phone number. 'Then I think you'll find that the only thing I'm guilty of is lying to my wife.'

'Mr Rigg,' said Mr Keene, echoing the sergeant. 'We had

the law office rubbish searched this morning, after it was taken away by the bin lorry. In that blizzard of document shreddings, we found shreddings of a photograph. We haven't seen it put together yet, but I believe in our forensics team. I have no doubt that they'll manage it, and that it will be an image familiar to Anna from her bookshelf. And they're handling it in such a way as to preserve fingerprints. I just thought you'd like to know, as this may inform your choice of solicitor. Perhaps someone experienced with serious crime.'

They were all staring at Nigel, as if they didn't understand him. But I understood him. I didn't want her in this house either, even just popping in. I didn't want her at Christmas dinners, and included in family holidays, and her picture up on the wall. I didn't want another sister. I didn't want Mum saying her name in the voice she was using now for her, as if Hannah-Claire were the only thing that ever mattered. I didn't want to reimagine family history to include where she was at the time, and catch each other up on all that we've missed. *Why couldn't she have stayed in Canada? Mum gave her up for a reason. Why couldn't she have taken the hint?*

I didn't know how much time was passing. I was the only one still sitting. I think I was leaning. *It must be time for my medicine again . . .*

The police both stepped towards Nigel, but Mum pushed him against the wall. They had to grab her instead, and hold her arms behind her. Nigel began to snap back at her, but she spoke over him, which I'd never heard her do before.

'She was *my child*!' Mum wailed.

279

'I *don't want children*!' he answered back to her, in the same echoing volume.

I felt a stabbing sensation in my gut, a sparkly kind of cramp, remembering all of the Christmas and Easter and summer holidays that I returned here, all of the books and clothes that Mum helped me buy, all of the ways in which I was present here despite being an adult. Mum had thought she was safe getting married after we were grown. She'd thought she was a single woman again, not still a single mother. That's what Nigel had thought too. I, and Hannah-Claire, had taught him otherwise.

'Listen!' Mum said. 'Listen.' She relaxed her arms and the police let go of her.

'I had Hannah-Claire at a very unpleasant "home" in Devon. We told everyone that I was going to France. The school advertised the programme, but ultimately it was up to each interested family to make their own arrangements with the agency. So long as my parents said that was where I was, the school had no reason to doubt it. Annalise was going, and I asked her to cover for me. We weren't close, but she was kind. When she came back, I tried a bit too hard to make a show of having been there together, hung around her a bit too much and told stories of things we'd supposedly done together. It was a fantasy, I suppose, of something much better than what I'd really been up to. I needed it desperately, but Annalise hated it.'

Mum sucked in a deep breath, then pushed out the rest: 'The day she, the day she . . . We argued about it. She told me to stop. She said that if I didn't stop, she'd tell everyone the truth. I couldn't yell at her – I didn't want anyone to hear – so I hissed it all out, that she was selfish and mean and awful and had everything, just everything, and why couldn't she share just a little bit? Why should it bother her if I made up stories about us in France? I never made a fool of her, or made her out to be mean. Both of us came off well, and to be honest I even sometimes made her out to be better than me. Braver. More special. They were just stories. And I would have stopped, eventually. I just needed them for a while.'

'So you were angry,' Mr Keene prompted.

'What?' Mum shivered, and the rhythm of her telling was broken. 'I was heartbroken. Humiliated. I had thought we were friends.'

'Mrs Rigg—' the sergeant began, seeming impatient to get on with Nigel, but Mr Keene interrupted him.

'What happened next, Cathy?' It was the first time I'd heard either of them address her by her first name.

She looked genuinely baffled. 'Nothing. Nothing. I left first. I got on my bicycle to go home but I knew that Annalise was faster than me. I thought it would be awkward if she caught up, so I went around the back of the school library and waited a while. Let her get home first. But she never did get home. And if I'd been with her then, maybe . . .' She covered her mouth with her fist. I didn't know if she was going to say that she might have been able to save Annalise from whatever had happened, or if she might have fallen victim to it too.

Mr Keene seemed frustrated, but he let the sergeant get on with what he had to do. They took Nigel away.

When Rosalie turned back around, she reached almost immediately to clear away the coffee things. The sergeant's untouched and childishly sweet coffee spilled halfway over as soon as she lifted it. She grabbed a cloth from the serving tray and moved it in circles to mop up the mess, but mostly just smeared it around. She was making these frustrated, squeaky noises, which I think would have been crying if she'd let it out. She'd worked for Nigel a lot longer than Mum had been married to him.

Rosalie dropped the cloth back onto the tray. The table was still a sticky swirl. She left.

Mum and I sat, with an empty chair between us.

I used to pretend that she had named me 'Annalise'. I used to tell myself that 'Sandra' was very near having done so, being reducible to the same nickname, if you squint.

Mum said to me, 'When we realised that something had happened to Annalise, of course we could talk of nothing else. And of course the police wanted us to talk, and the press wanted it too. I was free to tell all the made-up French stories I could have ever wanted, but I never told a single one ever again.'

That was all she said. We sat quietly. I waited for them to come back and take me, but they didn't.

CHAPTER EIGHTEEN

Morris Keene

The dining-room double doors thudded shut behind us: me, and DS Spencer holding Nigel Rigg by the arm.

Spencer calmly delivered the caution to Nigel Rigg and politely apologised for bringing out handcuffs, which he didn't mean in the slightest.

This was Spencer's case and his arrest; actually, I couldn't arrest anyone any more, as the Review Team's status is civilian. I thought I would hate it. I thought I would flinch at being addressed as 'Mr Keene' instead of by my former rank of Detective Chief Inspector. But it wasn't a demotion, not the way it came out in there. We had decided our roles beforehand: Spencer would be deferential to Anna, I would be sceptical. We got Cathy to agree to be there, 'for Anna's sake'. We planned the lie about Blake Ambrose confessing, which his mother had helped us concoct. We were doing what it took to get Anna to give up her mother, which she did . . . and then! I admit we were surprised by Nigel Rigg taking on the part

283

of chief suspect. We assumed that the photograph would eventually give us Cathy's fingerprints. From Nigel's reaction to it, though, I was confident that it would yield his. We'd done it, even if the 'it' we'd been aiming for had changed partway through. The throbbing in my rib cage was made equally of thrill and panic.

Coming down from that now, with an arrest and a reasonable case ahead, made a buzzing, humming satisfaction in my chest. Spencer turned at the front door, looked over his shoulder, and mouthed 'thanks' at me, which felt like we were high-fiving over Nigel Rigg's head. For my part, I nodded, and smiled, and sat on the edge of the reception desk, arms folded.

Rosalie the receptionist pushed through the doors, carrying a tray. She stared at Nigel Rigg's hands behind his back as he exited.

Her obvious agony penetrated my vindication. We solve things, but we don't fix them. A lot of things can't be fixed, only revealed.

'I'm sorry,' I said, standing up straight.

She sat at her desk. 'He's the one who should be sorry.'

I didn't have to follow Spencer, because we'd come in our own cars. I was tempted, though, to chase our moment of victory, in order to enjoy it a little bit longer. But I wasn't needed; I could hear Spencer's car already pulling away. It wasn't my case we'd solved here. Annalise, and whoever the girl was who'd been buried by the tracks . . . Those cases, my cases, were still opaque.

When Cathy had revealed that she and Annalise had argued the last afternoon Annalise had been seen alive, I had thought for a moment that . . . what? That young

Cathy Rigg had killed Annalise? I admit that had leapt to my mind. It was absurd. A teenage girl killing another teenage girl wasn't impossible, but to have hidden the body so completely was utterly unlikely. No, Cathy Rigg, emotional over her recent secret birth and feeling like her substitute fantasy of a summer in France was being taken away from her, might have lashed out, but I couldn't picture anything beyond that, certainly not such a successful burial. If I was right, and the body by the tracks in the schoolgirl uniform was not Annalise, then Annalise was still buried elsewhere. It's not as if we were beside the ocean in a yachting community; she had to be in the ground. I doubt Cathy Rigg on her own could have dug a grave deep enough. If she'd involved others, I doubt it would still be successfully secret now.

Unless . . . Charlie? Were we back to him? Would his loyalty have lasted so long, even when we were interrogating him over the semen on the skirt?

'Rosalie,' I asked gently, turning to her. 'Do you know Charlie Bennet?'

Rosalie wiped her cheeks and lifted her chin. 'Mrs Rigg's first husband? A bit . . .' she answered cautiously. No doubt Mr Rigg had rules about what she could and could not talk about. But Mr Rigg had been dethroned. 'I've worked for Mr Rigg for eleven years. I only met Mrs Rigg when they started dating. Mr Bennet's phoned a couple of times, and I met him at a Christmas gathering. He's her daughters' father, after all.'

'Did he . . . did he strike you as the sort of person who could keep a secret?' The skirt hadn't been a secret so much as an embarrassment. But could he have helped Cathy cover up an unintended death? Perhaps Cathy had impetuously grabbed some blunt object and swung harder than she'd intended? Or . . .

Stop, I told myself. *Charlie Bennet was in France.* He couldn't have assisted Cathy with covering up anything. If she did do it, and if she'd then had help, it was from someone we don't yet conveniently know.

Don't be ridiculous, Morris, I reminded myself, which is good advice every single day. I wanted to solve Annalise, but wanting it didn't turn the most convenient person into a viable suspect. The fact was, Cathy and Annalise had had an argument; Annalise headed home like we always knew, while Cathy waited behind the school library. That's why Annalise had been alone that day. *One mystery solved, at least*, I acknowledged. *I should write a book: 'Annalise Wood: the untold story of why she was alone on the way home from school'.* Something told me it wouldn't sell.

'Mr Keene?' Rosalie squeaked.

'Yes, Rosalie?' I said, sounding more impatient than I intended.

'Your colleague. Ms Frohmann? Detective Inspector Frohmann? She asked me for something. I didn't get back to her because . . .' Her eyes shifted towards the front door and then down to the desk. Ah, Mr Rigg had told her not to reply. 'But I have it now. I have it. I don't know if it'll do anyone any good, but . . .' She shrugged. She pulled an envelope out of her middle desk drawer.

I opened it.

There was no doubt in my mind that, for all his faults, Nigel Rigg had impeccable taste in personal assistants. Rosalie was a wonder of organisation.

'I knew a girl, Betty, who was engaged to a man who lived in this building, when it was a boarding house. She used to visit him here on weekends. She ended up not married to him and I think he might be dead. I haven't seen her in, oh, fifteen years but I found her on Facebook. She's friends with my cousin's best friend's daughter. Small world.'

'Small world,' I agreed, and turned to echo her leaning posture and tentative smile as well. There were names on this list.

She pointed to the paper. 'She tried her best to remember. It's a little map, see?'

So it was. It was the layout of the house. In one room, the surname 'Haskell'. In another, a first name, 'Gerald'. But mostly it consisted of descriptions: 'Bald man, briefcase, northern accent.' In another, 'Two women. Blonde and brunette. Sisters?' I turned it over to find the tower room.

There it was: 'Handyman. All hands.'

'Sorry, Rosalie, what did she mean by this?'

'Oh, him. She said he stared a little too hard, if you know what I mean. Betty didn't like him. He got the tower room because in addition to paying rent, he helped around the house. He was the one you had to ask if something needed fixing. She said she hated it when he worked on things in the common rooms. When the conference room – well, the dining room – was being rewired it took months. It was dusty and the portraits were all stacked up in the corner. She told me that he once backed her into the corner when her fiancé was in the kitchen, and the backs of her legs rubbed up against the edges of the frames. Betty's tights snagged and tore.' She suddenly sucked in a breath, and jumped from old murder to new. 'Mr Keene, what did Nigel Rigg do to that poor girl?'

'DS Spencer will get to the bottom of what happened to Hannah-Claire.'

'She was a nice woman. A nice woman. It's one thing to think of an unnamed upstairs handyman doing something bad, but can you imagine Mr Rigg, getting close enough to push her in?'

'I'm sorry, Rosalie. I'm sorry you had to witness this today.'

'I should look after Mrs Rigg. I mean, I should look after Cathy.'

A prophetic adjustment, no doubt. I couldn't imagine Cathy remaining a Rigg for long.

Rosalie pushed her chair back and walked towards the double doors of the conference room. 'You're not going to . . . ?'

I think she was asking if I was going to haul anyone else off. I demurred with a wave of my hand. Anna Williams was due something, but it didn't need to be taken care of today. If Spencer wanted her, he'd come back for her.

I had my own work to tidy up. I was no longer supposed to be moving the Annalise case forward (which, I was coming to accept, might be impossible); but it seemed all right to put a bow on what we'd already done. Maybe this – I held up the paper, deciphering Betty's handwriting – could identify the man who buried the body by the tracks, and lead us to identifying her. Instead of being disappointed by the possibility of putting a different name to that body, as I'd been dreading feeling, I was excited. I felt righteous. Whoever she was, she deserved to be named. That no one was looking for her, that no one had written books about her . . . That was something I was going to make right.

I thanked Rosalie and stepped outside the front door. It was a chilly, sunny day, and I turned away from the sun to cast a shadow on my phone screen.

I phoned Chloe. Maybe between this little map and the promised list of names from former cleaner Ginny Russell, we could identify the handsy handyman who'd lived in the tower.

Chloe answered, but didn't have much to report. 'I visited this Ginny Russell, but she seems to have changed her mind about the list. I offered to sit down for a chat and write the names down myself, but she just mumbled an excuse.'

'Some witnesses respond better to one gender or the other; apparently Ginny is the type to prefer male police.' I said this instead of assuming it was my personal charm that got something out of her; Chloe would have had something to say about that. 'Or maybe she was worried about disturbing her father. She looks after him and she seemed worried about him seeing me there yesterday.'

Chloe murmured a possible agreement. 'Suspicious, I say,' she said in an exaggerated tone.

I laughed. 'You sound like me earlier. I had a brief, bright-shining fantasy that Cathy Rigg had killed Annalise Wood and was about to confess it in front of witnesses.'

Chloe laughed too. 'We're getting silly.'

'But not completely ridiculous. We're not going to solve Annalise; I've accepted that. But we have a real chance with this handyman person. Look, I'll go and see Ginny Russell myself, see what I can get out of her. Maybe her memory's just going and she felt embarrassed when you asked.'

'Enjoy!' she said cheerfully. 'Ooh, I just got an email from the Dog Man. I'll—'

'"Dog Man"?'

'Our man Clemmy. The dog walker who found the body. Ugh, he's a talker. He wants me to phone.'

'All in the line of duty.'

'Well, I'm off. Nothing more for me to do around here. Enjoy tea with Ginny. I'm picturing doilies, a lace-edged tablecloth, and possibly porcelain dolls as guests. Watch out for metre-long hairs in your cup.'

That was just mean. 'She was alert yesterday; you caught her at a bad time.' A buzz; I glanced at my screen, then put it back to my ear. 'Oh, an email for me too. Peter Gage.'

'Who?'

'The ex-cop who did interviews in 1992. He's a porter at Robinson now. I have a suspicion he may have been behind the leak to the press and I'm not happy about it. Well, we'll see what he has to say.'

'I hope you didn't accuse him outright.'

'No accusation; I simply asked.'

She sighed disapprovingly, hung up, and we each turned to our emails. I read Peter's while sliding into my driver's seat. He wanted a call.

I pressed the requisite buttons and we had a hands-free chat while I drove towards Ginny Russell's.

'DCI Keene . . .' he began, and I corrected him that I'm a Mister now, like him. 'All right,' he said. 'I was distressed to receive your message. I'm appalled that my taking an interest in a case was perceived by you as having an ulterior motive.'

'It was no judgement on your character, Mr Gage. There are simply very few people with the collective information to have made those specific leaks.'

I drove through Lilling. In the middle bits, if you took away the cars and the people you could be in any one of several centuries – your choice.

'I don't know what to tell you, Keene. We weren't speaking in a soundproof room. Someone could have heard us here at Robinson, and Jimmy tells me there was an organist practising upstairs when you spoke with him.'

'I doubt the organist could hear much . . .'

'So do I, but that's not the point. Maybe someone was praying in the chapel, did you ever think of that?'

No, actually, I hadn't. It's not something I'd done as a student. 'Fine. You're right. I apologise.'

'There! Now that you trust me again, why don't you fill me in?'

Sneaky bastard. Whether or not he shares the information, he surely does enjoy getting it for himself. I laughed. 'Sorry, Gage. I'm – shit, wait a minute.' I was out of Lilling, on the road to Bishop's Stortford, going the opposite direction of Annalise's last journey. I had to keep my eye out for the dirt track leading into Ginny Russell's neighbourhood. If I missed it, I'd have to go almost all the way to the school to find another turning.

Ah, here it is. I turned. 'All right, sorry, I've got it now. I'm driving.'

'I picked up on that. I was a detective, you know.'

I normally appreciate banter, but I really needed to concentrate. I wanted to find a place to park where the car wouldn't be visible to the Russell house; that way Ginny wouldn't have to worry about her father seeing it, if that made either of them uncomfortable. But having only been there the once, I needed to pay attention. 'Why doesn't Ginny Russell's father like company?' I asked. With Gage on the line, I might as well make use of him.

'Who?'

'Never mind.' I pulled over onto what was either the edge of the Russell property or the edge of their neighbour's, someone who wasn't at home when I came knocking yesterday. A wide willow tree seemed to provide reasonable cover.

'Wait, I've got it – Ginny and Jack Russell. No, seriously, his name was Jack Russell. Like the dog.'

'I get it. Like the dog.'

'They live off Lilling Road, don't they?' British street-naming conventions are very practical. From Bishop's Stortford going towards Lilling, it's Lilling Road; at the halfway point, with cars from the other direction heading out of Lilling, it's Bishop's Road.

'They do. You remember them?'

'Not a future I'd want for myself. I don't know what happened to her mum but she looked after her dad from the time she was a teenager. Maybe longer. Did she ever marry?'

'She still answers to Miss Russell.' Not that that's a certain sign, but perhaps it's a hint, in her generation. 'I have to go.' I wanted to get on with the investigation, not explain it.

'I did wonder, when I learnt he'd died, if she'd sell the

292

place. It's sad to think of her minding that big house all on her own.'

'Sorry, what?' I'd unbuckled my seat belt and it slithered through my hand with a buzzy *thwip*.

'It's a big place. She must be seventy-something. I wouldn't want it.'

'Her father's dead?'

'Have you ever seen a doornail? Dead as it. He'd be a hundred by now. It's not really a surprise.'

'I suppose not,' I said automatically. I apologised again, thanked him, and rang off. I looked out the windscreen at the willow fronds stroking the glass.

She's not living with her father. She's living with someone else.

I considered a lover. That would be an obvious option, and one that could explain secrecy and embarrassment, depending on who it is. Gage would be pleased for her, at any rate.

The wheelchair ramp could be leftover from when her father was alive; why tear it up when Ginny herself might need it in a few years?

This isn't important, I admonished myself. *She never said she lived with her father. I said she lived with her father. She just agreed and hurried me along.*

In the time it took for me to form those thoughts, a large blue car pulled into the Russell driveway about a hundred metres ahead of me. Ginny got out of the passenger side. The boot popped open, and she started to pull out shopping bags.

It was Thursday. Ginny's friend takes her shopping on Thursdays.

So Ginny hadn't been in.

I phoned Chloe.

'You won't believe this,' she said. 'I think I've got something from the dog—'

'No, me first. When were you here?'

'Where's here?'

'At Ginny Russell's house.'

'Oh. About an hour ago.'

Her description of the imagined tea party that awaited me here lit up in my mind. Lace, florals . . . These 'old woman' generics didn't fit Ginny Russell at all. She wore jeans, a pullover, a down vest. Her just-shoulder-length hair was held back in a clip. *What had Chloe said? 'Metre-long hairs' in my cup?*

'What did Ginny Russell look like?' I asked her.

'I'm pretty sure you know.'

My voice was urgent, but not loud. I hunched down in my seat. I didn't want to be noticed. 'What was she wearing? Describe her hair.'

'Flowered dress, long brown-grey hair, walker. Were you expecting something different?'

I watched Ginny take two grocery bags in each hand, and even lift one to wave thanks to her friend, who pulled away with a cheerful tap of the car horn. Ginny – the person I had spoken to as Ginny – brought the bags inside the house.

'One of us didn't speak to Ginny Russell. Did she say to you that she's Ginny Russell?' *Possibilities: Ginny has a sister. Ginny has a housemate. Ginny has a female lover. Or, maybe neither of these women is Ginny. Maybe two complete strangers have taken over the house.*

'She didn't say much of anything,' Chloe said. 'If you

hadn't told me before that she was cooperative, I would have wondered if she was even capable.'

'Capable? How limited are you describing here?'

'She could just be shy of strangers. It's really not something I can judge from here.'

'If you weren't being politically correct . . .'

'I would say mentally limited. She seemed childlike.'

All right, Ginny is looking after someone who needs looking after. Or is the one being looked after. Admirable. Nothing the police need to be involved with . . .

The front door slammed open. Ginny, the strong Ginny, secured the door open with a hook on the wall. She went back inside and pushed out a wheelchair containing the other Ginny, the flowery, childlike one, according to Chloe. In her lap was a hard suitcase, an old-fashioned one, not one of those ubiquitous wheeled cases that fits in the overhead bin.

Strong Ginny got the wheelchair down the ramp then scampered back to the front door to close and lock it. Childlike Ginny didn't object, but neither did she seem to participate. She allowed herself to be pushed. They were heading for the large, garage-like shed on the opposite side of the house from the outhouse and lawnmower storage.

'Tell Spencer to come,' I told Chloe. 'You come too.'

'I'm on my way to see Clemmy. Morris, what's going on?'

'I don't know. It feels wrong.' I rang off. I opened my car door as silently as I could. Unexpected sounds, even soft ones, can carry.

That worked in my favour. As I skulked around the

trees at the edge of the property, I heard the padlock on the shed rattle as Strong Ginny unlocked it, and the doors slide shudderingly. They sounded like they hadn't been opened in a long time, and she had to push first one with all of her strength, then the other.

Then I heard Childlike Ginny scream.

The sound was horrible, garbled and half-swallowed, as if, like the doors, her voice hadn't been exercised in years.

Strong Ginny put a hand over her mouth, which pushed Childlike Ginny's head back, over the top of the chair. I ran forward, not skulking any longer.

In the time it took me to get close, Childlike Ginny had raised her arms against Strong Ginny, pushing at her chest. Strong Ginny let go of Childlike Ginny's face to swat down her hands, then swung the chair around to face away from the shed. Childlike Ginny stopped her keening, perhaps from exhaustion, or from fear, or spinning her round had done the trick.

Strong Ginny dragged the suitcase towards the open doors. Now out in the open, but not yet noticed, I could see the inside of the shed, which contained a large car. It was goldish brown. No, once-white, and rusting. It listed to one side. On the corner of it that I could see, the tyre had deflated. Or rotted.

Childlike Ginny saw me first. She started screaming again, but not the howl as before; this one was more of a gibber. Strong Ginny looked up from within the shed. She had wrenched a car door open and was wrestling the suitcase into the backseat.

I held out my hands, surrender-like. I wasn't going to physically fight her. I needed her to trust me.

She was fast. She slammed the back car door and clambered into the front.

The car didn't move. It couldn't. But still I pushed Childlike Ginny's chair out of its path, in case it rolled, or lurched. I entered the shed at the driver's side.

The outside of the car was coated evenly with dust, and spotted with rust. The front, I saw, had been in an accident. The driver's-side headlamp had been smashed, and that corner was dented in. In the dim light of the shed, streaks of rust on the hood looked like purple stripes.

A green growth coated all the glass. I rubbed the window with my hand to see inside. Strong Ginny had stabbed the key in and stomped the clutch, and was beating the dashboard with the palm of her hand, asking why it wasn't working.

'Ginny,' I said. 'Ginny.' And in the moments that it took for her to turn her head and shout 'no!' at me, and lock the door and pound at her side of the window to warn me off, I thought of Cathy, and Annalise, and their fight on Annalise's last day. Cathy hadn't wanted to share the journey home with Annalise, so she'd waited it out behind the library. But Annalise wouldn't have known that. What if Annalise had had the same thought to avoid Cathy, but instead of waiting, she'd taken a different route?

There's only one route, I remembered knowing, from my highlighted map. *It's a straight line.* But if you're determined to avoid that straight line, you can exit Lilling Road before it becomes Bishop's Road. You can take the long and winding way round. You can end up out here.

Childlike Ginny was screaming again. When I'd moved her I'd turned the chair, and she was facing us. She extended one arm, pointing at us. At me? Did I frighten her? More likely Strong Ginny did.

Or the car.

I lifted my phone out of my pocket with my good hand. I turned on the torch app and shone it at the hood. It hadn't been a trick of the light, turning orange rust dark; the streaks there were purple.

Purple bicycle paint? I wondered.

Then the streaks seemed to move away from me, and I felt the answers slipping from my grasp. I wondered in a flash if I'd imagined them, if I'd wished them into being and fooled myself, and now they were receding, out of my reach . . .

No; reality overcame metaphor. The car was rolling backwards, inching out the mouth of the shed. There was no surge of power from the engine, no purring vibration; nor could there be, with the car in its decrepit condition. Ginny must have released the handbrake. The car slid out and, with one back tyre in worse shape than the other, it tilted in an unexpected direction. Its skewed path listed towards the wheelchair.

I scrambled around to get in front of its back. I had to choose between lurching at the wheelchair, to cast Childlike Ginny out of the car's way, or trying to make the slow but heavy car stop. I chose the wheelchair.

Childlike Ginny windmilled her arms against me as I tried to grab hold of the armrests, battering my face. The brake was on, and I couldn't get my left hand close enough to the lever to pull it up. I tried shoving the chair but it held firm, threatening to topple but not to slide. So I whipped around and chose the car, which had become frighteningly close.

I spread my feet and braced myself against its slow surge. I pressed my hands flat against the boot, and resisted. Even without power, even at its ponderous pace, it had an almost animate strength, and it had gained momentum. The wheelchair and its terrified occupant were just a few steps behind me.

Inside the car, Strong Ginny was leaning on the horn, as if I were the enemy and she were signalling for help. Behind me, another car's horn blared.

'Move back!' called Spencer over the din.

I fell out of the way, coughing from stirred-up dust. Spencer's car slid forward, tapping against a corner of the white car and stopping its roll. The aged car shuddered. Its boot sprang open.

Spencer pushed out, leaving his door hanging wide; I stumbled forward. We converged where the two cars met. Sunlight fell into the open boot.

Inside, the remains of a twisted bicycle frame sparkled. It was almost entirely flame-coloured rust now, but I could make out bits of the original purple, that glittery kind of paint job that young girls sometimes get.

Strong Ginny within the car had stopped sounding the horn, and was bouncing her head on the steering wheel. 'The police. The police. The police,' she said. 'We've got to get away before they come back.'

Spencer called for medics. This situation was beyond questioning or arrest.

I fell into a sitting position on the ground. Childlike

Ginny, safe and upright in her chair, was still making noises, though weaker ones than before. Every muscle in my body throbbed. I'd just used every bit of my physical self, the whole damn thing. It became suddenly obvious how much of me there was besides the defective fingers on my right hand. There was a whole world of me. There was a universe of me. *I think this is what they call endorphins. I think this is what they call shock.*

I closed my eyes. More cars, bustle, voices. Spencer telling people what to do. *Good lad.* I supposed his swooping in to stop the car that was perhaps about to take me down counted as much as would an apology I was never going to get.

Chloe's car arrived with emergency services. I waved paramedics towards the Ginnies (as I'd come to think of them, though I now had a suspicion of another name) and got up.

Chloe, talking animatedly, had a promising lead about the body by the tracks, thanks to Clemmy the dog walker; I had an idea for how we were going to identify the handyman from the boarding house, even without the list of names from Ginny, Strong Ginny, who I didn't think was going to be much good to us now. But both of those were distant obligations compared to the dirty white car, which loomed like an elephant. I waved Chloe towards the marks on the dented hood; I nudged her to look in the open boot.

She gaped at the bicycle inside. 'An accident?' she said.

'I think Annalise took an out-of-the-way route to avoid Cathy that afternoon. She got hit by a car. This car,' I said.

'And what? Buried here, or . . . No. Surely not.'

We both turned towards Childlike Ginny, who was acquiescing to a cursory examination by paramedics. She was in her fifties. Her hair had once been dark.

I said, 'I think Ginny might have looked after her.'

'But a hospital . . . Even if Ginny didn't want to get in trouble for hitting a cyclist, surely her father wouldn't have put up with a sudden, permanent, medically needy guest!'

I looked in the front of the car. The driver's seat had been pushed far back. Judging by the dust, it had been that way since the time it was garaged. 'Unless he's the one who had been driving.' Even if the engine had survived, Ginny wouldn't have been able to get far in that position; she wouldn't have reached the pedals.

Strong Ginny – the only Ginny, it turned out – was going to go to a psychiatric ward for evaluation. When she'd come home from shopping and been told by Childlike – *No, she has a name, Morris* – that a second police detective had come by, that must have prompted a panicked nervous breakdown in Ginny. She'd tried to get them away from here, to . . . where? And how? I'd bet that car hadn't been touched or even looked at since 1976. But it was all she knew. Her improvised best had been good enough for forty years.

I walked over towards the ambulance. The woman I'd first thought of as Childlike Ginny was still in the wheelchair, waiting. They had finished examining her as much as she would allow at the moment. She was quiet now, her hands clutching each other. I thought, *I do that.* It's comforting, as if one hand can take care of the other, and vice versa. As if you can take care of yourself.

I knelt next to her chair. She might have suffered brain damage in the accident. No helmets in those days.

'Annalise?' I whispered.

She turned her head to face me. Her mouth hung open. I think she smiled.

CHAPTER NINETEEN

Anna Williams, Mental Health Treatment Requirement client, transcribed by Dr Arthur Dean, National Offender Management Service

Thank you, Dr Dean. I really appreciate you being here.

Yes, I understand. I'm here because the court ordered it as a condition of my probation. I'm to undergo regular therapy to help me gain a better insight into the choices I made.

Ha! Yes! I'm quoting the judge. I'm impressed that you recognised the wording. I'm going to have to keep on my toes around you. [Laughs.]

You already know why I'm here. I really don't feel like rehashing what we both know. But there is something new I've found out, since the trial. I found out what was in the photo that Hannah-Claire took from me to show Mum. The one the police found in Nigel's rubbish.

I already knew what it was a photo of, obviously. It was Mum and two friends, as young teenagers. There's a copy in Mum's yearbook, in the back pages of candid shots. And in it you can see a long, thin scar on her chest. It just peeps out the top of her shirt. She got it when she was swimming in the river. You can hardly see it now, and she doesn't really show her chest now anyway, but back then it was pretty clear, if you knew where to look.

Well, the police got hold of Hannah-Claire's belongings in storage in Canada, and there with her old baby clothes was her baby photo, her only one. There's a gap in the hospital gown Mum was wearing and you can see the scar.

Hannah-Claire meant to show the teenage photo to Mum, to make her admit the real truth. But Nigel met her instead. I don't know what they said to each other, but one of them smashed the photo in its frame. Nigel swept it all up the best he could, took the frame and the picture itself, and destroyed it all at the office. Not destroyed it enough, as you know, but he refused to admit anything, which is exactly what you would expect from him.

Look, I hate this part. I hate it. They weren't able to convict. Convict him for what? That his step-niece-maybe-stepdaughter fell in the river while he was nearby? While they were having an argument? That he took a picture away from her? So what? Unless they could prove he pushed her, it didn't mean anything. None of it.

Which is why what I did is so important. I'm

pretty sure the goal of this therapy is to get me to see the error of my ways, but without me, he'd be a free man. That wouldn't be right. That wouldn't be right.

The police finished analysing the stuff under my fingernails and it turned out that Nigel had been the one to beat me after the funeral. He even has scratches on his arms to match. He saw Henry and me together and, knowing what people already suspected Henry had done to Hannah-Claire, he saw his chance. After Henry walked away he . . . I don't really want to talk about it. I was as bad as Hannah-Claire to him. He'd already done it to her, and I was a variation on the same problem: a child he didn't want and couldn't control.

Is he having to have therapy too? Because I think that would be a really good idea.

All right, sorry. This is about me. I understand that.

But don't you get it, that if it weren't for what he did to me, he wouldn't be in jail? And he is now, for five years. Five years. For what he did to me. He didn't get anything for Hannah-Claire, but he got five years for me. That sounds short but I bet it feels like for ever to him. What I did was important. What I did was worth it. I got him.

Actually, no, I don't feel bad about Henry. Hannah-Claire put up with him because she was lonely but he wasn't generous. He wasn't kind. He should feel guilty for how he treated her. The way people looked at him when he was accused, that's how he deserves to feel, because the point is that people were able to imagine he'd done it. How do you get to be the kind of person that people think, *Huh. Maybe he did kill his wife.* Right? If you're that kind of person, you need to own that. You need to face it. Maybe his brief stint in jail did that for him. Maybe that was a kind of therapy, right? Therapy for everyone! [Laughs.]

I don't think that's fair. I don't think Hannah-Claire deserved what happened at all.

What do you mean? My part? I wasn't at the river. I was trying to protect her. Mum had already made her decision to not tell her, to not tell any of us, and Hannah-Claire just didn't respect that. That's what put all of this in motion. Not me lying; it was her not being satisfied with the lie. I gave her a lie I would have loved to have myself. I gave it to her. That's a kind of love. And she just wouldn't be satisfied.

[Exasperated breathing.] Well, for the same reason that kids all over the world imagine that their 'real' parents are royalty or pirates or dinosaur archaeologists. Annalise is the closest thing to a princess where I was growing up. Of course I would have loved to be hers.

Of course I've heard. Everyone's heard. 'Annalise Wood Alive'. The headline font was like three inches high.

I don't know. It's weird.

Even Annalise wasn't Annalise. I mean, she was Annalise Wood before she disappeared, but that Annalise was just a teenager who was pretty and popular in a general way but not perfect. Not famous.

She only became the important 'Annalise' in the eyes of others, once she was gone. She became a kind of symbol, a kind of idol, to strangers, and to me, but she didn't get to experience being that herself. I don't think anyone ever gets to experience being that, even if they're alive and aware that it's happening in other people's minds. That's something you can think about others, but you can't ever be inside of it. When you're inside yourself, you know better.

No, I don't think she did know. From the way it's been described in the news, Ginny Russell kept Annalise isolated from all that was going on. Ginny was terrified that if the accident was discovered, her father would go to prison for driving after his licence had been taken away due to poor eyesight. She felt badly about what had happened and dedicated her life to making Annalise physically comfortable. The injuries apparently made her . . . compliant. It's horrible. Horrible. I can't . . .

Nothing. I just mean that I'm not . . . [Breathes heavily.] I'm not . . . There was even my picture online; did you see? The reporter asked me for one so I got to pick. I chose one from a couple of years ago. I didn't go back to the photos I used to fantasise about using; those would have been far too young; but it was from my second year at university. I was at a party, so there are other people in it too. They blurred out the other people's faces but you can see that I was in a group, and I'm smiling, and my hair looks great, and I look pretty. I look pretty. That's 'me' now, if you google my name. Maybe someone is fantasising about being perfect like me.

Annalise is in a care home now. She's the same age as my Mum. In a way she looks younger than Mum, actually, in that one picture the media have been allowed to use. Her face is childlike while her body is middle-aged.

I . . . No. That's not what the fantasy ever was. That's not what the fantasy . . .

Look, it's not even my fantasy any more.

Because it's not. Because I have my own story now. My stepfather beat me until I almost died. [Crying.] He killed my cousin. Who was my sister. He killed her and he almost killed me. And talking about that doesn't feel special, the way that it did when I was making something up. It feels ugly, and out of control.

Thank you, Dr Dean. I appreciate the tissues.

CHAPTER TWENTY

Laurie Ambrose

This time I went ahead and wore black, because no one would be looking at me. I wanted to pay my respects, and we were all strangers, so no one would sort and rank who was close enough to justify the colour.

A charity group had organised a candlelight vigil to honour the memory of the young woman who for years was thought to be Annalise Wood. Her name was Mara Webster. She'd run away from her home near Hunstanton, that town in north Norfolk with the beach and that tiny aquarium, and ended up addicted and dipping her toe into prostitution in St Albans.

Simon didn't want to wear a suit, but knotted a tie, at my request, so we wouldn't look out of sync. 'How did they figure it out, after all these years? Was it DNA?' he asked me.

It's not that Simon doesn't bother to read the news; it's that the police had kindly told me details that haven't been reported. 'It was the man who found the body, back in 1992.

He was walking his dog.' I tucked my hair into a hairslide.

'. . . and?'

'You know dogs. It brought him a piece of the body.'

Simon wrinkled his nose.

I felt the need to defend the animal. 'The body had been buried for sixteen years! Wait, no, thirteen years. Maybe twelve. Sixteen is if it had been Annalise. But any body in the ground that long isn't . . . whole. Not completely.'

'Why is this significant?'

I slipped on black shoes. We were ready. I sat next to him on the edge of the bed. 'It was her right hand. He saw a tattoo on it. Three little fish, in red, blue, and green. Maybe she liked the aquarium when she was younger.'

'And the dog walker didn't tell anyone?'

'The dog had chewed on it. He thought he might get into trouble. That's what he said. But really I think he knew that meant it wasn't Annalise. That's what she'd looked like at first, of course, to everyone: missing teenage girl, long dark hair, school uniform, near Lilling. He wanted her to be Annalise. He wanted to be part of Annalise's story. So he let the dog keep at the hand until it was gone.'

Simon leant away from me. 'That's terrible.'

'I know! He knew it too. When he got home, he drew a picture of the tattoo, to remember it. He knew it was important. Not enough to actually do something, but important enough to make sure he had it right. When he finally told police, he had a decades-old sketch to show them. Coloured pencils. I've seen the picture. He's not a bad artist. Mara Webster had been registered as a missing person by a friend of hers, another prostitute, not her family. That very specific tattoo was part of the description.

310

The police hadn't put much work into looking for her.'

'I'm sorry,' he said. It was an odd thing for him to say to me, but it was also perfect. He was sorry that some people were treated as forgettable while others were remembered too much. He was sorry that I had become part of a story with such sadness in it. He put his hand on my hand. Against my will, I imagined little fish swimming up from the base of my thumb.

'When Hannah-Claire went to the dog walker,' I continued, 'she asked him if he remembered anything distinctive about the body. She was hoping he'd mention a scar. He, of course, thought she was on to him about the tattoo. He panicked. He lied to her. It was only when he found out that Hannah-Claire was dead and a new Annalise investigation hit the news that he felt he needed to confess. He phoned that woman detective, Chloe.' I know her better now. She's not terrible.

'Is he in trouble?'

I shook my head. 'Not even Anna Williams is in trouble.'

'You and Blake have restraining orders against her. She can't contact you.'

'What if she's there tonight?' The thought just occurred to me. I felt sick.

'We don't have to go. But,' he added, when I vehemently shook my head, 'there will be hundreds of people. Hundreds. That's a good thing.'

'It's a shame that hundreds of people didn't care about her when she was alive.'

We went downstairs for coats, scarves, my handbag. My scarf was red. We were near Christmas, and the memorial candles were going to look oddly festive in this context, as if we were gathering to turn on the lights on the city tree.

'They know who killed her!' I deliberately added an exclamation mark with my tone. Trying to hold on to whatever is good.

'That Peterborough man, right? The one who killed those prostitutes in the nineties.'

'Will Teague. He'd apparently lived in Lilling when he was much younger, under a different name. The police found his fingerprints all these years later, can you imagine?'

'How could they possibly . . . ?'

'He'd partly paid his rent by helping out where he lived. He took down a bunch of old paintings when there was building work, and he rehung them when it was done. No one had taken them down since. His fingerprints were all over the backs and frames.'

'Well, he's paid for his crimes.'

He'd died in prison years ago. But, 'Being dead isn't a punishment.'

'Isn't it?' Simon asked me. He said it like it was a real question.

Is it? I didn't know. Was it worse to be Tom, or to be me missing Tom? Sometimes I couldn't tell.

It had been proposed to hold the event where Mara's body had been found, but it was too dangerous to bring that many people so close to the tracks, or to light hundreds of candles in a field. Lilling's nearby town centre had also been considered, but it seemed unfair to mourn her in the place known primarily as the home of the girl she'd been too long mistaken for.

In the end, they held it in St Albans Cathedral. About two hundred and fifty people gathered to acknowledge the brief life and terrible death of Mara Webster, Will Teague's first known victim. Candles were handed out upon arrival, and the flame itself was passed from wick to wick. It was a moving service.

I didn't see Anna. I hadn't asked Blake or Clara to come. I recognised the police, but they didn't seem to be on duty. They seemed genuinely respectful. The one with the dead hand – I'd only noticed it when everything was all over and I'd tried to shake it – had been in the news a lot. A paramedic had heard him call the woman in the wheelchair 'Annalise' and that was it, the story got its own legs in that moment. The press needed a hero to focus on in all of the sadness and he was chosen.

We were supposed to be thinking of Mara, and I tried, but other figures overshadowed her. Others were thinking of Annalise, no doubt. It was a subject of gossip to wonder if she would have been better off dead, if her last forty years as a brain-damaged secret prisoner had been worse than the ghastly but quick murder we'd all assumed. Other people argued that she had years ahead and would be able to appreciate them, even in the limited way available to her, and might have appreciated all manner of things in her constrained life with Ginny Russell. Perhaps her limited mental capacity would have made her captivity more tolerable. If her doctors knew how much Annalise truly understood what happened to her, it wasn't being shared with the public. *And thank God for that.*

I was thinking of Tom. Simon's question about death being the ultimate punishment rattled around, distracting me. I realised that for years I felt like the worse off of the two of us, me and Tom. The one left behind to go on. The one who had to feel the agony of grief.

Simon squeezed my hand. The building had been decorated for Christmas, and silvery things reflected the candlelight.

But there's so much else, I reminded myself. I'd had to feel the grief, which lingered far longer than I let on, but I also got to feel new warmth and love and anticipation. I was alive. I had time for new things to happen.

Near the end of the service, the priest asked us to remember Mara. We were to say her name, and then blow out our candles together, in what I suppose was a gesture of letting her go. This was for us, after all, not for her. She wasn't here any more.

The congregation took in a breath together, and we let it out together. Around me, hundreds of mouths shaped 'Mara' as they exhaled. But mine shaped 'Tom'.

I blew out the candle.

ACKNOWLEDGEMENTS

Thanks to Superintendent Jon Hutchinson for orienting me to the new organisational structure of the Cambridgeshire Police and Major Crimes; to former forensic investigator Steve Morgan, now a porter at St John's College, for insight into both his past and present roles; and to Rosemary Parkinson, for sharing her experience working for the University Counselling Service and with privacy issues. Their generosity and experience were real gifts. Any errors or literary licence in the above areas are on me, not them.

Thanks to Rebecca Fitzgerald for getting me into Trinity College when it was closed, and to Jake Dyble for showing me around Robinson.

Thanks to Amanda Goodman for writing with me so many Thursday mornings, and to Jason Scott-Warren for being my writing challenge buddy as we both neared our finish lines.

Thanks to Katy Salmon and Neil Robinson for their thoughtful nitpicking; to Amy Weatherup for astute first impressions; and especially to Sophie Hannah for her invaluable insights.

Thanks to Chloe Moffett in New York for a brilliant edit; to Susie Dunlop in London for continuing support; and to Cameron McClure, agent and friend.

Thanks to Matt Wise, for helping me clarify Morris's emotional arc.

Lastly and always, thanks to Gavin and the boys, for their patience and support.

EMILY WINSLOW is an American living in Cambridge, England. She trained as an actor at Carnegie Mellon University's elite drama conservatory, and has a master's degree in museum studies from Seton Hall University. For six years she worked for *Games* magazine, creating increasingly elaborate and lavishly illustrated logic puzzles. In addition to writing her Keene & Frohmann crime novels, Emily has published a memoir, *Jane Doe January*, of her involvement with a real-life court case. Together, she and her husband homeschool their two sons in a house full of books.

emilywinslow.com

ALSO BY EMILY WINSLOW

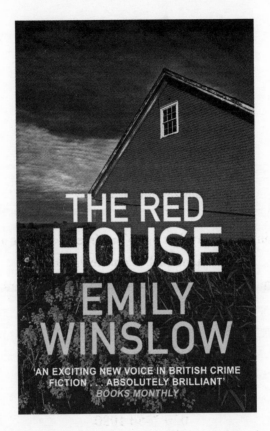

THE RED
HOUSE
EMILY
WINSLOW

'AN EXCITING NEW VOICE IN BRITISH CRIME
FICTION . . . ABSOLUTELY BRILLIANT'
BOOKS MONTHLY

Maxwell is living his worst nightmare when he begins to question whether his fiancée Imogen is his own sister, separated by adoption. While DCI Morris Keene languishes at home, struggling with a debilitating injury and post-traumatic stress, his former partner DI Chloe Frohmann is following a suicide case in which Morris's daughter Dora is suspected of assisting the death.

When buried skeletons are discovered next to an old barn the suicide is linked back to Imogen's childhood, revealing horrors of the past and new dangers in the present.

To discover more great books and to
place an order visit our website at
allisonandbusby.com

Don't forget to sign up to our free newsletter at
allisonandbusby.com/newsletter
for latest releases, events and exclusive offers

Allison & Busby Books
@AllisonandBusby

You can also call us on
020 7580 1080
for orders, queries
and reading recommendations